NEIGHBORHOOD

WATCH

BRUCE F. KATZ

ISBN: 979-8-9875634-4-1 (paperback)
ISBN: 979-8-9875634-5-8 (ebook)

Also from Bruce F. Katz

Fiction

The Family Jewels

The History Lesson

The Filthy Five

Non-Fiction

When Your Name is On the Door

Prologue

Had they been forced to fly commercial, the entire trip would have literally taken days. But Michael Capshaw didn't fly commercial anywhere, ever. At least not since he was promoted to his current position as senior vice president for external affairs with the North American division of Dommerich Worldwide, one of the world's largest pharmaceutical and pesticide conglomerates. These days when he needed to travel for any reason, to any destination, he had a fleet of Gulfstream jets at his disposal, and he had the budget to take advantage of this valuable perk.

While he thoroughly enjoyed this benefit, it seemed his traveling companion, the lithe, lean, and lovely Nancy Kuo, did not. She removed her hand from his, turned to gaze out the window, then turned back to look at him.

"What's the matter, Nancy?" he asked, knowing what was coming.

"I love you, Michael," she said, "but I can't stand having to make this trip whenever you need to go to that godforsaken place. Why do you need to go there? Why do I need to go with you? What kind of place in the civilized world doesn't even have an Olive Garden? There's nothing for me to do there, and what we do do there, we can easily do at home way more comfortably and without all this exhausting time in a plane, even a nice plane like this."

He looked at the woman who served as his executive assistant in the office and his lover away from work. "It's something I need to do from time to time," he said patiently, as if addressing a five-year-old. "And, yes, it's a long and perhaps boring trip, but I know you enjoy the beach. I know you enjoy getting away from work and from Minneapolis. So, I bring you with me. Is it really all that bad?"

"There's nothing to do there, Michael, for me at least," she said. "The beach is fine, but otherwise it's so boring. There are no good restaurants, no decent shopping . . . Can't we go someplace that isn't so . . . remote?"

He smiled. "For my purposes, Nancy, it's the only place. Now, can we please put this conversation to rest? Please?"

They had been what she referred to as "together" for almost three years. In that time, they'd made this trip nearly a dozen times, interrupting the nearly eighteen hours in the air only to refuel. Including going there and coming home, these trips always lasted a little over five days.

He paid her very well for her duties at work and fully expected her to respond favorably to any reasonable request he might have at any given moment. Except for these trips, about which she could be counted on to complain, she always met his—some might say, unreasonably high—expectations. She also knew that when he asked her something and managed to say "please" more than once, the conversation was over.

They sat together in silence until the flight attendant whispered that they should fasten seat belts to prepare for descent into Minneapolis–St. Paul International Airport. Michael reset his wristwatch to central daylight time.

"I need to go into the office for a couple of things," he said, "and I need you to come with me. How about, after we finish a few quick chores, I take you to dinner?"

She mustered a smile. "Can we go to Olive Garden?"

He shook his head and tried to suppress his exasperation. "Jesus," he said. "Yes, Nancy, we can go to Olive Garden."

She smiled, put her hand back into his, and kissed him on the cheek.

• • •

Michael placed the handset into the charger that sat alone on his glass-topped desk. He'd been on the phone since they'd returned to the office from MSP an hour earlier. It was nearly 4:00 p.m. on Friday. He buzzed for Nancy to come into his suite.

"Yes, sir?"

"Call GSA. See if they have people in Central Florida. If they do, I need someone picked up tomorrow afternoon at 2:00 p.m. and flown here."

"Tomorrow is Saturday."

"Don't you think I know what day of the week tomorrow is, Nancy?"

"What if Global Security doesn't have people in Central Florida?" she asked.

"If they don't, have the office in St. Paul provide two agents," Michael said. "Have them on the MSP tarmac at 6:30 a.m. tomorrow morning."

"Is this about that annoying man?"

"Not your concern, Nancy, but yes, it's about Mr. Censell."

"That's a funny name," she said.

"Nothing about him is funny, Nancy. He's a pain in my ass, and I need to deal with him once and for all," he said. "His bullshit has been going on for too damn long." He gave her the necessary information and instructions regarding the acquisition and delivery of Mr. Jordan Censell. "I want him in my office tomorrow at 8:00 p.m."

"What will happen after—"

"Tomorrow evening, 8:00 p.m., Nancy. The less you know about him and the nonsense he's peddling the better. One way or another we will be rid of Mr. Censell after tomorrow evening."

She looked at him. "Does that mean we'll be able to—"

"Sunday is all ours, Nancy," he said. "Yours and mine." He dismissed her with a smile.

Minutes later, she buzzed her boss. "Yes?"

"All set, sir," she said. "The jet will be fueled and ready for a 7:00 a.m. departure. Two GSA agents will be on hand at 6:30 a.m., awaiting instructions."

"Thank you, Nancy. You can head home if you like. I'll be right behind you."

"I know," she said. "See you later, Michael. Olive Garden, right?"

• • •

The man who called himself Jordan Censell stared into the blank screen on his laptop computer. The machine held virtually everything he'd done to date attempting to track the movements of his only child, his daughter, Christy, who'd been missing for ten months somewhere in South America.

"Okay," he whispered. "Okay." He turned and stared into the doleful eyes of his sole companion. Lady, his nearly two-year-old brown-and-white Basenji, looked back at him. She cocked her head slightly, in Jordan's mind, encouraging him to go on.

"Okay, I know you think I've lost it, and that this whole . . . exercise is a waste of time when we could be at a park somewhere, and you could be peeing and pooping and frolicking to your heart's content. But consider this: this guy, this . . . guy, wouldn't give me the time of day if he didn't know something about what happened to Christy. Why would he? Right? He's been blowing me off for months, so why take a meeting now?"

Lady laid her head down, sighed, and closed her eyes.

"Look," Jordan said, "I don't expect you to have anything to say about this. First, you're a dog. Second, you're a Basenji, so, you don't talk, or bark, or, whatever. But I have to believe that sometime tomorrow, we are going to know more—maybe much more—than we do right now." He paused. "Which, as we both know, amounts to absolutely nothing."

Jordan stood. So did Lady, sensing a trip to the backyard was, for her, now a distinct possibility.

"No, baby," Jordan said, "no, not right now. The game is afoot and we—I—have work to do."

For the next two hours, in the single room he'd been living and working in for months, Jordan Censell purposefully staged the scene under Lady's occasion-ally watchful eyes. He wasn't entirely sure why he'd decided, upon learning of Christy's disappearance, to leave every other room of the house bare and unlived in. But he had. His brilliance and his eccentricities often clashed, but for most of his life these conflicting attributes seemed to have worked in his favor.

He suspected, sometime after he was visited by representatives of Dommerich Worldwide, someone—or several someones—might surreptitiously enter his house on Susie Q Court. On the one hand, if it was a friendly incursion, he wanted certain information findable, just in case he was walking into a carefully constructed trap. On the other, if it wasn't friendly, he needed to keep a lot of what he'd accumulated in his search for his daughter as hidden as possible from those particular prying eyes.

The contents of the master bedroom suite, which included a large bathroom and walk-in closet, constituted virtually everything Jordan needed to live his life the way he'd been living it since relocating to Florida. Since the good-sized room had become the only one in the house he used, he installed a Murphy bed and a couple of hutches he'd customized to keep everything he needed close at hand while he worked, day and night, to find his daughter.

Little by little, piece by piece, he placed certain books in certain places. He recorded a brief video message using his laptop, saved it onto a flash drive, deleted it from the computer, and placed the drive in his pocket. Before leaving on Saturday—he assumed he'd be leaving, but for how long, he didn't know— he'd place it somewhere visible to curious, hopefully friendly eyes. He'd hide the laptop, but he suspected that, ultimately, it would be found. He placed some photo albums strategically, so they'd be accessible, but not too obvious. When he was as satisfied as he could possibly be, he turned to Lady.

"Right now, you and I are the only ones who know what's going on here," he said. "And I know I can trust you to keep our secrets." He filled Lady's bowls and prepared himself a light dinner: a can of Chunky New England Clam Chowder and a few slices of buttered loaf bread. When they both were done eating, he took Lady to the sliding glass doors in the empty living room and let her out to do her business while he stood silently contemplating possibilities.

. . .

SATURDAY

Michael Capshaw met the two GSA agents at the company's hangar at MSP in the morning.

"He's expecting you around 2:00 p.m.," he told them. "He doesn't know where we're meeting, only that we're meeting. As far as he knows, I'm coming to him."

"So, you're not joining us today, Mr. Capshaw?" the senior GSA agent asked.

"No. The best outcome is that he gets on the plane with you without incident, and you bring him to me at my office tonight around 8:00 p.m."

"Copy that, sir."

The two agents, the pilot, and a single flight attendant boarded the plane, one of several the company kept based at Minneapolis–St. Paul airport.

Michael watched the jet taxi to the runway and take off, bound for Orlando Executive Airport.

Just do what you're supposed to do, Mr. Censell, Michael thought. *I promise you'll live to regret it.*

• • •

Early Saturday morning, Jordan went outside to play out the last couple of elements in preparation for whatever good or bad awaited him later in the day. When he finished laying some groundwork with his neighbor, he and Lady spent the rest of their time together in his room.

"Sometime soon I'm going to have to go off, baby," he said, sitting in his office chair while Lady occupied her place on the shag-carpeted floor next to him. "I don't know where I'm going. I don't know how long I'll be gone." He paused. "If I'm honest, I don't even know if I'll be coming back."

Lady stood and placed her paws onto his legs. This was not one of her predictable Basenji behaviors. He hugged his best friend. In response, since barking wasn't a part of her vocal repertoire, she gave him a robust yodel.

He remembered the flash drive in his pocket and affixed it to a location where it was, effectively, hidden in plain sight.

All he could do, he'd already done. Whatever was going to happen was going to happen, and that was that.

A few minutes after 2:00 p.m., his doorbell rang. He closed and locked the door to the room he and Lady had been living in for almost a year. He hoped she wouldn't be locked in alone for too long.

He answered the door and stepped outside to face his destiny.

Chapter 1

Ronnie Levitt was up early on Saturday morning only because he needed to go into the newsroom for a few hours. He saw Jordan, the neighbor he often referred to as "the Professor," mowing his lawn.

Ronnie's job no longer sentenced him to specific days at the newspaper. Being the *Orlando Chronicle*'s enterprise investigative reporter meant he chose his own leads, story ideas, and hours. This day he was doing a favor for a colleague, filling in on the breaking news desk.

Most weekends Ronnie was technically free to sleep in with his wife, Jennie, but that was little more than a hope because almost every Saturday, along with the rest of the folks sentenced to life on Susie Q Court, Ronnie got to enjoy the exhilarating experience of being roused at around 7:30 a.m. by the sound of the Professor's lawn mower. It was, he believed, one of the few downsides that came with living on a cul-de-sac in a large, planned development in suburban Orlando.

Ronnie opened his garage door, eased his Prius into his driveway, and took a moment to behold the man at work directly across the cul-de-sac. He shook his head.

One never knew what to expect in the way of sartorial choices from the Professor. On this occasion, Jordan was dressed in a pair of vintage Doc Martens over heavy black woolen socks that covered his calves to just below his knees. The strategy here, no doubt, was to avoid the gravel-like projectiles thrown up by the mower in the absence of any real grass-like surface.

Then there were the lederhosen. The leather shorts were suspended over a well-worn Mickey Mouse T-shirt. On the Professor's face sat a pair of tinted wraparound safety glasses. Atop his head, he sported the full Desert Rat top hat, angled so as not to allow the blistering June sun to redden his delicate ears or the back of his closely shaved neck.

"What ho, young Lochinvar," Jordan hailed, stopping the noise of his mower in order to enrich Ronnie's life. He disengaged a pair of heavy Koss Pro headphones, allowing the cans to hang from his neck. He wore these not to listen to music, a podcast or two, or NPR. No, he wore them to deaden the noise he so willingly inflicted on the rest of his neighbors. He walked over and said, "Don't typically see your smiling face this early on a Saturday, Squire Ronald."

Unable to avoid falling into his rhythms, Ronnie tipped a nonexistent hat. "Without wishing to offend, good sir, doesn't one require first an actual lawn, that is, one containing something green and perhaps at least resembling grass before cranking up the old Snapper at this ungodly hour on a weekend day?"

Jordan left the mower where it was and approached Ronnie in the middle of the cul-de-sac. The semicircle of homes defined their tiny subset of the neighborhood, inside a larger community within the overall development. He leaned in, looked from side to side, and whispered, in unaffected speech and with a degree of urgency, directly into Ronnie's ear. "If anything strange happens today involving me, I hope you'll take care of my Lady." His eyes darted as if he expected something strange to happen involving him right then and there.

Conversations with the Professor were always unpredictable. They ran a topical gamut from history, warfare, and literature to politics, the environment, and even the man's informed and closely held opinions on America's healthcare system, which he didn't care for at all. Clearly, he was an intelligent life-form. This day, though, it appeared his discourse was culled from *The X-Files*.

"Exactly what do you think might happen?" Ronnie asked, with a sarcasm he had not meant to exhibit.

"Just because I'm paranoid, Woodward," he said,

ignoring Ronnie's tone, "doesn't mean they're not out to get me. Tread carefully this day. There are dangerous activities taking place in this part of our gentle forest."

Jordan had arrived in Orlando nearly ten months earlier. He'd scooped up the last new home built on the last available lot on Susie Q Court. The Astoria Woods development mirrored the cookie-cutter suburban subdivisions within larger planned communities that had sprouted up by the dozens in and around Orlando since the world's most famous rodent decided to build a second home in Central Florida. Walt Disney World's influence in Orlando was confirmed on this day by the Professor's wardrobe choice.

There were thirteen homes on the Susie Q Court cul-de-sac. There were slightly more than seven hundred in all of Astoria Woods. To Ronnie's knowledge, none of the occupants of any of those homes had ever set a single foot inside his neighbor's three-bedroom, two-bath-with-a-bonus-room house. It also occurred to Ronnie that it was entirely possible neither he nor his neighbors on Susie Q Court were aware of Jordan's last name.

Any time Ronnie or any of the neighbors broached what for others would constitute an innocuous line of inquiry, Jordan would deflect it in some offhand, literary manner.

"You may call me Longfellow, my good fellow," or "What's in a name? A rose by any other name . . ."

This cloak of mysteriousness was certainly a part of his charm, along with the way he engaged all of them in the dying art of person-to-person conversation in the age of smart phones and Twitter.

Since the Professor had arrived, Ronnie had seen some of the others housed on Susie Q Court make thoroughly ridiculous guesses regarding the man's biography. This was done in the manner of people sitting in an airport, waiting to board, making things up about fellow passengers as a means of passing time.

"I'm thinking he's ex-military, maybe with a pension and the occasional off-the-books 'odd job,'" Doug offered, putting air quotes around "odd job." Doug and his wife, Stacy, lived next door to Ronnie, in the big house second from the center of those on the actual cul-de-sac. Doug was in finance and Stacy freelanced in pharmaceutical sales.

Mikey had the Professor writing novels under assumed names. Mikey was a big, good-natured guy, but not the brightest light in the harbor. He lived with his mom and worked as a personal trainer. "Maybe he's an author, like Donald Balducci or Ronald Lublum," he once suggested.

A couple of others thought he might be in witness protection, or maybe recently released from prison. What Ronnie knew was that one day he arrived in a rental truck after paying cash for the house.

Alberto, who lived at the corner of Susie Q Court and Delaney Drive, was certain he was either some kind of intelligence agent or possibly even a working criminal. This was how Alberto's mind worked. He thought everyone who didn't have a regular job with regular hours was either a no-good spy or a no-good drug dealer. "I'm telling you, this guy is bad news," Alberto once said, with the kind of certainty born of total ignorance. For reasons of his own, Alberto didn't like Jordan, and Jordan took occasional pleasure in exploiting Alberto's discomfort.

Ronnie had hung the "Professor" tag on him because of the way he sometimes quoted literary classics to their group of pop-culture heathens. They referred to his house as the Lecture Hall. Most Susie Q Court residents were Gen Xers. To them, culture was *Star Wars*, a Grisham paperback, or 1980s rock music.

"I promise to watch my back, Professor," Ronnie said. "And you should do the same. Will you be attending our little neighborhood shrimp boil later this afternoon?"

"If I'm here, I'm there," Jordan said. "But today could be . . . well, let's just call it . . . interesting." His eyes softened a bit. "Ronnie, seriously, promise me if anything happens, you'll look after my little girl."

"Of course," Ronnie said instinctively. *First, it's "my lady," now it's "my little girl."* "Gotta go defend democracy and uphold our glorious First Amendment. Catch you later, Professor."

As Ronnie backed into the cul-de-sac, Jordan rushed back to the Prius' driver's side window. "Look for clues,

Ronnie" he said. "Look up and look down beneath." And then he whispered urgently, "No police—under any circumstance, no matter what. No police!" His face softened again, this time into a kind of sad plea. He turned and walked back to his yard.

Ronnie gently stepped on the gas with the man's last words marinating in his brain. Jordan waved at him as he drove away and returned to mowing the patch of dirt and weeds that passed for his lawn.

• • •

Ronnie finished his fill-in duty at two o'clock. He made sure all news of potential value was in the hands of the reporter responsible either for the beat or the geography. He returned home a bit after two thirty. When he made the turn into the cul-de-sac, he noticed Jennie and a couple of the other women who lived on Susie Q standing in front of Ronnie's house, staring across at Jordan's house. He pulled into his driveway, got out of his car, and, with a dollop of trepidation, approached the gaggle.

"What's up?" he asked.

"He's gone, Ronnie," Jennie said.

"Jordan?"

"Elvis has left the building," announced Hallie. The latest move-in on Susie Q Court, a freelance textbook editor, had recently been named official cul-de-sac smartass.

"Where did he go?" Ronnie asked, staring at the

house as if it might, in some metaphysical manner, communicate directly with him.

"I know what this is going to sound like, but a half hour or so ago, a black Suburban showed up," Jennie said. "There were two guys with buzz cuts, wearing identical black slacks and short-sleeved white shirts. They knocked. He opened the door, closed it behind him, and walked out. Then he got in the back seat of the SUV. I don't think he ever even looked at me, and as far as I could tell, he never looked back. He was, as the expression goes, gone in sixty seconds!"

Ronnie looked at her. "Stop it," he said. "You can't be serious. Were black helicopters hovering over the house?" Ronnie was immediately sorry for the sarcasm and for his tone. He knew his wife. She was serious.

"We were waiting for you to come home so we could go see if . . . if everything was okay. We knocked," Stacy said, "but no one answered." Stacy was supermodel material, came from money, and was very sweet, but she presented as just a bit slow on the uptake.

"Is my knock somehow going to work better than yours?" he asked. By their collective look, Ronnie surmised they apparently weren't thinking about him actually knocking. *Okay*, he thought, *let's go over and engage in a little neighborhood B and E.*

They walked across the cul-de-sac. Ronnie knocked anyway, but no one answered. He tried the knob. The front door of the Professor's house was unlocked. He looked at the three of them as if to ask, *Did you even try?* They stepped inside.

"Hello?" Jennie called out. No response. "Anyone home?"

Ronnie didn't know what to expect when they walked through the front door. He'd lived across the street from his neighbor for nearly a year and had never been invited inside the house or the garage or the Professor's backyard. Still, he wasn't prepared for what was in front of them.

Nothing. Zero. Every room in sight was completely empty.

The living room, kitchen, and dining room were all visible from the small vestibule and appeared exactly as they might have on the day Jordan moved in; there was no furniture, no light fixtures or ceiling fans, no TV. Nothing. Ronnie called out, but, as before, there was no answer.

There was some noise, like paper rustling, coming from one of the back bedrooms. They all heard it. They cautiously made their way down the hall, past a spotless bathroom and two equally empty bedrooms before arriving in front of what looked like a locked door at the end of the hallway. Ronnie knocked. Again, no response, but this definitely was the source of the rustling noise.

This door wasn't like any bedroom door Ronnie had seen. It was heavier, possibly some kind of composite, perhaps even reinforced steel. He tried the door. Surprise. It was locked.

"Why don't you three go outside and check the windows into this room. Let me know if you see anything inside," Ronnie said. "I'm going to look around for a key to this lock, and while I'm at it, I'll take a peek in the garage. Someone or something is in that room."

The women turned and left as one, looking at each other but saying nothing.

To Ronnie, weird didn't begin to describe the scene. Had his neighbor really known something was going to happen? Weirder yet, could Alberto possibly have been right?

Ronnie opened the door leading from the house to the garage. He discovered that, while it looked like an ordinary garage, there was no car inside, nor was there any evidence of one ever having been there. His eyes, searching the details as was his nature, took in a red Craftsman double-deck rolling tool chest, a steel work bench, a rusted Char-Broil grill, some garden hoses, two bright red gas cans, and that damn Snapper lawn mower. There were also a couple of bicycles, nice ones. On occasion, the Professor had been spotted pedaling around the neighborhood, oblivious to his surroundings with buds in his ears, either listening to something or talking or singing to himself.

He scanned the garage once more, then went back inside the house and pulled open the drawers in the kitchen. They were all empty.

He returned to the locked door and stared at it until the women came back. "You're not going to believe this," Jennie said. "There's aluminum foil on the insides of the windows. They're sealed tight and . . ." she hesitated. "The windows, at least those windows, don't appear to be made of glass."

"Not made of—Do I want to know how you know this?"

"Hallie tried to break one," Stacy said. Hallie offered a tight smile and lifted her eyebrows twice, Groucho-style.

"Hard plastic, the kind you'd find on an indoor racquetball court," she said. "Like Plexiglas. Unbreakable, is my guess."

Ronnie sighed and recounted his conversation with Jordan earlier that morning. Since everyone on the block suspected their neighbor's elevator maybe didn't quite reach the top floor, there was shoulder-shrugging and eye-rolling but not a lot of surprise.

"The last thing he told me was 'Look up, look down beneath,' and 'look for clues,'" he said.

"Maybe we should call the police," Stacy said.

Before Ronnie could tell them what Jordan had said about police, Hallie weighed in.

"Bullshit. We need to get inside that room. Someone or something is in there. We all heard it."

They were silently evaluating their options when, being the sharp-eyed investigative reporter he was, Ronnie caught a glimpse of something that should have been obvious; the door opened out, not in. He ran back to the garage, opened the massive tool chest, and grabbed a hard rubber mallet and a flat-head screwdriver. In less than a minute, he had the pins knocked out and the two parts of the hinges separated. He gently slid the door out and laid it against the wall to his left.

A hyperactive dog leaped out, momentarily scaring the devil out of all of them. This was a dog that clearly needed to get outside. It galloped into the empty family room, to the slider that opened to the back yard. The dog stopped dead and stared at it, breathing in that way dogs do that sounds like they might be hyperventilating. Hallie followed quickly behind and opened the slider. The dog ran out and immediately did her business.

Jennie, Stacy, and Ronnie stared into the room. Unlike the rest of the Professor's house, this room was definitely not empty.

Chapter 2

It was hard to imagine a more cramped and cluttered room. It was clear both man and dog lived together pretty much full time in this relatively small space It appeared that the Professor's and the dog's wants and needs were accounted for, except the taking-the-dog-outside part.

"What kind of friggin' tornado went through this place?" Hallie asked as she returned with the dog. Books and papers and who knows what else were strewn all over the floor. Clearly the room, as cops would say, had been "tossed."

Questions bounced around in Ronnie's head: *Who would have done it? Why would someone do it? When could it have happened? What were they looking for?*

Stacy took a step in, but Jennie grabbed her by the arm. "Wait! Don't touch anything."

A former ER nurse, Ronnie's wife was always prepared for any contingency. She reached in her pocket and extracted four pairs of blue latex gloves. "Put these on," she said. "For all we know, we may be entering a crime scene."

"Good thinking," Hallie said.

"Oh, right," Stacy said, earnestly. "I saw that on *CSI*."

"Let's all just wait one second," Ronnie said. "This is not our stuff, and we don't know what we're looking for. I know he told me not to call the police, but—"

"We don't need no stinkin' police," Hallie said. "Let's just look around and see what we see."

The dog walked across the room and found a place on the bed. It was part of a unit that took up most of the only wall in the room without either a window or a door. She curled up and watched them with casual interest. Directly overhead, a ceiling fan turned lazily.

"Well," said Stacy, "at least we know there's no wife or child involved." She looked lovingly at the dog. "I wonder what her name is."

After a moment, Ronnie said, "Lady?"

The dog's ears perked up. They all looked at her and then at Ronnie.

"He asked me to take care of 'his Lady' in case anything strange happened. I guess this qualifies as strange." He looked a question at Jennie. Before she had a chance to vote, Hallie stepped up.

"Look . . . I don't have kids, and I'm mostly stuck in the house," she said, referring to Ronnie and Jennie's nine-year-old daughter, and Stacy and Doug's work and travel schedules. "I'll take care of Lady. Besides, I'm not 100 percent sure, but she looks to me like she's a Basenji. They don't bark and won't disturb the neighbors."

Hallie scratched the beautiful brown-and-white dog behind her ears and on the top of her head.

"I think she likes you, Hallie," Ronnie said.

"Yeah. That's only because she doesn't know me yet," she said, smiling while still petting the dog.

"So, how do we make sense of all this mess?" Stacy asked.

"Jennie, remind us how it went down when he was taken," Ronnie said.

"Well, you know, I'm not sure it's even fair to say he was *taken*," she said. All eyes turned to her. As one, they questioned why they'd gone through this whole breaking and entering exercise.

"No, no, listen," she said. "I was bringing the garbage can back to the garage when the SUV pulled into his driveway and the two identically dressed guys I told you about walked to his door. As soon as they knocked, he opened the door. It was like he was waiting for them. He walked out and they talked for less than a minute. I couldn't make out what anyone was saying. He closed the front door—obviously, he didn't lock it—and they all walked to the SUV. I think it was a Suburban, or maybe a Tahoe—I know it was one of those—and it was black. They got in and drove off."

Ronnie processed Jennie's words through the lens of what he'd been told earlier that morning. "Clearly, he knew something was up. He left the front door open—for us, I believe—but this door was locked, the dog was inside, and the room had been trashed."

For a moment they all ruminated over what Ronnie had said. Hallie put into words what they all were probably thinking. "He did this himself," she said, waving her arm at the clutter. "But why would he do this and then go away and leave it—"

"For someone else to find?" Ronnie finished for her. He didn't have an answer. None of them did. Not yet.

Ronnie guessed that before Jordan had trashed the place it was well organized. The whole room was lined with bookcases, matching shelving units, file cabinets, and other office-type furnishings. It appeared the bed would fold up into the wall unit when not in use.

The bathroom suite was off to the right and contained a good-sized walk-in closet. Lady's bowls were on the floor of the closet. Just above, on a shelf, they saw the dog's food, leash and collar, and a few chew toys. Jordan had four or five changes of clothes. There were no suits, ties, or dress shirts. Instead, there were jeans, T-shirts, a couple of golf shirts, and a single pair of khaki slacks. Dockers. His lederhosen hung from a hook on the inside of the closet door. Underneath, there was a laundry hamper.

He'd created a pantry of sorts along a wall inside the closet, with cans of soup and other packaged food, a box of cereal, some cookies, some crackers, three boxes of granola and energy bars, and a couple cases of Ensure. Stacy found a utensil tray with four sets of stainless-steel knives, forks, and spoons.

Inside the bathroom, Ronnie saw a kind of field kitchen. It featured a small dorm fridge. Inside, they found a carton of fat-free milk, a half-pound of butter, and two six-packs of Diet Coke. A two-burner hot plate, with an empty saucepan on one burner and a small Teflon-coated fry pan on the other, occupied a low shelf that ran around the three walls of the closet. There was a stacked washer and dryer inside an adjacent linen closet. All but one of the upper shelves had been removed. The remaining shelf held about a half dozen towels and two identical sets of bed linens.

"What was he wearing?" Hallie asked.

"I don't remember what he had on his feet, but he was wearing jeans and a T-shirt," Jennie said. "I'm not 100 percent sure, but I think the shirt said, 'Drugs Suck.'"

"Anything else you can remember?" Ronnie asked. "Was he holding or carrying anything?"

"He wasn't," she said. "Not that I noticed."

Hallie removed her phone from her back pocket and started taking pictures of both rooms. "Jennie's right," she said. "At some point, this place could be viewed as a crime scene. If we're going to start rooting around, we need to know how it looked. That way, we can put everything back pretty much the way we found it."

Stacy sighed. "Listen, guys, I'm sorry, but I've got about thirty pounds of shrimp to clean, and only two hours to get it done. Maybe Doug's home and can help. Can you . . . ?"

"No problem, Stacy, but please, please, for now don't say anything to Doug about this," Ronnie said. "And try not to let anyone see you leave."

Stacy nodded and walked down the hall. She quietly opened the front door, peeked out, then stepped outside.

The curiosity that helped earn Ronnie his current employment started to kick in. *Why would anyone buy a three-bedroom, two-bath home, around 2,500 square feet of living space, and then cram everything he owned into one room? And then share that one room with a dog? Who is this guy? And what has he gotten himself into?*

Hallie started going through the books that were strewn all over the floor. Jennie carefully picked up and put back every individual piece of paper, pad, or writing tablet. Ronnie concentrated his efforts searching for a power cord or a storage battery, hoping maybe to find a laptop or a desktop computer or an external hard drive or some other piece of technology. If he could locate such a treasure trove, he knew who to call on to gain access to whatever secrets it held.

The three of them went on with their business quietly. Jennie came across a couple of pictures of Jordan with a young woman. She was, Ronnie thought, too young to have been a wife. She could have been the right age for an adult daughter, maybe college age, maybe older. One picture appeared to have been taken in some kind of a forest or jungle setting. Jennie carefully removed the photograph from its frame, but nothing was written on the back to indicate who it was or when or where it had been taken.

Most of the loose stuff appeared to be scratch papers with phone numbers and other scribbles that surely meant something to Jordan but didn't offer any insights for Ronnie, Jennie, or Hallie. Four identical notebooks contained pages and pages of handwritten prose. *Maybe he's working on a novel or some other kind of book.*

"He read good books," Hallie said. "These are classics—*Bleak House, The Count of Monte Cristo, Les Misérables, Leaves of Grass.* They've all been read, a lot." She held up the Dumas book. "This one's almost falling apart."

There were popular fiction books by Nelson De-Mille and Tom Clancy; music CDs, mostly jazz; a few DVDs of movies, boxed sets of *M*A*S*H*, and one of the *Law & Order* concepts.

"He has a few travel guides to some pretty exotic far-away places in Africa and South America," Jennie said. "Some political nonfiction, and it looks like a handful of *National Geographic* magazines." She reached under the bed.

The dog jumped off as the bed pivoted slowly upward, folding into an alcove within the line of shelves.

"All I did was bump this front leg thing here, and there it went," said Jennie, almost apologizing.

"Those things are cool," said Hallie. "But there's only room in the bed for one person."

As soon as the bed was in its storage position, Lady took up residence on a part of the green-and-ivory shag carpeting that covered the floor of the room, directly under where the bed previously sat.

Affixed to the underside of the Murphy bed were additional homemade storage compartments, all containing photo albums. All other investigatory efforts came to a halt as they began poring over photographs.

"I'll be right back," Hallie said. "I have an idea." She bolted through the front door before Ronnie could remind her to be circumspect. "Hallie" and "circumspect" were, in his mind, contradictory notions.

Jennie sat studying a photograph in one of the albums. "Come look at this, Ronnie," she said. "Is this him?"

It was indeed. They were looking at a much younger version of Jordan; he was in military fatigues, standing in front of a tent with what appeared to be another soldier. In another shot, three soldiers—none him, and none of them smiling—were sitting on the ground, smoking. They came across a good one of a stone-faced Jordan, alone, wearing fatigue pants and a white crew neck T-shirt. He was standing in front of a troop transport truck.

"It's definitely him," Ronnie said.

"Would that have been Vietnam?" she asked.

"I don't think he's that old, Jen," Ronnie said. "But it appears to be military, and it looks like someplace hot or at least warm. First Gulf War, maybe?"

They reviewed several similar pages of pictures from that stage of the Professor's life. Another album contained photos of a child in dozens of progressively maturing stages, from one of a pale-skinned baby girl to a graduation photo of an attractive, freckle-faced, red-haired, green-eyed young woman. The same young woman in the picture Jennie had discovered earlier.

Hallie bolted back into the room. "Jordan Censell!" she said. "I can't believe none of us did this sooner."

"Jordan's not here, and—" Ronnie said.

"The name of the owner of this house is Jordan *Censell*." She spelled Jordan's last name. "He bought it new from the builder just over a year ago," she said in that sing-song voice middle schoolers use when they know something you don't. "The rumor was true; he paid cash for it!"

"How could you possibly know that?" Jennie asked.

"No mortgage holder on the property appraiser's record," Ronnie said. Checking out someone's property record on the internet was a relatively simple and oft-used tool of his trade. Apparently, Hallie had figured this out as well. "Okay," Ronnie said. He stood, stretched, and stepped over some of the mess on the floor. "Let's see what we know. The Professor, excuse me, Jordan Censell, owns his home, free and clear. He's lived here for a little less than a year. He paid cash for the place. Until today, none of us knew his last name or that he had a dog. None of us had been inside his house. He was suspicious this morning about something that might happen today, and he asked me to take care of Lady. He either was taken by or voluntarily left with some muscle in a black Suburban. And he left his place in a shambles on purpose. He likely served in the military, and he has an adult daughter. Does that about cover it?"

"He also likes crossword puzzles, anagrams, and other word games," Jennie said, holding up a pair of paperback puzzle books.

"We need to let this all marinate a little," Hallie said. "Let's get out of here because the boil starts soon, and it would be front-page news here on Susie Q if we were seen exiting this place together without the man himself."

Utilizing Hallie's phone photography, they got things back to a point where the mess looked pretty much as it did when they first entered the room. They hadn't technically broken in because the front door had been left unlocked. But, if they ever needed to explain the locked bedroom door now leaning against an adjacent wall, well, that might prove a bit problematic. Ronnie quickly reattached the door to its jamb but left it unlocked and open.

Ronnie snapped a few images of the scene onto his own phone. He also took a visual inventory of the place and tried to commit as much as possible to memory. He couldn't find a computer, a printer, a modem, or any other piece of technology except for a nice thirty-two-inch LG flat-screen TV mounted to the wall. *He probably watched it from his bed*, Ronnie thought. He made a mental note to look inside and outside for cable wiring or any kind of internet connection when they returned.

The women walked out first. Ronnie turned off the overhead light. He thought he'd come back after dark since there wasn't much chance the light in the room would be seen from the outside through the aluminum foil on the windows. Then, remembering the ceiling fan was still on, he stepped back inside and reached up for the on-off cord. It had a fancy-looking pull attached to the chain. Upon closer inspection he saw it wasn't just a fancy pull.

It was a fancy flash drive.

Chapter 3

A sudden jolt woke Jordan in what were, for the moment, unfamiliar surroundings. He thought he heard a woman's voice.

"I'm sorry, sir, just some turbulence. We'll be through it pretty quickly. Please fasten your seat belt. It will pass shortly. Thank you."

So polite, he thought. As if he wanted to be seven miles up hurtling six hundred miles an hour inside a slim metal tube heading who knows where, all the while being bounced around like the last Cheerio in a bowl of milk.

"So, my dear," he asked, "which airport are we putting down at?"

She smiled and walked to the front of the Gulfstream, leaving his question hanging in the sweet-smelling air along with all his other disorganized thoughts. *Okay, so far so good. At least I'm not dead. Maybe I'm finally making progress.*

• • •

It had been two years since an insurance company agreed to pay six million dollars to settle the civil suit surrounding his wife's death. She'd been on an operating table in an Indianapolis hospital when the drunk with an MD after his name botched the delivery of anesthesia in what should have been a routine partial hysterectomy. He had finally been stripped of his license to practice medicine and ultimately took a plea on criminal charges. The medical director at the hospital took one for his team by choosing early retirement. Still, Leslie was gone, and no amount of money would bring her back. Jordan wasn't the litigious type, but he had been way beyond angry when the hospital refused to take responsibility.

Settlement in hand, he'd sold his property and disposed of most of his belongings, placing whatever he thought he might possibly want sometime in the future in a storage unit near the Indianapolis airport. He left Greencastle in a rented RV and traveled around the country for a year in an attempt to clear his head and try to make sense of things.

He visited Christy, his daughter, and the light of his life. At the time she'd been serving in the Peace Corps in Mali, an empty pocket of desolation in sub-Saharan Africa. She was part of what he affectionately referred to as the granola Birkenstock brigade: a gaggle of do-gooders assigned to find a reliable source of drinking water for about thirty thousand people living—or more appropriately, barely subsisting—near the southern edge of a forest bordering the Sahara Desert.

For a month, he worked at helping her and her band of brothers and sisters locate shallow wells. He tested samples to ensure the water was or could be made potable. Another group attempted to devise what to him were ridiculous contraptions designed to get whatever water was discovered out of the ground and delivered, as close as possible, to where it was needed.

During that time, he and Christy bonded as never before or certainly since the rock of both of their lives had been taken from them.

After Leslie died, Jordan had lost his balance. Then, Christy decided to chuck a fledgling but promising career practicing public interest law in Chicago to go and live in the middle of nowhere, where the simple act of taking a shower was viewed as on par with a Caribbean vacation.

For most of her time on the African continent, she and her team had been treated well and, against all odds, managed to feel safe. Her last correspondence from Mali included troubling news. Following some territorial dispute involving a large multinational corporation, the local provincial government suspended work on their water project. Days later, two members of her team—a man and a woman—were found savagely murdered, Christy believed, by a band of well-armed thugs from Mauritania.

Jordan had shot her a note begging her to come home, but she'd wanted to wait until the water project team was able to finish its work. *Thousands of lives*, she had written, *depended on it.*

Days after he learned about the deaths of her two colleagues, Christy sent her father an email announcing that without even requesting it, she was being transferred out of Mali. She had been reassigned by the Peace Corps to help create a microloan-based economic development platform in the South American nation of Paraguay. Jordan, then believing her to be safe, pulled the trigger on his earlier plan to resettle in Florida.

While finalizing the logistics of his relocation, his world once again spun out of control.

It wasn't unusual for Christy to be out of touch for a week, or sometimes even longer. When three weeks had passed without hearing from her, he reached out to her Peace Corps management in DC. After a day or two experiencing the federal government's well-known bureaucratic bounce from one paper pusher to another, he checked in with his local congressman's office. Three days after that, he got a troubling phone call.

According to someone on the Latin American desk at the State Department, Christy was reported two weeks earlier to have been "cozying up"—their words—to some people in the region who were protesting a large private investment project. Following a demonstration in Asunción, Christy had failed to return to her compound.

Her Peace Corps colleagues had attempted to locate her or at least find out what might have happened to her, but nothing surfaced. The guy on the Latin American desk assured him they'd continue seeking both information and contact, but also let him know they had no evidence or even reason to believe there was any foul play involved. It wasn't unusual, Jordan was told, for Peace Corps volunteers to leave the service and move on without reporting in with anyone. He'd been reminded that the Peace Corps wasn't the US military.

Jordan knew his daughter. He didn't think she would just up and leave, but if she did, even if she didn't tell anyone else, she'd definitely inform him.

The congressional district office had also made assurances to him, but time passed, and other pressing priorities pushed the disappearance of a Peace Corps volunteer down on their list. During that period of time, he'd completed his move to Florida and had made his daughter's disappearance his new life's work.

It had been ten months since Christy dropped off the face of the earth.

• • •

The men who had picked Jordan up at his house had been polite, respectful even, but didn't answer a single question. He believed he knew who their employer was and felt if he wanted information about Christy, he didn't really have a choice about whether or not he should go along with them.

They didn't know, of course, but going along with them was exactly what he'd wanted in the first place. Before they'd driven away, he'd caught the eye of Ronnie Levitt's wife, Jennie, as she pulled her dark-green Astoria Woods–authorized community refuse container back inside her garage. He believed—he hoped that moment of recognition, along with his earlier conversation with Ronnie, would lead them to wonder what might have happened. If so, he was confident Ronnie's finely tuned professional curiosity would take over. Jordan believed he was a pretty good judge of people.

The flight attendant returned to tell him they were approaching their destination and would he please stay seated and keep his seat belt fastened. "We'll be on the ground in approximately fifteen minutes, sir," she said.

"What time is it, please?" he asked her.

She hesitated before answering. "Well, I guess it's all right to tell you." She looked at her wristwatch. "It's nearly 8:05 p.m.," she said, adding, "central daylight time."

He'd been gone from his home for nearly six hours.

. . .

Jordan's move to Central Florida was originally designed to resemble an active retirement. It would include some travel, or maybe a return to school to get that MFA he'd always wanted. He'd even given some thought to writing a book about his ordeal following Leslie's death, focusing on the trial and on his dealings and interactions with insurance companies, lawyers, drunk physicians, and healthcare administrators.

Christy's disappearance, his frustration at contending with bureaucrats and other government weenies, and his sense of helplessness at not being able to do anything about her circumstances had led to the pivot point that found him where he was today.

First, a healthcare institution had failed, and his wife had ended up dead. Now his daughter was missing, and he was once again an angry and motivated man. This time the institutions of government, which he believed from personal experience should have been trustworthy and helpful, were of absolutely no use.

Before he left Indiana, and because he really didn't have any idea where his search for the truth might lead, he made an impulsive decision to leave his past behind completely. He put his household goods into a storage locker and paid for a year in advance. He turned his financial resources into cash and other easily convertible assets. He methodically distanced himself from friends and colleagues. With the help of the internet and a book he picked up at an independent bookstore, he created a new identity for himself. Over time, and with the help of a former work colleague, he obtained a Social Security number, two credit cards, a driver's license, a new banking relationship, and even a voter registration card. At the time, he'd promised himself he would never tell anyone how easy it was to do all of that.

There was no practical reason for him to do it, other than to insulate his prior life, the memory of his wife, and his relationship with his daughter from any deeds or misdeeds in which he might engage while resolving Christy's disappearance.

He viewed it all in simple terms: he would do whatever he needed to do, and he would leave the consequences of his actions for later consideration.

• • •

The Gulfstream touched down, a perfect landing by the crew up front. Then one of the gents who'd visited him earlier in Florida invited him to deplane.

"Still not telling me where we are or where we're going?" he asked.

The young man smiled. "You'll know soon enough, sir."

They descended the staircase. He immediately noticed the temperature was a lot cooler than when they'd left Orlando. In addition to being early evening, it was also way north, but then most of the rest of the country was way north of Central Florida.

He was given a windbreaker to wear over his T-shirt. As he got into yet another black SUV, he wondered for the first time that day where he might be sleeping that night, and when, or even if, he would ever return home.

He assumed he was where he needed to be because he'd managed to get the attention of someone he believed knew something about or was even directly involved in Christy's disappearance.

To Nelson J. Calder, now identified as Jordan Censell, finding Christy was the only thing that mattered in his entire world.

• • •

This room is fucking freezing, Jordan thought.

The office in which he found himself was spare, just a few pieces of modern furniture and what looked like two Rothko prints. He sat in a white leather captain's chair in front of a clean glass-topped desk. There was a phone, a laptop computer, a single leather coaster, and a single blue file. He consciously tried not to twiddle his thumbs. After what felt to him like several minutes, Jordan concluded he was being left cool his heels.

"Mr. Censell, thank you so much for coming to Minneapolis today." Someone moved from somewhere else in the oversized office and seated himself behind the desk. Jordan hadn't heard anyone enter the room.

"I had a choice?"

"Life is all about choices, Mr. Censell," said the smiling, splendidly dressed, dark-haired, dark-complexioned man now seated before him. "In fact, that's what your journey here is all about, I believe: choices." The man held onto his smile, showing a row of large, perfectly aligned, perfectly white teeth. "I'm Michael Capshaw, senior vice president of external affairs here at Dommerich North America."

Jordan nodded. He was exactly where he'd hoped to be. He had, over the past year, done everything he believed possible to get the attention of people in the hierarchy of the Munich-based chemical, pharmaceutical, and pesticide behemoth. The company produced everything from food additives and pills claiming to resolve symptoms of psychological disorders in children to liquid-, granular-, and dust-style products that kill termites, insects, and rodents. As his T-shirt so indelicately proclaimed, Jordan believed many of those products also killed or injured all kinds of other living things for which they probably weren't intended, including human beings. As best he could, he peeled away layer after layer of hard, fact-based knowledge, along with rumor, innuendo, suggestion, and wild-ass guesswork. Jordan now believed beyond any doubt that Dommerich was involved up to its avaricious neck in his daughter's disappearance, and maybe a whole lot more.

"I trust your trip was comfortable," said Capshaw.

"For a kidnapping, I suppose it was," Jordan said, just to see what kind of response the word got him. It got him a head shake and a snarky smile.

"Mr. Censell, you could have either refused to answer or closed the door of your house on"—he looked inside the blue file folder—"Susie Q Court. You could have gotten out of your ride at any traffic light or stop sign on the way to the airport. You could have decided not to board the ten-thousand-dollar-an-hour jet that brought you here to Minneapolis, or you could have left this building at any time since you arrived. I believe you know all that. It appears you wanted to visit with us as much as, if not more than, we wanted to visit with you. Now isn't that the truth?"

Jordan stared at Michael Capshaw.

"Oh, by the way," Capshaw said. "Interesting T-shirt you're wearing. Is it intended to be purposely provocative? Or just in bad taste?"

Jordan looked down, as if he didn't know what he'd worn on his trip. He smiled and spread his palms. "Just something I grabbed when I got out of the shower this morning," he said.

"It's beneath you, I believe."

Jordan leaned in. "Mr. Capshaw, what have you done with or to Christy Calder? Answer me that one simple question and this will have been worthwhile, perhaps for both of us."

Capshaw maintained eye contact while shaking his head from side to side. "As I—and, as I've come to understand things, several of my colleagues—have attempted on numerous occasions to convey to you, Mr. Censell, not only have we not done anything to or with Miss Calder, but I also don't have any idea who Christy Calder is, other than your claim that she's your daughter and that she's missing and that Dommerich is somehow involved."

"So, we're still in the same place today we've been in for the past several months, Mr. Capshaw? Is that also the truth?"

Capshaw leaned forward also. "I can't and won't manufacture information simply to feed your mistaken beliefs, Mr. Censell. Dommerich is a wealthy, multifaceted global conglomerate with a market capitalization of nearly sixty-five billion dollars. We have fifty-five thousand employees and contractors; forty-two hundred patents; and a competitive, if not dominant market position in every segment in which we operate. We simply don't engage in the kind of behavior you continue to suggest. We don't have to! I am sorry that your daughter is missing, but Dommerich has had absolutely nothing to do with that, and I believe some of the things you've been saying and doing in furtherance of your obsession regarding our alleged role in this matter are both slanderous and threatening." He paused for effect and leaned back. "I would like nothing better than to put a stop to it once and for all, here and now. Everyone in the world knows it's difficult to prove a negative. I promise you, sir, if

I had something to tell you on this subject, I would, just so we could both move on."

Jordan sat, processing Capshaw's words, willing his face into a stoic mask. He ticked off in his mind the coincidences he was being asked to ignore by someone he viewed as a smarmy asshole in a very expensive suit. When Christy had been in Mali, Dommerich had been in Mali. Within days of the murder of two of her Peace Corps colleagues, Christy had been unceremoniously transferred to Asunción in Paraguay. Dommerich had been in Asunción. Within weeks of her arrival there, Christy disappeared. If Michael Capshaw truly had no idea what happened, he and his company were either terribly uninformed or woefully unlucky. Jordan smiled at Dommerich's senior vice president for external affairs.

"Mr. Capshaw, when you boil it all down, you're a PR guy, so manufacturing information is what you do. I get that, and I believe that you believe some of the garbage you just unloaded. Here's what I know—not what I suspect, surmise, or guess—but what I know to be absolutely the unvarnished truth: Dommerich is everything you said it is and more. Right now,"—Jordan made a show of looking at his wrist, even though they'd taken his watch and his phone when he'd boarded the plane—"it's in a race to get a dandruff shampoo called SaniScal to market. It's a foray by Dommerich into a new business space, involving prescription health and beauty formulations, like shampoos, lotions, and creams, as well as nutrition and dietary supplements. It's a brand-new, multibillion-dollar segment ripe for a flashy new entry. Now, the FDA is skittish because field tests—at least one that I know about—have been, let's just say, inconsistent. Wall Street isn't in a very happy place over this move, either."

Capshaw sat back in his chair, crossed his arms in front of his chest, and sighed. He started to speak but was shut down when Jordan launched into the second chapter of his diatribe.

"Add to that the fact that a large and growing number of the good people of west central Paraguay don't particularly care to have twenty-thousand-plus acres of their pristine jungle destroyed just so you can send in crews to scrape bark from a tree to be used in the manufacture of, let me see . . . What's it called? Oh, right, Veracozen, a new pesticide you're waiting on the EPA to approve. Now, my daughter relocated to Paraguay precisely ten months and seventeen days ago. Just over three weeks after she arrived, she went missing from the nation's capital following an event that occurred near the presidential palace. A few locals—no, it was over a thousand locals—had come together to protest Dommerich's plan to wipe the forest clean. The nearly simultaneous timing of those occurrences, along with a couple of interesting and decidedly unpleasant events that took place in southwestern Mali two months prior . . . it's all just very interesting to me, in terms of timing, Mr. Capshaw."

Capshaw rose from his chair and turned to gaze out at the Minneapolis skyline from the window of his twenty-seventh-floor office. He was, in Jordan's mind, obviously straining to keep from vaulting across his desk and strangling his guest, who was silently praying he'd try to do just that. Jordan was in the best shape of his life and would have liked nothing better than to hurl Michael Capshaw through the floor-to-ceiling window behind his desk just to see what new Rorschach design he would create on the chilly Minneapolis sidewalk below.

"You don't have to say a word, Mr. Capshaw. Any idiot hearing this conversation would know that you're full of shit, and I'm full of verifiable information. Information, by the way, that came from highly reliable sources of mine and that has already been transmitted to leadership of both the FDA and the EPA. In case you're interested, my next step is—"

Capshaw turned and held up a hand. "Your next step may very well be down a deep, dark legal hole from which you might never again see the light of day, Mr. Censell. I don't know what you think you know or what nonsense and misinformation you've cobbled together from who knows where and shared with our friends at the FDA and EPA. And yes, they are our friends. I also don't know if you realize both the folly of what it is you are suggesting and the . . ." Capshaw paused, seeming to choose his words carefully, "the highly negative ramifications that may result from your misplaced anger and actions."

Jordan had gotten the exact reaction he'd expected. Capshaw was, in Jordan's estimation, a possibly off-the-reservation functionary, a wildcard in the enormous profit machine that was Dommerich. But he also knew things would probably get worse, maybe even much worse, for him and for Christy before he'd get where he needed to be. He stood so as to be on equal footing with Michael Capshaw.

"And I'm here, having been brought in this manner, because you and your masters aren't just a wee bit worried that I'm about to upset your whole nasty little cart of apples?" asked Jordan. "Maybe I should just take you up on your previous offer." Jordan turned and moved toward the closed door. Two young, strapping security types, eerily similar to those who'd picked him up that morning, appeared from beyond Jordan's line of sight and placed themselves in front of him, blocking his departure.

"Ah, as I suspected." Jordan said, turning back to Capshaw. "Exactly how many people is Dommerich going to disappear because of its greedy misadventures, first in Mali and now in South America and then who even knows where else?"

"You'd be well advised, Mr. Censell, to carefully consider any further misstatements and misadventures of your own. Dommerich will do whatever is necessary to protect its brand, its investments, and its interests.

"I think we're done for tonight. Gerald," he said to one of the guards, "please take Mr. Censell to his accommodations. Mr. Censell let's pick up this conversation in the morning if it's necessary to do so. Good night, sir."

Jordan stood. He offered his host a small bow. "And to you, Mr. Capshaw."

Chapter 4

On Saturday afternoon, the third annual Susie Q Court shrimp boil went off without a hitch. Twelve of the thirteen homes in the cul-de-sac were represented, along with friends, relatives, and a few nearby neighborhood freeloaders. Not even one of the nearly six hundred shrimp Stacy had meticulously cleaned with her own delicate, professionally manicured hands, along with a boatload of Jennie's world-famous conch fritters, and about five gallons of Publix coleslaw escaped consumption. Jennie, Hallie, and Ronnie casually fended off inquiries from Mikey and Alberto regarding the Professor's absence. They simply shrugged their shoulders and shook their heads.

"I bet he's doing some research for a new book," said Mikey. "You know, he disappears for weeks at a time, sometimes."

"Probably laundering money somewhere or capping some rival crime family lieutenant," said Alberto. "I'm telling you; this guy is serious bad news."

Hallie couldn't stay still. She wanted to get back inside Jordan's house and see what else they could uncover. Ronnie wanted to get his hands on that flash drive but knew he may need to enlist assistance just in case the data was encrypted or otherwise protected from being seen by the wrong people.

"Well," Stacy said to the few hearty souls still milling around, "I'm going to clean up and get some sleep. I just found out I need to fly to Phoenix on Monday."

Jennie gave Stacy a hug and assured her that the boil was a smashing success due to her hard work and Doug's excellent secret Louisiana spice recipe.

"I'm heading inside also, guys," Hallie said, stifling a really badly executed fake yawn. "Still got about a hundred-plus pages of a high school biology book to clean up before Monday." She made eye contact with Ronnie and mouthed, "Call me," adding the thumb-and-pinky gesture as she walked to her front door.

Alberto and Mikey said their respective good nights and headed home as well.

. . .

While he waited for Hallie's call, Ronnie considered the path that had taken him to who and where he was today.

He'd made up his mind to become a newspaper reporter when he was nine years old, after seeing his first Superman movie.

When he finished Edgewater High School in

Orlando's College Park neighborhood, his family could only afford to send him to Valencia Community College. His goal there was to make it impossible for top journalism schools to turn him down. Ronnie took every writing, media, journalism, government, criminal justice, and US history course he could. When he'd finished, he'd amassed over eighty credit hours, twenty more than necessary, and had collected several awards for work on *Valencia Voice*, the huge community college's digital media outlet.

He was accepted as a transfer student at Columbia University. By the time he'd graduated—as he often said, on the three-year plan, because he had to work to support himself in New York City—he'd obtained magna cum laude status, nearly eighty thousand dollars in student loan debt, and an entry-level job at his hometown newspaper, the *Orlando Chronicle*.

While working the crime, cops, and courts beat, Ronnie met Jennifer Kaplan, an ER nurse at Orlando's Florida Hospital. He was attempting to persuade Nurse Kaplan to allow him access to a crime victim in order to get her first-person account of a brutal home invasion. He didn't get the interview, but he was able to convince the nurse to have coffee with him. They'd been married for thirteen years and had a nine-year-old daughter, Kimberly.

Six years ago, he'd moved from the CCC beat to a suburban bureau, where he covered one of Orlando's adjacent county governments. While collecting information for another piece he'd been working on, he caught wind of what, on the surface, seemed to be a pattern of arbitrarily scattered development applications. They were all beyond urban service boundary lines and had been approved by planning and zoning officials and county commissioners over the course of the eight previous years. The votes were always close and always involved the same governmental players and the same group of developers, planners, transportation engineers, landscape architects, and development lawyers.

It had taken Ronnie two years and hundreds of hours poring over documents and interviewing current and former government officials and development consultants before he'd amassed sufficient, inescapable evidence of what he and his editor believed constituted a criminal conspiracy. His story had won local, regional, and national accolades and led to the newspaper's first Pulitzer Prize for investigative reporting on the local level. It had also cost several public sector employees their jobs, resulted in more than a dozen criminal indictments for bribery and corruption, and led to changes on both the county and state levels regarding the process for evaluating applications for development.

Two years after the prize had been awarded, in the face of more than a dozen offers for Ronnie to move to various major-market dailies, he was given a nice raise, along with freedom by his editors and the publisher at the *Chronicle* to pursue stories that piqued his interest and were worth the investment of his energies.

While he didn't expect it to take two years of his life, as it had for him to wrap up what came to be known as the Scarlet Lake development affair, his Susie Q Court neighbor's odd disappearance had, without question, piqued his interest.

Jennie put Kimmie to sleep and joined Ronnie on the sofa for a moment of quiet and a glass of wine. He was dialing Hallie's number on his mobile phone when he heard a light, persistent tap on the front door. Jennie let Hallie in.

"We need to get back over there," she said. "I have a bad feeling about this whole thing. It's clear, at least to me, he's not coming back tonight, and I want to get Lady out of there and over to my house, and—"

"There's a flash drive hanging from the ceiling fan in the bedroom," Ronnie said.

"Didn't he tell you to 'look up, look down'?" Jennie said. "The more we get into this the more I think we need to call the police. Ronnie, you must have someone there you can trust, don't you?"

Hallie started to jump in, but Ronnie cut her off. "He also told me, emphatically, no police, under any circumstances, and for now I think we need to respect that. We have no evidence at all that any kind of crime has been committed."

"Abso-friggin-lutely," said Hallie. "Local cops come in and who knows what happens. I think we need to know a whole lot more about Mr. Jordan Censell and what his deal is before we let Orlando's finest mess things up."

Ronnie thought for a moment, then said, "I need to borrow Kimmie's laptop."

"Take ours," Jennie said. "It's much newer and has a zillion more features than Kimmie's old Dell."

"You're right, of course. Our Mac is definitely more machine than Kimmie's," he said, "but Kimmie's is a PC, and most of the world still uses PCs. I need to get a peek at what's on that flash drive and I just want to make sure there are no viruses or translation problems."

He tiptoed into his daughter's room, carefully disconnected her laptop from the wall and returned to Jennie and Hallie.

"Something Mikey said tonight, about the Professor sometimes disappearing for weeks at a time," Ronnie said. "He's right about that, isn't he?"

"I'm not sure, but if he is right, I wonder what he did with the dog on those occasions," said Hallie.

"There are a number of pet boarding places in the area," Ronnie said. But that left them with the question of why he'd enlisted a neighbor to care for Lady this time. Maybe this time the Professor wasn't sure whether he'd actually go anywhere or when he'd return.

Jennie got up and started pacing. "I seem to recall him not being around for a while some time ago, because his garbage can stayed at the curb for a long time," she said. "It was when landscapers were putting in those azaleas in front of his house."

"I wonder where he was," said Hallie.

"Maybe," Ronnie said, "the answer to that question can be found among those travel guides and *National Geographic* magazines we found."

"And that's why you're Mr. Crusading Reporter," Hallie said, punching him in the arm.

"Right now, I'm just like you, a curious neighbor with no idea what kind of mess he's walking into."

Jennie stayed home with Kimmie even though she was old enough to be by herself. Ronnie and Hallie would take the brief walk on the wild other side of Susie Q Court by themselves.

"Just be careful over there," she said, kissing Ronnie on the cheek. "And don't forget to wear your gloves."

• • •

After making sure the coast was clear, Ronnie and Hallie left Ronnie's house and walked slowly in different directions before ending up together at the front door of Jordan's home.

"Why do you think he's living all in one room?" Hallie asked, standing in the doorway to the master bedroom suite that had been converted, for all intents and purposes, into a tiny one-room apartment. "That's not a rhetorical question."

"I honestly don't have a clue, Hallie," Ronnie said. "Maybe . . . I just don't know."

"What were you going to say?"

They eased inside, carefully stepping around the restored piles and messes that constituted the original scene. "Maybe he lived in a small space before and just feels more comfortable," he said.

"What . . . like a prison cell?" she asked with a smirk.

"I don't know. It's weird."

"True that, my friend. So, what now?"

Lady was curled up on the floor exactly where they'd left her earlier. Hallie moved closer, kneeled, and started dog whispering. Ronnie carefully removed the flash drive dangling from the ceiling fan pull.

"I'm going to look at the contents of this thing," he said. "It must mean something. He went out of his way to tell me to look up, look down, and this was up."

After disconnecting the flash drive Ronnie noticed it was an old version and not very robust, containing only 256 megabytes, although it could still have a lot of data on it. He plugged it into Kimmie's old Dell laptop.

Exactly one folder showed up on the desktop. Inside, there was a single AVI file.

"Well, if we were expecting answers . . ." Hallie said.

"Let's not prejudge," Ronnie said. "A single file could be really significant, if it contains the right information."

"What type of file is it?" Hallie asked.

"A video, I think," he said.

He clicked on the file. Their enigmatic neighbor appeared, talking right to them. "Since I don't know who is seeing this, I must be circumspect. By now I am likely not in Florida, unreachable, and perhaps in some danger. This is not paranoia. This is fact.

"Elsewhere in my office, which is where you are likely watching this, you will find additional information relating to some very important questions I am seeking the answers to.

"I know you have questions. Who is he? Where is he? Why is he living like this? None of that is as important as the simple fact that at least one life is at stake—and perhaps more lives will be at stake if I don't get answers of my own to these very important questions.

"I have no way to communicate right now, and truly, I'm not even sure if I am still alive. I know that sounds dramatic and mysterious, but as you become more resourceful and more aware of exactly what's happening, you'll understand. And perhaps, you'll even be able to help, if you're so inclined.

"I really hope that someone will take care of Lady. She's the best friend—the only real friend—I have in my life right now, and she's a wonderful companion. She's not a lot of work, and a little love and attention goes a long way with her.

"Look at her. Watch her. Look closely at where she was when you first found her. Look for clues. They're here. They won't tell you everything because I don't know everything yet. But they'll help you at least to begin to investigate, along with me.

"I hope . . . I pray that whoever you are, you're able and willing to assist me in finding the truth that's so important to me and perhaps to others. Be vigilant. Be resourceful. Most importantly, be careful."

Hallie and Ronnie looked at one another. They watched the video again and then again. Ronnie searched to see if there was anything else on the drive. It was empty, save for the cryptic message left by their neighbor.

"I have no friggin' idea what any of that means," Hallie said. "Do you?" She was almost accusing in her tone.

"Well," Ronnie said, "I think it's safe to say that the guy in that video is communicating in a markedly different manner than the guy we've seen puttering around on Susie Q."

"Yeah, I guess," Hallie said, "but he's still not making a whole lot of sense."

Ronnie found himself staring at the blank screen on Kimmie's computer. He was considering how much he wanted to share with Hallie. He liked her; she was smart, and she was funny, but what did he really know about her? Not a whole hell of a lot.

"He doesn't even know if he's still alive," Ronnie said. "Jennie said he wasn't taken by force, but this sounds like at least he knew he was going to see someone who had the means and possibly the motivation to place him in significant danger."

"I'm going to go through these photographs to see if anything jumps out," Hallie said. She assumed a lotus position on the floor and, with Lady's head comfortably in her lap, started turning pages.

Ronnie returned to the four notebooks filled with precisely formed penmanship to search for order amid the growing sense of chaos he was feeling. First, he determined he had all the notebooks, and there were no other significant repositories of information or data. The room's disarray made that conclusion uncertain. If nothing else, Ronnie was accustomed to wading through bunches of otherwise irrelevant data and arcane material before locating the nugget necessary to move him closer to the answers he sought.

This tenacity served him well. He'd moved into the investigative reporting slot at the *Orlando Chronicle* following the retirement of the paper's only two-time Pulitzer nominee. In the four ensuing years, Ronnie had earned two nominations of his own, and he owned his home outright thanks to the bonus he'd been awarded following the paper's win three years ago.

Every now and then, while he was reading, Hallie would show him a picture that, for one reason or another, interested her. She'd found two entire albums of what they both believed were family pictures. They included Jordan, the daughter, and what must have been his wife or, at the very least, the mother of the young woman. The similarities in terms of facial features, hair color, and body type were as close to conclusive as anything in this whole strange affair. Jordan, this woman, and the younger woman were a family. After viewing several pages in the album, the older woman, literally, ceased being in the picture. The rest were all of Jordan and the younger woman.

One picture Hallie zeroed in on showed the girl—she was probably of high school or early college age at the time—in the uniform of a server, perhaps in a Mexican restaurant based on the outfit she was wearing. There was a nametag on her uniform that they both tried to decipher in hopes of getting at least a first name.

Ronnie pulled open drawers one at a time until he found a pair of glasses, perhaps Jordan's readers, and tried to manipulate them over the photograph. Hallie took them and placed them on her face.

"Christy!" she said. "Her name is Christy. Christy Censell."

"Already this night is a success, I guess," he said, yawning. "Let's close up shop and come back tomorrow when we're rested."

"I'm not tired," Hallie said. "I want to go through more of these photographs and see if there's anything else that gives us any insights. You go get some sleep. I'll take the dog home with me when I'm done."

Ronnie wasn't totally comfortable leaving Hallie alone in the room. He understood he had no leverage to tell her not to stay, or any reason to, for that matter. Even though she was the newest member of their little cul-de-sac family, Hallie Garard had become a part of the neighborhood in a hurry, and everyone seemed to like her except Alberto. *He probably thinks she's a narc or a vampire*, Ronnie thought. Now that he thought of it, Ronnie guessed Alberto really didn't much like anyone unconventional. *Must be part of having been a cop*, he thought. Hallie was kind of in your face but in a friendly way, and she didn't take crap from anyone, including Alberto. She'd moved in about six months earlier, a few months after Jordan. No kids or pets, worked from home as a freelance textbook editor, she'd said. She'd kept pretty much to herself and didn't push herself onto anyone else, at least not onto Ronnie, Jennie, and Kimmie. Probably, next to himself, she was the neighbor Jordan seemed to get along with best. *Maybe because she's single?*

"Okay," Ronnie said. "Just make sure you . . . you know."

She smiled up at him. "I'm an adult, Ronnie. I know how to turn off lights, close doors, and slink off into the night, all the way across to my own house, even with a sweet, quiet dog in tow. Go get some sleep."

Chapter 5

They'd taken Jordan's phone, wallet, and keys before putting him on the plane earlier that day. They'd snapped a photograph of him. He had no idea why. They also took his iPod, ear buds, and his wristwatch. Even though he manipulated things to get in front of someone from Dommerich, all of this reinforced the obvious conclusion that his trip to Minneapolis was neither entirely voluntary nor necessarily over.

It had only been a day and a half since he'd received the invitation to visit with a Dommerich executive. But here he was, late on a Saturday night, in a suite of rooms inside a complex of town homes somewhere within the Twin Cities metropolitan area.

When he learned he'd be picked up and brought to meet with people who would allay his concerns about Dommerich's possible involvement in Christy's disappearance, he thought they'd meet in Orlando. Now, in hindsight, there was really no basis for him to have had that assumption.

Why have they brought me here, he wondered, *only to continue to deny any role in this? And what do they have planned for me?*

. . .

Michael Capshaw crossed the nearly empty row of offices on the executive level and knocked on his boss's door. As was typical, Nathan Becker, president, and CEO of Dommerich North America, was still at work and on his phone. He waved Michael inside and finished up his conversation with Dommerich's regional manager for the western United States.

It had been less than half an hour since Michael had the man they knew as Jordan Censell secured in a residence that Dommerich kept for visiting customers and the occasional government bureaucrat or member of Congress. In Capshaw's estimation, Censell only knew what was, if not technically public knowledge, then information relatively easy to obtain. Although he did demonstrate some level of awareness regarding Dommerich's recent troubles, both in Mali and in Paraguay, which, Michael had to admit, constituted closely held information.

"How does he know about Veracozen?" Becker asked. "Specifically, I mean. That name is only known to the working group inside Dommerich and to very few inside the EPA. Hell, registration of that name is still pending."

"I guess it's interesting he knows the name, but it's not material to anything involving his daughter or the negotiations going on with the Paraguayan government for access to the forest," said Capshaw. "And just so you're in the loop on these things, Nathan, the girl is safe and is living under our control. That's how you want it, isn't that right?"

Becker raised an eyebrow. "Nothing's changed that I'm aware of, Michael," he said. "But she's not our current concern. Mr. Censell needs to be reined in, and we need the EPA's blessing on Veracozen and FDA approval on SaniScal before our next quarterly call. Wall Street doesn't like uncertainty, and we don't need some punk analyst straight out of Wharton deciding what our profit picture is or should look like."

Or some obsessive parent desperately concerned about a missing daughter and who might do something screwy, Capshaw thought. He had given the matter some thought and decided to put his plan on the table for his boss.

"I know it's got some small potential downside, Nathan, but I wonder what you think about a nice family reunion slash vacation down in South America for Mr. Censell," he said, standing at the window of his office, looking down at the lights and motion of a summer Saturday evening in Minneapolis. "It will get Mr. Censell out of the way for however long we require for Dommerich to receive these approvals, and it should serve to calm his fears or concerns about his daughter's well-being." He hesitated, and then added, "Frankly, it sounds like a win-win to me."

"That's an interesting, even intriguing, suggestion, Michael," Becker said. "I need some time to process it. It's too early over there for me to call Munich, but I'm going to run this by the chief as soon as I know he's awake. Meanwhile, make sure Mr. Censell is secure and, at least for the moment, reasonably comfortable. If we decide to do this, we should do it sooner rather than later. Make sure the plane and the crew are ready."

• • •

Michael Capshaw had been born Michael Antonucci, the only child of Teresa and Michael "Big Mike" Antonucci. His parents called him Milo. His father had been a lieutenant in the notorious Patterino crime family operating out of St. Louis, Missouri. His mother had owned a pastry shop in the Italian neighborhood St. Louis natives called "the Hill."

When he was a boy, his parents had taken him on trips to Italy at least four times each year until his father's bullet-ridden body was discovered in a burned-out car. Milo was fourteen years old and ready to begin high school when that happened. Following her husband's funeral, Terry Antonucci and her son relocated to Milford, Pennsylvania, a small town in the Pocono Mountains, where she had family.

He attended Delaware Valley High School. At seventeen, he was arrested for possession of marijuana. He pleaded no contest and received thirty days of community service. At eighteen, and with no additional issues, his record in Pennsylvania was expunged.

He went to college at Lehigh University in Bethlehem, where he barely scratched out a BA in finance. While at Lehigh, Michael demonstrated a growing disdain for almost any kind of supervision. He also continued to enjoy the attention of local law enforcement.

He was charged with possession of jewelry stolen from a girl he'd dated for a while. She reported him, but without empirical evidence, he managed to evade both prosecution and responsibility.

He also pushed the boundaries of acceptable behavior by facing and then escaping charges of plagiarism for an upper-level term paper. He was caught with marijuana in his automobile but bribed a campus security officer before a report could be filed.

While Michael could never honestly say he felt any deep affection for his father, he had learned lessons from him that were endemic to organizations engaged in questionable or even criminal behavior. He came to understand that laws and rules were for civilians, not for those who grew up in a culture that rewarded getting things done, whatever it was, by whatever means necessary.

He charmed his way into a job right out of school

as a securities analyst with a focus on the pharmaceutical sector with Chadwick and Dillon, a respected investment bank operating in Philadelphia.

As he gained experience and was promoted at C&D, he made the acquaintance of people associated with Dommerich Worldwide. One of those, Nathan Becker, took an interest in the gregarious young analyst. Two years later, Michael was twenty-five years old, unattached, ambitious, and growing restless in Philadelphia. He reached out to Becker, who offered him a position in external affairs if he would relocate to Minneapolis.

Earlier, when he was about to graduate from high school, his mother had met and married attorney Charlie Capshaw, who, following Michael's high school graduation, moved the family to New Brunswick, New Jersey. Before uprooting herself and Michael, Teresa had insisted Charles adopt her son and give Michael his name. She didn't want him carrying the baggage associated with his father's tarnished reputation for the remainder of his life or even through college.

Michael Capshaw, in addition to full documentation in his new name, also held on to his passport, Social Security number, driver's license, and birth certificate in the name of Michael Antonucci. He'd updated the passport, driver's license, and the Visa credit card he'd secured while he was in college whenever each neared expiration. He was never certain as to why, but he thought having a second identity to fall back on couldn't possibly be a bad thing.

. . .

Hallie watched through the front door peephole of Jordan's house as Ronnie nonchalantly walked around the cul-de-sac and through the front door of his own house across the street. After he was safely inside, Hallie pulled a mobile phone from her back pocket and punched a single number. She walked back inside Jordan's bedroom.

"Macaluso 629," a voice said at the other end.

"Secure transmission, please. Garard 11235."

There was a pause of approximately ten seconds.

"Secure, 11235. How's it going, Hallie?"

"Curiouser and curiouser down this rabbit hole, Tommy. Are we rolling yet?"

"We. Are. Rolling."

"FBI Special Agent Hallie Garard, voiceprint identification 11235. Interagency Task Force, action file delta hyphen Nancy hyphen Charlie, Orlando 32812."

Hallie Garard's job with the FBI had her investigating alleged criminal activity impacting multiple, meaning two or more, US government agencies that didn't maintain their own robust criminal investigative capabilities. This focused on allegations made by a single individual, code name Arrow. That individual, Jordan Censell, formerly Nelson J. Calder, had contacted both the US Environmental Protection Agency and the US Food and Drug Administration. Mr. Calder alleged, among other crimes, the kidnapping of his daughter, either directly by Dommerich

Worldwide or by agents in service of Dommerich. On his own, Arrow had learned that Dommerich was on a fast track toward obtaining FDA approval on a new prescription pharmaceutical named SaniScal. SaniScal's active ingredient came in part from the flowers and leaves of the *Grewia villosa*, a shrub-like plant indigenous to certain parts of western North Africa. At the same time, the EPA was in the final stages of testing Veracozen, a potentially game-changing pesticide made from the bark of Verawood, a subspecies of a tree found, to date, only in the forest region of, and adjacent to, northwestern Paraguay.

A common thread inside both applications involved one Christy Calder, daughter of Arrow, missing from her Peace Corps compound in Paraguay for nearly a year.

• • •

Hallie Garard had received her law degree from Northwestern, passed the Illinois and New York State bars, and then was recruited by the FBI. Out of training at Quantico, she'd been sent to the New Orleans field office.

After years of confusion and questioning, she finally came to terms with who she was when Emily Berkowitz, another newly minted special agent, made a pass at her at a welcome mixer put on by her new FBI colleagues. They'd been a couple for nine years.

Hallie had grown up in Queens, New York, attended Forest Hills High School, and made her First

Communion at Our Lady Queen of Martyrs. She'd celebrated her confirmation at twelve, with about a hundred other preteen candidates from throughout the five boroughs at St. Patrick's on Fifth Avenue in New York City. She'd decided on her own to leave Catholic school after eighth grade. She'd had enough of the nuns and their nonsense and wanted something resembling a normal social life in high school.

Her parents, a NYC firefighter, and a middle school teacher, didn't try to stop her when she took her 3.97 high school GPA and near perfect 1,570 SATs to St. John's University in Queens. They'd hoped for Fordham or maybe even Villanova down in Philadelphia, but, for reasons of her own, Hallie had wanted to stay at home a little while longer. They were fine when she chose Northwestern for law school.

Until he passed, her father had bragged on her recruitment and appointment to the FBI. When she was tapped to join the newly minted Interagency Task Force, which had brought her to the current case she'd been working on for nearly seven months, she saw it as a validation of how good she was at her job and how she'd been accepted within the FBI's notoriously conservative, buttoned-down, straight white male–centric culture.

When the house on Susie Q Court went up for sale, Hallie first attempted to rent it. When the realtor balked, she requested and was granted a withdrawal from a Bureau account established from funds seized during criminal prosecutions and bought it for the asking price just days after the listing hit the Orlando MLS. She made the sale contingent on a fast closing so she could move in as soon as possible. The Bureau did this so their agent could keep a closer watch on Arrow. Her cover story, that she edited textbooks for a specialty publishing company, was one she'd used on previous assignments since the formation of the IATF.

• • •

Hallie began her recorded report. "Here's what's known. Arrow was visited early afternoon on Saturday, June 7, by two white men traveling in a GM SUV, could have been a Suburban or Tahoe. Arrow's neighbor, Jennifer Levitt, wife of Ronnie Levitt, an investigative reporter for the *Orlando Chronicle*, observed the meeting. She observed Arrow leaving, apparently voluntarily, with the two men. No one entered Arrow's home at the time. Later in the afternoon, when Ronnie Levitt returned from work, he; Jennifer; another neighbor, Stacy Peterson, wife of Douglas Peterson; and I entered Arrow's home. We observed rooms devoid of furniture and fixtures except for a locked back bedroom suite. Ronnie Levitt removed the door from its hinges revealing a combined living area and workspace. Arrow left behind a dog, a Basenji named Lady, for whom I am currently caring. The room appeared to have been thoroughly searched and left in a shambles, although we have reason to think Arrow disheveled the room himself for currently unknown reasons."

Agent Garard continued her report, outlining her review of photographs and confirming the existence of a daughter, Christy. She reported that Ronnie Levitt had taken several notebooks home with him to review, and to this point there was no additional information clearly revealing any new facts about Jordan Censell's circumstances or whereabouts.

Finally, she revealed the existence of the flash drive disguised as a fan pull and reviewed the contents of the communication left behind by Arrow, almost verbatim.

"Here's what's not known. I don't know Arrow's current whereabouts. I don't know for certain whether his current whereabouts has anything to do with our investigation. I don't know the whereabouts or circumstances of his daughter. I don't know yet what the neighbors are going to do next. I don't know why Arrow chose to live in a single room of a much larger home or if that has any relevance. I'm not sure who trashed the room.

"Here's what I presume. I presume Arrow is either in or is going to be in Minneapolis at Dommerich North America headquarters. I presume he is alive and safe, for the moment. I presume he is trying to determine the location and status of his daughter, who has been missing for perhaps as long as a year, and I presume he blames Dommerich for her situation, or at least he believes they know something of his daughter's whereabouts.

"I presume Ronnie Levitt, the reporter, is going to get more deeply involved in attempting to locate Arrow, and that he will pursue these events independent of our investigation, possibly as a story for his newspaper. I presume this can work to our advantage in having a skilled professional investigative reporter doing additional and, for the purposes of our investigation, disinterested research. He's bright and highly capable. I will report again in twenty-four hours or sooner if events dictate. This is Special Agent Hallie Garard, voiceprint ID 11235. Out."

There was a momentary pause, then, "Wait one moment, please." There was another brief pause. "Okay, we've got it. Secure transmission terminated. Macaluso 629 out. Be safe, Hallie."

Hallie broke the connection and returned the phone to her back pocket. She collected the dog, her food, and her bowls and turned off the light. Moments later, she and Lady slipped from Jordan's house and walked to hers.

Chapter 6

Sunday

It was 6:15 a.m. when Jordan heard the knock at his door. It was immediately followed by the sound of a key turning in the lock. "Mr. Censell?" a man's voice called. "Hope you're up and ready. We need to get going."

Jordan was indeed "up and ready," having been awakened by his internal clock, as he was virtually every day in Florida, at 5:45 a.m. This morning, due to the time zone change, he'd awakened an hour earlier. He'd found cereal, milk, fresh fruit, and his own pot of coffee in the small, nicely appointed kitchen. He had to admit, if only to himself, while this company might very well be responsible for all kinds of bad acts, including criminal behavior, they did know how to make a guest, even an unwilling one, feel comfortable.

"In here," he called out. "Just cleaning up breakfast dishes. Can I get you—"

"If you would, sir, we need to take you to the airport. Just leave things as they are. Someone will be by to freshen the place up," the man said. Jordan stopped his cleanup and dried his hands.

"Do I have time for a quick shower?" Jordan asked.

"Sorry, sir, but we have to get going. I'm not certain but you might be able to take a shower on board the jet."

"Wow! And where might we be going after we go the airport?" Jordan asked.

"Above my pay grade, sir. I'm sure you'll find out soon."

"Well, I hope it's back to Florida. I obviously wasn't prepared for an extended trip."

The driver and his associate delivered Jordan directly to the staircase of what appeared to be the same Gulfstream jet he'd arrived in last evening. This, he thought, was confirmation that he was, indeed, heading back to Orlando. Unfortunately, he hadn't accomplished much of any real substance.

Less than fifteen minutes after boarding and strapping in, the plane was in the air, flying south, as indicated by the position of the sun in the morning sky. Jordan was served a second breakfast by a different attendant, who, like the earlier one, wouldn't answer questions with anything other than a lovely smile.

After the meal and a second cup of coffee, Jordan settled in for the flight to Orlando. Despite having enjoyed a relatively good and sound night's sleep, he could not seem to keep his eyes open.

• • •

Jordan was awakened by a slight bump when the Dommerich Gulfstream jet touched down. The windows on the plane were shuttered; he had no idea how long he had dozed. He had an urgent need to visit the bathroom. Before he was even fully awake, the smiling flight attendant brought him a tray containing a plate of fresh fruit; a croissant stuffed with chicken salad, lettuce, and tomato; and a small pot of decaf coffee.

"Did you have a nice nap," she asked.

"Where are we?" Jordan asked, yawning. "Are we on the ground? In Orlando?"

"A brief refueling stop," she said. "Enjoy your lunch." She turned and walked back to the front of the aircraft.

"You didn't refuel on the way up to Minneapolis," Jordan shouted. "Why on the way back to Florida?"

The attendant didn't respond. Jordan tried to open the window shade but was unable to do so. One of the security guards approached.

"Sir," he said. "We're not even opening the aircraft's door. We're just refueling. We'll be airborne again in less time than it takes you to eat lunch. I promise, it won't be much longer."

Jordan was disoriented and a bit hungry. He didn't understand why. He'd had a good night's sleep, and he'd just eaten breakfast. He was permitted a quick, escorted bathroom visit.

The plates in front of him appeared appetizing. He took a bite of the croissant. His appetite kicked in, and he proceeded to eat everything on the tray, including a bowl of cantaloupe, honeydew, pineapple, and kiwi. Then he poured himself a cup of coffee, expecting the caffeine to give him a bit of a jolt. Instead, after two more bites of the croissant, his eyes grew heavy again.

When he next opened his eyes, they were on the ground again. This time the window shades were open. He didn't recognize the airport and thought perhaps he was at a private airstrip somewhere else in Florida. As the plane taxied, a phone rang. A satellite phone had been placed alongside him while he slept. Jordan answered the call.

"Mr. Censell? This is Michael Capshaw. I have some very good news for you."

"What very good news could you possibly have for me?" Jordan asked. "And where the hell am I?"

Capshaw chuckled. "Ah, Mr. Censell. In less than an hour, you'll be reunited with your daughter."

"You son of a bitch," Jordan said. "You've had her all this time? What kind of people—"

"Mr. Censell, please. Give me a moment to calm your concerns and maybe, just maybe, you'll feel better about things. You first contacted us, I believe, almost five months ago. At that time, we began employing our considerable resources in South America, specifically in Brazil, Bolivia, Argentina, Chile, and Paraguay, to see if we could locate your daughter. You provided valuable essential information. We did the rest."

"Where is she? Where was she? Where are we?"

Capshaw laughed again. "I know. It must be overwhelming. You told me she's been out of touch for nearly a year, correct? Well, right after you and I finished our visit last night I was alerted to the wonderful news that Christy had indeed been located at an encampment under the control of a local Paraguayan insurgent militia. I'm sorry I couldn't share any of our efforts with you earlier, not until we had definitive information. And to be quite honest, you were hurling some awful accusations at me and at Dommerich."

Jordan was caught off guard. "I . . . I . . ." His brain tried to put it all together. The flight attendant and the security guard stood by, watching him, and smiling while he tried getting his head around what he was hearing.

"Look, Mr. Censell, I'm sure, in just a little while, she'll tell you herself all about what she's been going through for the past several months. This morning, while you were in the air, I engaged some people employed by contractors who work with Dommerich Worldwide. They have had some . . ." Capshaw paused, obviously choosing his words very carefully. "They've had some firsthand experience, I guess I should call it, with these kinds of people all over the world. They paid the camp a visit and negotiated for Ms. Calder's release into our custody. We brought her to Asunción this morning and placed her in a residence we maintain in the capital for visiting Dommerich officials. We gave her some time alone to clean up and find her footing. You should know before you see her that she's still a little disoriented from her ordeal with the militia."

How convenient, Jordan thought. *I'd confronted Capshaw less than twenty-four hours ago and now this.* "I'm not sure what to say."

"Well, 'thank you, Michael,' might be a good start," Capshaw said.

Jordan's emotions conflicted with his knowledge. He knew what he knew about Dommerich, but if Christy was okay, and if they had a real hand in bringing her out of something bad, then, well, maybe . . . but he wasn't quite ready to thank him just yet. "Look, Mr. Capshaw, I do appreciate what you've done on Christy's behalf," he said, "but after the dust all settles and Christy and I are able to return to our normal lives, maybe then you and I can, I don't know, find some equilibrium."

"Jordan . . . May I call you Jordan?"

"Sure."

"Jordan, listen. Dommerich is not what you thought we were. Yes, we are a big international business, and yes, we do enjoy making a profit on the products and services we create and provide for our business partners and for consumers. But we don't kidnap people and we don't intentionally hurt people. I hope you can become comfortable with those fundamental truths about us."

Capshaw had one more card to play. He needed to be careful; Jordan Censell had demonstrated that he wasn't stupid. Capshaw was playing a long game and needed to keep Mr. Censell and Ms. Calder as far away as possible from the SaniScal and Veracozen approval processes. That was job one. After that, well, there were many options moving forward. Some were good, some not so good.

"I've got an idea, Jordan. Please understand that I have no need nor any desire to sell you a bill of goods. Your daughter has been missing for a long time. Now, she's safe, as you'll see for yourself very shortly. You've been carrying this with you for that same long time, and it's caused you to come to some inaccurate conclusions that I hope you'll be able to put behind you."

"I promise, Mr. Capshaw . . . Michael," Jordan said, "if she's good and if we're able to decompress at home for a while, I'll be the first to let you know that Dommerich will be part of my portfolio, limited though it may be, moving forward."

Capshaw laughed. "I'm delighted to hear that, Jordan. Do this. Not for me but for yourself and for your daughter. Spend a week, maybe two. Enjoy Asunción and the natural beauty of the surrounding area. Visit Buenos Aires, Rio, maybe La Paz in Bolivia. These are all beautiful and interesting places. I can arrange transportation, lovely private accommodations, even a little spending money for the two of you to begin healing from the ordeal of the past year. Don't answer me now. Talk to her, think about it, and let me know."

"I . . . I don't know, Michael," Jordan said. "I'm not

sure any of that is necessary, or, for that matter, appropriate. I don't have my passport with me, as you know. I'm not sure if Christy has hers, either. We're going to have to visit the embassy in, where are we?"

"Asunción," he said. "It's the capital of Paraguay. Why don't you let us handle that for you? We do this sort of thing all the time."

Jordan wanted, needed to get this call done so he could get to wherever Christy was currently being kept. Finally fully awake, he was beginning to feel little twinges of concern at the hospitality being thrown at him by a guy who a day earlier had threatened him with all sorts of legal grief and whom he'd happily have strangled.

"I'll be in touch, Michael," Jordan said. "Again, I appreciate you finding Christy and, I suppose, the unconventional manner in which you are bringing us together."

"So long, Jordan. And please, be at peace."

• • •

Michael instructed his man on the ground to take their guest to the small house the company made available to visiting VIPs when they were in the Asunción area. Then he called Becker, his boss.

"Yes, Michael."

"Mr. Censell is in South America, sir," he said. "I'd like to discuss next steps with you before proceeding."

"What next steps?" Becker said. "We need to keep

him and the girl under wraps until the FDA moves approval on SaniScal, which should happen in the next week. You told me the EPA is about to approve Veracozen, perhaps as soon as tomorrow or Tuesday. Is that still the case?"

Capshaw marveled at how a person could ascend to business leadership without a shred of long-range strategic vision or the ability to keep more than one thought in his head at any given moment in time. "To my knowledge it is, sir," he said. "But I'm thinking about the strategic issues involving Mr. Censell, the girl, our associates on the ground in Paraguay, and yes, the impending schedule of government activity. After the EPA and then FDA actions occur, what do we want to do with Ms. Calder and her father?"

"I assume you have some thoughts on the matter, Michael?" Becker said.

"Well, sir, I don't wish to overreach here." Capshaw said. "While we technically did not commit any illegal offenses on either American or German soil, there's a chance Ms. Calder might see things differently. That said, I think our friends in South America will be sympathetic to our point of view."

Becker said nothing, so Capshaw continued. "As I see things, sir, we have two, perhaps three options. First, we can bring Mr. Censell and Ms. Calder home to the USA, perhaps with some . . . incentives to help them get reestablished. There's a chance they'll simply forget their most recent unpleasant circumstances.

Money typically helps with that. Or we can turn them loose in Paraguay and let them fend for themselves and wonder whether any of the things that happened to Ms. Calder had anything at all to do with Dommerich. This might allow us to continue denying any complicity in their circumstances. I think we've prepared nicely for that contingency in terms of what can be proven should they get vocal. Or," Capshaw said, thinking aloud, "we can return Ms. Calder, along with Mr. Censell, to Col. Negron and let nature take its course."

Becker was silent for a moment. "What's your recommendation, Michael?" he asked.

Capshaw shook his head, smiling to himself. *Not only is Becker not wise but he has no balls, either.* "For now, sir, I think we maintain the status quo and keep Ms. Calder and Mr. Censell comfortable but within our control and incommunicado, at least until our friends at the EPA and the FDA get Veracozen and SaniScal approved. Once that occurs, we can revisit next steps for both of them." Letting Becker off the hook for now could pay dividends for Capshaw when it came time for his compensation review.

"Good thinking, Michael, as always," an obviously relieved Becker said.

Michael understood that where Becker was concerned, making no decision was often the safest decision in difficult circumstances.

Chapter 7

Ronnie spent most of Sunday poring over the four journals Jordan had left for them to find. He wished he had a way of reaching him, but he had no idea where he was or how to connect. Ronnie wondered if he was doing all of this for his neighbor or for a story. At the end of the day, it didn't matter.

In the first journal, he learned what happened when Jordan visited his daughter, Christy, while she was serving in the Peace Corps in Mali. According to the journal entry, they both were still reeling from the death of Leslie, his wife, and her mother. In their grieving they found their father-daughter relationship, which had mostly eluded them while Leslie was alive.

Ronnie didn't want to tear pages out or mark them up in these journals. Jordan likely had a plan for them if or when he returned from wherever he was. Instead, he made copies of certain pages and then highlighted passages that caught his attention.

The journals revealed Jordan's role in helping Christy and her cohort find sources of drinking water and figure out how to get it to the people in the region who desperately needed it. They enjoyed some small degree of success; instead of individuals having to transport relatively small amounts of water for two days over brutal terrain, they managed to design a rudimentary infrastructure that would help get it to within six hours of those in need.

Were it not for some Mauritanian militia that seemingly sprang up overnight keeping them from crossing a dense forest in the southeastern part of the country, they could have tapped directly into the Niger River. That would have brought the water all the way to the string of impoverished desert villages. After filtration, citizens would have had the means to meet both the human and agricultural water needs of tens of thousands of people.

A few pages later, Ronnie uncovered the first of an increasing number of references appearing in all four journals to Dommerich Worldwide. Christy believed Dommerich likely either controlled or financially supported the militia that held the part of the forest through which they were prohibited from extending a water line from the river to the desert villages. She saw vehicles carrying Dommerich's logo, three trees connected by intertwined root systems, with Dommerich Worldwide printed in small type below.

● ● ●

Michael Capshaw went to a single-drawer lateral file cabinet disguised as a plant stand on the far side of his corner office. Using a key he kept in a locked drawer of his desk, he opened the cabinet and took out a manila envelope containing a single file. It was unmarked. He took it back to his desk and reacquainted himself with who he thought of as the single biggest pain in the ass he'd had to deal with over the past twelve months.

Christy Calder had come to his attention following a formal request she'd made with Mali's central government in Bamako. She and her do-gooder group of volunteers had wanted permission to cut a narrow trail through a dense patch of jungle in order to bring water to some ignorant villagers who, in his view, chose to live a hundred miles from where Jesus left his shoes. At the behest of his corporate masters, Capshaw had generously greased the palms of both the local and provincial government functionaries alleged to have oversight over natural resources in that godforsaken place, along with several insurgent gangs, militias, and warlords, all hell bent on taking the entire nation and making it their own.

Michael had discovered some years ago that money either solved or helped manage most logistic issues that surfaced in the impoverished areas of the world that were rich in the resources Dommerich required for its compounds. Money didn't necessarily work with what Capshaw viewed as "soft" problems, like the Peace Corps.

There was no way he was going to permit some hippie commune to gain even minimal access to that forest. He'd do whatever he had to do, up to and including some form of removal or, if necessary, elimination of anyone and everyone who, in even a small way, attempted to get in his way.

Part of the billions Dommerich spent each year sending biologists and earth scientists all over the planet searching for material with potential for being developed into something they could bring to market was at stake. If some bug, bush, leaf, land or sea creature, piece of tree bark, or arcane plant had some element they believed might possibly have developmental potential, they'd spend money to obtain it, test it, and, when possible, develop it into a pharmaceutical. If they couldn't do that, they'd create an ailment that could be treated by whatever it was they'd discovered in the world's jungles, oceans, forests, and deserts. Failing that, they'd see if it could be modified into something that might kill or control rodents, termites, or other pests.

As Michael Capshaw thoroughly understood, selling drugs, and killing bugs were Dommerich's core businesses.

One such discovery, bark from a bushy plant indigenous to an isolated forest in southeastern Mali, showed early promise in countering some of the more painful symptoms associated with rheumatoid arthritis. Several years of compound testing on lab animals, primates, and, ultimately, in controlled studies on humans, revealed that, in concert with the right combination of additional ingredients, the product could in fact produce pain relieving results but only sufficient to generate a marginal profit against competing pain relievers already in the marketplace. The company was about to jettison the effort and write off the development costs. At the urging of a Dommerich scientist, Munich green-lit a test, at the time unauthorized by the Food and Drug Administration and known to only a handful of Dommerich scientists and leaders. The test was performed on a sampling of adults with chronic dandruff. It had come to the company's attention that natives in the region had used it for this purpose in its raw form. It had demonstrated spectacular symptomatic results. It wasn't a cure, and that was fine with Dommerich.

Dommerich recalled its original application for the pain reliever and reapplied to the FDA for approval as, what the scientists called, "a giant step forward in dealing with the scourge of seborrheic dermatitis." The marketers concentrated on its ability to control dandruff. SaniScal, when approved, would constitute a windfall for Dommerich.

So no, Capshaw couldn't have the Peace Corps and their water project get in the way of what could be a game changer for Dommerich and, by extension, its shareholders. And since Michael now had significant personal holdings in Dommerich stock, he wasn't about to let anything stop the company from taking SaniScal to market.

He reached out to a contact in the State Department to see what could be done to have someone in the Peace Corps reassigned and make it look like a promotion. He quickly learned that in exchange for political support or other considerations, pretty much anything, including much bigger, more difficult obstacles could be overcome. Moving a single Peace Corps volunteer required little more than a phone call, followed by relatively small, quietly dispersed, cash incentives. It cost Dommerich under $250,000 in payments to a single Peace Corps bureaucrat and a dozen Malian officials to get Christy Calder reassigned to Paraguay.

Christy's new assignment would be to help establish a continental economic development initiative, working as a volunteer in the same locale where Dommerich was negotiating rights to erase twenty thousand acres of nearby forest and jungle. This way, he could keep an eye on her. However, he underestimated her impulse to help right wrongs where she could. Three weeks into her new assignment, Christy became aware of what was happening in Paraguay. Despite Peace Corps policies to the contrary, she engaged with local dissidents opposing Dommerich's plans to harvest the bark from the Verawood tree, as locals called it, and combine it with elements of Dommerich's existing termite control product.

The bark from Verawood had been used by indigenous Paraguayan people to help address painful stomach issues, but when added in higher concentrations to the earlier termiticide, the new formulation could attack the digestive systems of a plethora of household insects, including both major varieties of termites. This gave it excellent product potential, and it also could be marketed as organic. The tree, to Dommerich's knowledge at the time, didn't grow anywhere else in the world. Until the formulation could be synthesized, securing a substantial stockpile of Verawood bark had become an extremely high priority.

With the addition of what Dommerich was tentatively calling Veracozen, the new, improved product could have a revolutionary impact and could place Dommerich in an unassailable position at the top of the massive global pest and termite control industry.

Chapter 8

According to the journal Ronnie was wading through, Jordan had been with his daughter for almost a month, during which time he'd adapted to the rhythms and pace of their volunteer project. She'd been happy when her father came to visit her in Mali. Her mother's death was still an open wound and she'd found it comforting to be able to commiserate with someone she loved and who loved her unconditionally.

Their compound, where they lived and where they did a lot of the planning for their drinking water projects, was actually a converted local jail in a small village near the city of Koulikoro. Each of the dozen volunteers had their own cell, which served as sleeping quarters and bathroom facilities, and they cooked and ate their meals in the jail's former kitchen. The Interior Ministry of the central government in Mali supplied their food. They also had three vehicles, access to as much fuel as they needed, and enjoyed a safe, mostly peaceful, if only occasionally productive existence. She knew, she could have been in much more challenging circumstances, even by Africa standards.

Peace Corps and World Health Organization biologists helped locate and map potential sources of water between the villages and the Niger River. Engineers charted potential pipeline routes across and through desert, jungle, and forest in the same vicinity. They concluded what was needed was an almost thirty-four-mile-long pipeline. It would employ mostly straight-line piping with minimal disruption to plant and animal habitat. If the Bamako government would supply workers, the US Agency for International Development would fund the costs associated with pulling the water from the river and running it through the necessary filtration infrastructure to ensure potability. Then, together, they would build the subsystems necessary to dead-end supply lines in each of the villages along the path.

Jordan loved all of it. Plus, it had the added, most desirable benefit of bringing him and his daughter closer together.

All the Bamako government needed to do was approve the submitted plan and provide approximately one hundred workers. They would be compensated through a fund established by the Malian government and USAID.

The plan was submitted on a Tuesday, approximately two months after Jordan had completed his visit with Christy. He'd been in the early stages of relocating from Indiana to Florida at the time.

Sixteen days later, two Peace Corps volunteers were dead, and Christy Calder had been on a plane headed for Asunción, Paraguay. Once there, she was to take over leadership of an established Peace Corps team on the ground.

That's how fast Michael Capshaw was able to halt what had become known on the ground as the Koulikoro Water Relocation Project to protect Dommerich's access to the source material for its prescription dandruff shampoo, SaniScal. Ronnie assumed that Dommerich, as with other multinational companies in the pharmaceutical and pesticide segments, maintained a slush fund under some name like "government and community relations" or "business development" for use in lubricating the often-complex machinery of international commerce.

At first, Christy didn't seem to know Dommerich was behind the attempt to denude potentially thousands of acres of Paraguayan forestland. As a former public interest attorney in Chicago, she would have understood the risks associated with taking on powerful interests accustomed to operating with virtual impunity in pursuit of profits. What she hadn't known, or hadn't taken the time to learn, was that outside the United States, protections she'd come to expect at home often were nonexistent.

In large part, Peace Corps volunteers served in

places with authoritarian, autocratic, or military regimes. The work was typically humanitarian in nature, and while the governments tolerated the American presence, they didn't usually operate in anything close to a democratic system, and human rights were whatever local authorities determined they were at any given time. Christy most likely hadn't fully realized the real and potential consequences associated with what she was doing whenever she found herself at odds with the local power structure in Mali or in Paraguay.

• • •

Jordan had written in the journal about Christy's relocation to Asunción. She was also promoted to project coordinator, but as far as Ronnie had read, there was nothing indicating whatever became of the Koulikoro Water Relocation Project in Mali.

Ronnie put down the last of Jordan's journals. He tried to stop his head from exploding. This constituted something of a revelation for a guy who, while doing his job, had brought down corrupt developers and government officials, broken stories exposing dirty cops, and publicly shamed a once revered ballet school operator who'd turned out to be a serial pedophile.

He made notes regarding Jordan's revelations about Dommerich Worldwide, the new products named SaniScal and Veracozen, and trips his neighbor had made to exotic, dangerous locales, like rural Mali in Africa and Asunción, the capital of Paraguay.

Ronnie strongly considered how much of this information to share with the others, especially with Jennie. She always expressed concern whenever he started on some new investigation. Ronnie often investigated powerful people with a whole lot to lose. He did this without the benefit of a badge or a gun.

Chapter 9

Skeeter Bates was seated at a console inside his reconfigured, air-conditioned, forty-four-foot trailer when his phone rang. At the moment, the rig was in a Walmart parking lot in Saddle Brook, New Jersey, as far as possible from the store itself. Honey had filled the tank on the seven-year-old Kenworth that pulled the rig with 150 gallons of diesel and re-connected to the trailer. This left them positioned to jump on the Garden State Parkway in either direction as quickly as whim or circumstance required. Honey checked the caller ID, nodded her head once, and handed him the modified iPhone.

"Skeeter," was all he said.

"Ronnie Levitt."

"Still in the same job?"

"Yep."

Skeeter nodded to Honey, his best friend, part-ner, driver, and protector, freeing her to do whatever needed doing to keep their little operation of supplying hard-to-find information to a select group of friends going. No police, no military, no defense contractors. Certain news reporters were okay, as were principled white-hat hackers; dissident groups opposed to war, military buildups, and exploitation of women, minorities, or the disabled; and what had begun to be called aggressive environmentalists. Skeeter wouldn't consider working with big business under any circumstance, regardless of the money involved.

He pushed his wheelchair away from the console. "What do you need?" he asked.

"Two names. Jordan Censell and Christy Censell." He spelled the last name.

"Okay, let's see, we've got some driving to do. I'll call back tonight, around ten eastern time." He broke the connection.

• • •

Ronnie only used Skeeter's services when he came up empty on his own. All he knew was Jordan Censell owned a house in the Conway neighborhood of Orlando; he had a Florida driver's license, but it seemed he didn't own a vehicle; he was eligible to vote in Orange County, Florida; and he was registered without party affiliation.

Ronnie wasn't quite ready to talk to his editors. Frankly, he wasn't sure what kind of party his neighbor had invited him and his Susie Q Court neighbors to crash. And, at least until he knew more, he needed to honor the man's plea to keep law enforcement out of it. *Maybe*, he thought, *Skeeter would be able to open some new avenues of investigation.*

For the time being, Ronnie decided to keep whatever it was that was happening to the man who lived on the other side of the cul-de-sac between himself, Jennie, Hallie, and maybe Stacy.

. . .

Jordan walked down the stairs of the sleek pale-yellow G-5 and climbed into the back seat of an unmarked black Hummer. One of the security guys from the plane got in the front passenger seat. Another got in alongside Jordan.

"Seat belt, please, sir," he said, smiling.

"Where are we headed?" Jordan asked, also smiling.

"I could tell you, but it wouldn't mean anything to either of us," he said. "The local driver is the only one who knows how to get us from here to there." They drove off, heading, Jordan hoped, to Asunción and a reunion with his daughter. They'd not bothered clearing customs, and Jordan wasn't counting on Capshaw being truthful about getting passports for them so they could go home as soon as possible.

Jordan realized he didn't know for sure what day or what time it was. The sun was low in what he believed was the western sky, so it must be around dusk in Asunción. He wasn't tired but he was hungry. He considered the distinct possibility that he'd been dosed with some sleep aid on the plane, but he had no real idea how long he'd been gone from Minneapolis.

"Can I please have my watch and my phone back?" he asked.

The security guy looked genuinely upset. "Oh, I'm sorry, sir. They must have been left on the plane. Soon as we get you where you're going, I'll go back and pick them up for you, although I doubt the phone will work down here."

"Right." Jordan nodded his head. He'd never considered the notion that he might need to convert his mobile phone for international use.

After a drive of what he estimated was a little over an hour, including passing through the center of Asunción, the Hummer came to a stop in front of a small home in a quiet residential neighborhood on the west side of the city. From his seat, Jordan noticed the white stucco house had a red barrel-tile roof, a small shed, and a four-foot-high white stucco-covered wall around the property. There was an ornamental wrought-iron gate, a brick walkway, and some lovely low-scale landscaping. A bushy hibiscus did not quite hide a TV satellite dish on one side of the house. It was aimed toward the northern sky. A wooden archway overhung the one step up to an ornate front door. *Gotta say, these Dommerich people run a very good game.*

Jordan's traveling companion from the back seat led him up to the front door. He knocked and yet another security guy opened the door to let them in.

Christy was seated on a small floral-upholstered love-seat. When she saw Jordan, she smiled, then started sobbing, and rushed into his waiting arms. As they hugged one another, Jordan whispered, "Don't say anything; don't say a word. Follow my lead, baby."

"Oh, I'm so glad you're safe, baby," Jordan said, fully aware the guards were still in the living room, watching. His controlled paranoia involving all things related to Dommerich Worldwide led him to the certainty that the entire place was peppered with listening devices and possibly even cameras.

"I'm fine, Daddy, I'm fine," Christy said. Jordan brushed her long red-auburn hair from her freckled face. Her green eyes were puffy from crying, but she was smiling now.

"You think you guys could give us a little privacy?" Jordan asked. "We haven't seen each other for a year, and we have a lot of catching up to do."

One of them, who had told Jordan his name was Mack, said, "Sure, sir. We'll be right outside. We can talk later about—"

"Thanks, Mack," Jordan said. Mack and his partner backed out the way they'd come in and closed the heavy wood door. Jordan noticed the single-cylinder, handle-set door lock. There was no deadbolt or any other mechanism for keeping out someone with a key. The windows, at least those in the living room, couldn't be opened. But there were curtains, and as far as he could see, no one was peeking in.

"Come on, baby," Jordan said, "let's look around this place." He looked her directly in the eyes, pointed to his ears, and then put a finger in front of his lips. She nodded her understanding.

The house was larger than it appeared from the street. There was a living room, three bedrooms, a modern kitchen, a small dining room, two complete bathrooms, and a small, tiled patio in a courtyard off the kitchen. The house was furnished modestly but with everything one or two people might need to live, at least for a brief period of time. The refrigerator and pantry were stocked with groceries. There was a quiet AC system powered by a Trane heat pump, and flat screen TVs were in the living room and all three bedrooms. There was no landline phone and, unfortunately, there was no computer.

"Look, baby," Jordan said, scanning the pantry choices available to them. "Maybe we'll make some pasta. There's a jar of red sauce, some olive oil, and some good-looking bread. How about that?"

"That'll be great, Dad," she said. "Any wine anywhere?"

Jordan opened the door that led from the kitchen onto the back patio. Before walking out, he said, "We'll eat dinner out here, Christy." He paused for a moment, looking into his daughter's eyes. "God, I wish I had some clean clothes to change into."

Within seconds there came a knock at the front door. Jordan smiled broadly at Christy, winked at her, and walked back into the front room to open the door.

"You know, sir, I'm pretty sure I forgot to tell you," Mack said. "Mr. Capshaw had us pick up some things for you and the young lady as soon as he knew you'd be coming here." He started for the first bedroom. "May I?"

Jordan made a sweeping gesture for Mack to lead the way. In the first bedroom closet there were two pairs of blue jeans, two white guayabera shirts, two changes of underwear, two pairs of socks and a pair of Sperry docksiders in his size, ten and a half D. The bathroom was stocked with towels, shampoo, a toothbrush, Crest toothpaste, and a bar of Dial soap. There was even a hair dryer. The second bedroom was similarly equipped, along with some women's apparel and a pair of white Birkenstock sandals.

"Mr. Capshaw?" Christy asked of no one in particular. Mack began to say something, but Jordan interrupted.

"Mr. Capshaw is the reason you're here, the reason we're all here, Christy," is all Jordan said. He looked into her eyes, conveying, he hoped, the message to not pursue this line of discussion.

"Well," she said, "whoever he is, he sure thinks of everything."

"Indeed, he does, baby," Jordan said. "Thanks so much, Mack."

Mack smiled, nodded, and dismissed himself. Jordan made the hush sign once more and signaled Christy to follow him back to the kitchen. He wasn't sure if they were being watched, but he now knew for certain that their hosts were able to hear everything.

"I want you to tell me everything, Christy," Jordan said. "Where have you been for the last year?" He moved her to a corner, where she was facing out and he was facing into the corner. He mouthed "Nothing about Dommerich" and nodded, indicating it was okay for her to speak openly.

They walked back into the living room and sat on the sofa. She told him that shortly after she'd arrived—a few weeks at most—she got caught up in a demonstration in front the Palacio de los López, where Paraguay's president lives. Locals were protesting something; at the time, she wasn't sure what. She reminded her dad that she'd learned French for her assignment in Mali, but her Spanish, while better than it was when she'd arrived, was still limited. And she told him and whoever else was listening, her original Peace Corps assignment had been to help the Paraguayan people with economic development, nothing controversial.

"So," Jordan said, "you were on the street protesting—"

"No," she interrupted. "No, I wasn't protesting; I was sightseeing. All of a sudden, a car pulled up and someone grabbed me, put a hood over my head, and pushed me into the back seat. She said they'd driven for at least a couple of hours to somewhere outside of Asunción.

"I'm not sure I was even still in Paraguay. For all I know, where they took me might have been across the border in Argentina or maybe even Bolivia. It was some kind of camp where men with guns kept me in a tent with a bunch of other women who spoke almost no English. I was there until early this morning, when those two came." She pointed to the front door.

Jordan put his head down and took a couple of deep breaths. "They didn't . . . did they . . . did they hurt you?"

She shook her head. "No," she said. "Not at all. It was weird, Dad. They fed me every day, pretty well, in fact. The women took me with them a couple of times a week to a nearby stream where I was able to bathe. To this day, I have no idea where I was or who those people were, except the head guy; he was called Negron, Colonel Negron, I think. I seldom saw him in all the time I was there . . . ten months.

"The worst part, except for the fact that I couldn't leave, was that I was bored to near insanity. There was nothing for me to do. Occasionally the women let me help in the kitchen or with laundry, but there was nothing to read, no radio. I don't know if these people were really soldiers or a militia or just some kind of commune, living in the jungle. I'm just really glad to be out of there."

Jordan nodded throughout the telling. She smiled at him, stepping in to give him a hug.

"Oh, Dad, I can't tell you how good it is to see you," she said. "Did you get settled in Florida?" She put her hand to her mouth, but he smiled and waved her off.

"I did," he said. "When you see it, you'll laugh your head off. Lady and I are living in a pretty nice home in a nice community in a suburb of Orlando, but I couldn't find a way to get comfortable in such a large space."

"I know," she said. "Even this is way more than I've been living in for the past couple of years. But I have to admit, I could get used to more than one room."

"Yeah," he said. "Maybe I will, too, someday, when you come home with me." Jordan hesitated. This next part was going to be tricky.

Chapter 10

Ronnie joined Hallie at Jordan's to go over his cryptic message yet again. "You know, he said something about looking where Lady parked herself," Hallie said. "When we opened the door, she bolted, but when she came back, she went right to the bed, here." She pointed to a place near where the foot of the bed would be when it was opened. She looked up and pointed to a handle at the top of the built-in but couldn't reach it. Ronnie pulled the Murphy bed down into position.

"She was here, right?" Hallie asked, patting a spot near the foot of the bed.

"Looks right to me," Ronnie said. "Do you think . . . ?" He put the bed back up and looked closely at the underside of the bed, but there was nothing there except the apparatus the bed sat on when it was in the down position.

"After Jennie tripped the bed into the up position, the dog settled right here," he said, pointing at a spot on the shag carpet that lined up with where the dog had curled up on the bed and watched them all work. Hallie got onto her hands and knees and started feeling around.

"Whoa," she said. "What's this?" She started feeling around on the carpet and then started knocking on the floor. Ronnie watched her with renewed interest.

"Underneath the carpet, there should be a quarter- or half-inch of padding, and underneath that, a solid concrete floor," he said. That's the way it was in his house. He stared at her. *Textbook editor? I don't think so.*

"What are you looking at?" she asked, smirking. "You never saw a hot girl on her knees before?"

He got down on his own knees and put his own face close to hers. "What do you think you've discovered, Hallie?"

She ran her hands over the carpeted area. She stopped, looked at Ronnie, and smiled. She pointed to a spot on the floor. "You do the honors, Woodward."

Ronnie found a clear plastic ring sewn into the carpet. He carefully pulled on it. The carpet pulled away, revealing a piece of plywood approximately eighteen inches square. He lifted the plywood.

"Bazinga!" Hallie said. Ronnie looked at her and laughed.

"Seriously?" he asked. "*Big Bang?*"

"Yep," she said, smiling. "And you, my friend, are Dr. Sheldon fucking Cooper!"

Under the half-inch piece of plywood, which had

been altered to fit over a recessed area, was a thin Microsoft Surface Pro tablet. There was also a single blue file folder.

Ronnie was about to comment about the ingenuity of carving out a hiding place in the concrete floor under the carpet pad when his phone rang. "Ronnie Levitt."

"Skeeter."

Ronnie walked out of the room. He wasn't about to share Skeeter with anyone. Besides, he was now pretty sure Hallie wasn't quite what she presented to the folks on Susie Q Court. He signaled her that he'd be back in five minutes. She was already trying to get into the tablet.

"Whatcha got?"

"I'm sending you two files. Not a whole hell of a lot on the girl, except that she's . . . a disrupter. You know, my kind of people," Skeeter said. "And you've got her name wrong. It's not Censell, it's Calder. Christy Calder." He spelled the last name.

"What about Jordan Censell? Am I wrong about that, also?"

"Yes and no," Skeeter said. "Hang on a sec, I'm distracted."

There was some muffled talking. "Could you at least put some clothes on?"

Ronnie tried not to laugh. "Anything you want to share, Skeeter?"

"Sometimes Honey gets a little frisky at just the

wrong time." Having never met Honey, Ronnie couldn't know what kind of distraction she might be. "It's late, and we're . . . supposed to be in bed."

"You were saying, yes and no," Ronnie said.

"Seems your Mr. Jordan Censell arrived on planet Earth a little over a year ago," he said. "Nothing at all before that."

"Okay . . ."

"The second file will introduce you to one Nelson J.—that's for Jerome—Calder," Skeeter said. "Now, our Mr. Calder is a *very* interesting dude. I don't want to go any deeper on the phone because, you know."

"I know," Ronnie said. "Can you take on one more little project for me?

"Not until tomorrow morning, probably," Skeeter said. "She's messing with me again."

"Okay," Ronnie said. "Just two words. Dommerich Worldwide."

"Oh, yeah, I already know about that. I'll talk to you when I can talk to you." Skeeter was gone.

"Have fun, buddy," Ronnie said to the dead phone line.

"Something important?" Hallie asked.

"What did you come up with?" Ronnie answered.

Hallie was sitting in Jordan's desk chair with the tablet on her lap. "First, you and I need to talk, Sheldon."

Ronnie pulled the Murphy bed down and sat on the end of it. "I'm all ears, Leonard."

Hallie smiled and reached into her back pocket. She tossed her credentials to him.

Ronnie looked at her gold badge and photo identification. He nodded and smiled at her. "I thought . . . not a textbook editor. Not sure I saw this."

"I've been on this case since Jordan first contacted two government agencies, trying to get a lead on the whereabouts of his daughter," she said. "I'm sorry . . ."

Ronnie put up his hand. "You've got nothing to apologize for," he said. "So, is this 'you tell me yours, I tell you mine' time?"

She got up, walked over, and sat down next to him. "We're both in uncharted waters here, Sheldon," she said. "First, I believe you probably know I'm under absolutely no obligation to share anything with you. This is an ongoing investigation involving a couple of large federal agencies and an enormous, very influential, well-connected international conglomerate, and allegations of a shitload of wrongdoing in multiple national and international jurisdictions. As I see it, there are now at least two lives at stake and . . . I really can't say more than that until I get some clearance from my folks in DC."

"Don't government agencies have their own investigative capabilities?" Ronnie asked.

Hallie nodded. "They do, but when two or more are involved, we sometimes get called in to avoid jurisdictional posturing," she said. "This unit I'm a part of exists to avoid or at least minimize those petty issues."

"So, this whole time you've been living here as our neighbor, you've been investigating Jordan?" Ronnie asked. "We're off the record right now, Hallie."

"All I can say is that we're not investigating Jordan," she said. "But he's like the linchpin in what could turn into a huge criminal conspiracy. We've been—I've been monitoring him and his activities."

"What do we do, Hallie?"

"First, I need to ask you a question," she said. "Do you know anything I may not already know? I know that's a stupid question because you don't know what I know. Can you tell me what you know? Please? I'm sure we're on the same side here, but you're maybe chasing a story, and I'm chasing some potentially really serious crimes and, by extension, some really bad people. And we both want to see Jordan and his daughter get home safely." She looked at him. "Can we maybe work together on this, Ronnie?"

Ronnie took out his iPhone and opened the first email that had pinged in while this little drama was playing out. He didn't even bother looking at it. He gave it to Hallie.

She read for a moment. "Fuck . . . fuck . . . holy shit." She kept reading and cursing, reading and cursing. She finished the email up on her feet, walking in circles, reading, and cursing. "Where the hell did you get this?" Ronnie thought that if Hallie had been carrying, she might just have drawn down on him.

"I know a guy," he said, smiling. "He's a source, so

don't even ask, Hallie. That's just not going to happen." He gestured for her to hand him back his iPhone.

"I'd like to see what got you so wound up that you'd use such . . . colorful language," he said, smiling again. "Oh, and like I asked before, did you learn anything else new tonight from the tablet?"

"Yeah, but nothing that trumps what's in that document you got from your 'source,'" she said, putting air quotes around the word.

"Well," he said, "at least you're still the same smartass we've all come to know and love. I want to read this for myself and look at what Jordan wanted us to see when we finally found the tablet, and then we should probably talk tomorrow in the light of day before doing anything else. You need to talk to DC, and I need to talk to the third floor at my place." He stood up and looked at her, differently now. "I think we need to keep all of this to ourselves for the time being."

"Yeah," she said. "Absolutely, even Jennie."

He nodded. "Especially Jennie." They locked up and went their separate ways.

• • •

MONDAY

The next morning, Jennie hustled Kimmie off to school and reminded Ronnie she was having lunch with her old boss at Orlando Health's level-one trauma center. She asked him about the night before across the street. Ronnie said that nothing much new had surfaced, except for the fact that he hoped she was okay with him and Hallie working so closely together on this.

She smiled. "First, I know numerous ways to kill someone without getting caught," she said. "But no, Ronnie, I know you, and even though Hallie is . . . well, I'm not sure what she is, but I honestly don't think you're even on her radar. Not that way, anyway."

"Should my feelings be hurt?" he asked. She laughed out loud.

"No, babe, they shouldn't. Pretty sure Hallie bats for the other team," she said. "You should be more worried about her coming on to me." She shook her head. "I swear, I guess on some things, sometimes, even Pulitzer winners don't have a clue. See you later, babe."

Ronnie stared at her. "Really? Really?"

She left through the door to the garage, laughing all the way.

• • •

Ronnie gave his editor a broad outline of what he was working on. His stories sometimes took weeks or even months to be fully realized. When they were finished, invariably, they were on page one, above the fold, and constituted a multipart series on something of significant impact and reader interest.

Joe Hill, editor of the *Chronicle*, was not president of Ronnie's fan club, but the publisher was, and in most newspapers, including the *Orlando Chronicle*, publisher trumped editor.

"So, let me get this straight," Joe Hill said. "You've got a guy who may or may not have been kidnapped by a major multinational corporation. Said corporation also may or may not have kidnapped the guy's daughter. Said daughter may or may not have crossed paths with said multinational in Africa and then South America. And said multinational may or may not have a couple of drugs imminently pending government approval."

Ronnie smiled. He understood his editor's skepticism. It came with the territory. But Joe Hill hadn't seen what Ronnie had seen, both in Jordan's house and in the cul-de-sac on Saturday morning. Besides, Ronnie's gut was pretty finely tuned.

"Close enough, Joe," Ronnie said. "One drug, one pesticide."

Joe shrugged his shoulders. "What do you need?"

"Right now, except for some baksheesh to spread around to a couple of sources, I've got everything I need, Joe. Thanks for asking, and thanks for the confidence. I just want you to know I may or may not be reachable for what may or may not be a week or two."

Joe Hill couldn't help but laugh. "Ahhh, another fucking smartass in my newsroom. Maybe or maybe not you'll keep in touch?" Ronnie left the *Chronicle*'s editor's small office and returned home.

• • •

Ronnie's doorbell rang and he was surprised when he saw Stacy at his front door. "Hey, Stacy, how's it going? Jennie's not here right now."

"Actually, it's you I want to talk to," she said. "Do you have a few minutes?"

"Sure," Ronnie said. "Come on in. You want a cup of coffee or something?"

She walked over to the dining room table and sat down in one of the chairs. "Just a glass of water, thanks."

Ronnie made himself a cup of coffee and brought Stacy a cold bottle of Zephyrhills water and a glass.

"What's up?" he said.

"I just want to find out what's new with him," she said, making a gesture in the direction of Jordan's house. "I know he hasn't come home yet, and I know you and Hallie have been over there a time or two. Do you know anything yet?"

He wasn't sure if or how much he really wanted to share with her. *She's a sweetheart*, he thought, *and really, really good looking*. But he didn't know what, if anything, she could contribute to what he and Hallie were into.

"We really . . . I really don't know much more today than we did on Saturday, Stacy," he said. "He hasn't been back, and to my knowledge no one has heard from him. I guess Mikey told us at the boil—super job on the shrimp, by the way, to both you and

Doug—Mikey told us that he disappears for a while every now and then."

"I know, but that whole thing with the black SUV and those guys Jennie saw. I don't know; I guess I'm just worried," she said. "I know he's a little strange, but mostly he seems like a nice guy and a good person."

Ronnie thought that unless Stacy saw someone carrying a bloody axe away from a dismembered corpse, she'd give the benefit of the doubt. A thought flew into his head.

"Hey, Stacy, listen," he said, trying to put together, on the fly, some context for what he wanted to ask her. "I'm actually working on something for the paper on prescription drugs. Are you still"—he smiled—"dealing drugs to doctors and pharmacies?"

"Yeah," she said, smiling, "like I've never heard that one before. Yes, Ronnie, I still do freelance pharmaceutical sales to the medical profession.

"Have you ever done anything with . . . what the hell's the name of that company? It's German, I think . . ."

Her smile disappeared. "Dommerich?" she asked.

"That's it, right, Dommerich. What can you tell me about them?"

"I can tell you that I did do some rep work for them but no more, no, never." She was dead serious.

"Wow," Ronnie said. "I don't think I've ever seen you angry, Stacy. If you don't mind telling me, what happened?"

"Well, I can't . . . I'm not sure what I'm able to talk about, Ronnie, and you being a newspaper reporter, I'm just not sure, but I can say they're just not very nice or trustworthy, and they're not very honest."

Ronnie didn't want to point out the redundancy, but he knew he'd love to hear more from someone who actually did work for them.

"Can you just, you know, maybe give me some big picture stuff? Did they stiff you on commissions or something like that?"

"Oh, no, nothing like that," she said. "Let me just say, without being specific, Ronnie, that Dommerich makes claims about some of their products—How can I say this? Some of their pharmaceuticals might over promise and under deliver if you know what I mean. You didn't hear that from me, and I can't tell you about any particular products."

This was an interesting little nugget, but he didn't want to push her too hard. "Okay, Stacy, thanks, a lot," he said. "I don't even know if it will impact what I'm looking into, but . . . listen, I promise, soon as I know something about Jordan, I'll let you know."

She smiled again and moved toward the front door. "You know, Ronnie, you should talk to Doug about Dommerich," she said.

"Doug?" he asked. "Isn't Doug a stockbroker or something like that?"

"I'm not sure exactly what part of high finance Doug's into. His company is so huge, they're all over the world, and he doesn't really talk to me about it all that much. But he was the first person to tell me to maybe not rep Dommerich's pharmaceuticals because they were having some . . . issues. I'm looking for a word . . . liquid issues? Something like that. He wasn't very clear, but I trust his judgment. You should talk to him."

Liquidity issues. Ronnie wanted to give her a hug, but they didn't have that kind of neighbor relationship. Instead, he thanked her and told her he'd be in touch. He needed to get back with Hallie.

Chapter 11

For Jordan, and probably Christy as well, showers and fresh, clean, new clothes felt almost as good as being back in the USA and done with this whole Dommerich affair would feel. Almost, maybe. But not quite.

As they boiled up a pound of some kind of pasta, Christy said, "I haven't had any pasta, or anything really that I'd had back home, for nearly a year. At the camp, I was well fed, mostly stews and stuff that didn't taste awful, but I had no idea about the ingredients and wasn't sure I wanted to know."

While they prepared the pasta, Jordan located a pencil but found no writing paper. Christy pointed to a roll of paper towels standing upright next to the sink. They talked about nonsense while they scribbled notes to one another on more important things.

He wrote notes to her about his name change and about his trip to Minneapolis. He wrote about his ongoing conversations with Michael Capshaw.

I'm convinced, he scribbled, *they're about as bad as any organized crime enterprise I've ever read about.*

She shared a few details of the demonstration in front of the Palacio de los López. It had everything to do with Dommerich's designs on thousands of acres of pristine forest to scrape the bark of off the Verawood tree so they could produce and market some product to kill termites.

They drowned the spaghetti in a jar of locally packaged red sauce and ate out on the back patio. Christy was voracious. Later, in the living room with the TV on, they watched a soccer match between a Paraguayan team and one from Brazil, turning up the volume—even though neither of them spoke Spanish—so they could whisper things to each other. Jordan tore the paper towel scribblings into shreds and flushed it all down both toilets in small deposits. Every now and then Jordan would look outside and notice either the Hummer or another unmarked black SUV parked directly in front of the house. *These guys aren't subtle.*

For the moment, at least, this was not the exciting vacation Michael Capshaw had attempted to seduce them with. The accommodations were better, but Jordan was sure he and Christy were still being held against their will.

Jordan wished there was a way he could get a message to Ronnie Levitt.

• • •

Michael Capshaw was sensing a victory lap in his near-term future. His retainer inside the Environmental Protection Agency expressed confidence regarding a first-round preliminary approval for Veracozen, sometime in the next seven to ten days. The name had cleared intellectual property hurdles and Dommerich now owned all conceivable itcrations of the created word, Veracozen. The Dommerich North America marketing division was in the process of readying trial samples for shipment to the hundred largest pest control operations in the US and Canada. Marketing copy and artwork were already finalized and approved internally. They were with Dommerich's ad agency in Minneapolis awaiting a go for production and shipment. The Dommerich PR machine, another direct report of Capshaw's, had video and print press packages produced and ready for release. Company spokespeople had been prepped and teed up for bookings on local morning TV news shows throughout North America. The company already had nearly forty-five million dollars invested in getting Veracozen to market. Projections showed initial orders could recoup over 80 percent of development costs.

The Paraguayan government had blessed Dommerich's deforestation program despite significant opposition from environmental groups. Sufficient financial incentives had been invested in important people in Paraguay so as to render President Acosta's current political opposition little more than background noise.

FDA approval for SaniScal awaited a single staff sign-off following double-blind tests in fifteen American cities. The results were remarkable. The groups testing the actual product, as it would be taken to market, demonstrated a 75 percent greater symptomatic relief than the control group, which had been given a well-known over-the-counter dandruff shampoo. Capshaw wished it had been a lower number, somewhere closer to 60 percent, because, while still very impressive, 60 percent raised way fewer eyebrows than did 80 percent, but the number was the number, and Dommerich's R&D division was doing handstands. *All this*, Michael thought, *for a dandruff shampoo.*

Reports from the field regarding Mr. Censell and Ms. Calder, in Asunción only a day, indicated both seemed thrilled at seeing one another and with their accommodations. So far, Capshaw's security team reported, they were making no noise regarding a quick return home. Capshaw wasn't worried. Even if they did try to get home quickly, he believed the fates were working overtime in Dommerich's favor. He was of a mind that they probably wouldn't require the five hundred thousand dollars he was ready to offer for them to let the past be the past. He was confident he could convince them to move on into a much more appealing future than might otherwise have been the case.

He'd spoken to Becker earlier in the day and made clear a willingness to ensure neither Christy Calder nor Jordan Censell ever saw the light of another day if things unfortunately deteriorated to a point that might threaten either SaniScal or Veracozen from moving forward. Becker expressed satisfaction with the status quo but took pains to make certain Michael understood how anything less than complete success would reflect on his compensation and future advancement within Dommerich. Capshaw didn't let Becker know that the big boss, Gunther Soldinger, had personally called him earlier and told him that up or down on SaniScal and Veracozen, Becker might be reassigned to a less strategically significant business unit, and Dommerich North America might be ready for some new, younger, more dynamic leadership.

Michael received the message loud and clear. He interpreted it as the global CEO's supreme confidence in the way he was handling this whole affair.

In his mind, nothing would stand in the way of Michael Capshaw fulfilling the promise of his own bright future.

• • •

At home, Ronnie picked up a call from Doug Peterson just as Hallie knocked at his front door. He opened the door to let her in and told her who he was on the phone with. She hissed, "From next door? What are you doing?"

He pointed to her and then his other ear, signaling her to listen.

"Hey, neighbor, to what do I owe the pleasure?"

"I just got off the phone with Stacy and she told me you had some questions about Dommerich Worldwide. You gonna bring those assholes down?"

Hallie went borderline apoplectic but managed to do it without making noise. Ronnie muted the phone, put his hands on Hallie's shoulders, and walked her into the kitchen. He stood her in front of the coffee machine. "Calm the fuck down! I'm not stupid," he whispered.

Ronnie unmuted the phone and said, "Yeah, I don't know about that, Doug, but Stacy told me you had mentioned to her that it would be a good idea for her to stop repping their products. Is that right?"

"Not for the record, Ronnie. Okay?"

"Absolutely. Strictly on background." Hallie was slamming cabinet doors, ostensibly in search of a coffee mug. Ronnie pointed a finger at the correct cabinet door.

"Maybe seven, eight months ago," Doug said, "our analysts whispered a strong buy on Dommerich to our clients. They had a couple of seemingly nice things in their pipeline, and we felt their stock was, at that moment, marginally undervalued."

"Okay," Ronnie said, sitting down so Hallie could put her ear to the other side of the phone. "So, what happened?"

"This is just for your ears, Ronnie, and not for publication, right?"

"Doug, I've already gone off the record with you. This is just you and me." Ronnie looked at Hallie, who nodded once.

"We obtained information that, on at least three occasions, Dommerich contracted with what I would call inappropriate test facilities," Doug said. "These facilities apparently had a knack for making sure the results were exactly what the company needed. Don't ask me how we got this information because I don't know. That kind of intelligence is typically obtained by people working well above my pay grade. But we dropped Dommerich like a bad habit. Their stock went down but has pretty much leveled since then."

"How widely known is this information, Doug?"

"I have to believe not very," he said, "otherwise the stock probably would have tanked even more than it did."

"That's interesting, Doug. I appreciate you sharing that with me. Honestly, I'm not sure it's germane to what I'm working on, but as promised, I won't breathe a word of it to anyone."

"You know, two of the three drugs where the results might have been fudged were drugs Stacy repped in the southeast. She was really, really upset, and, as you know, she's usually an upbeat person."

"Do you by chance recall the drug names?"

"No, but I'm sure she does."

. . .

After a good night's sleep, Jordan and Christy got dressed and headed out from their vacation villa. One of their security detail approached them. "Is there anything at all we can do for you, Mr. Censell?" he asked.

"I'm sorry, I don't know your name," Jordan said, smiling.

"I'm Tim, sir."

"I don't think so, Tim," Jordan said. "We're just going to walk around the neighborhood, maybe check out downtown Asunción, visit the tourism office. You know, that kind of stuff."

"We're happy to take you and . . ." Tim hesitated, obviously unsure of their relationship.

"My daughter," Jordan said.

"Yes, right," Tim said. "We'd be happy to take you and your daughter anywhere you'd like to go."

Yeah, Jordan thought, *I bet you would.* "Oh, thanks, Tim, that's very thoughtful, but we don't even really know where we want to go just yet. I do need to visit a bank branch to see if I can get my hands on some money so we can do some things, buy some stuff. You know, just be tourists as long as we're here."

"Oh, right," he said. "Hang on a second, okay?" Tim

walked back to his SUV. Jordan just shook his head and smiled at Christy. "These guys . . ." he whispered to her.

Tim went to the window of his SUV and huddled with his partner. He came back with an envelope. "Mack meant to give this to you yesterday," he said, handing Jordan the envelope. "Mr. Capshaw told us to get you some cash and that he'd arrange for an American Express card in your name in the next couple of days."

Jordan opened the envelope. There was a stack of maybe fifty twenties in US currency and a much larger amount of Paraguayan guaranies.

"We've only been here a few days ourselves, Mr. Censell," Tim said. "To be honest, these folks love American money way more than their own stuff."

"How much is this?" Jordan asked, looking at Christy.

"Inflation is crazy down here, Dad," she said. "You've probably got yourself a couple million guaranies there."

Jordan stuffed about half the money in his pockets and gave the rest to Christy, who did the same.

"I hope this isn't a problem for you, sir," Tim said, "but we're supposed to keep you two pretty close. You're not . . . prisoners, or anything like that, but as your daughter knows, there are some dangerous people here, and some rebel groups are operating in and around Asunción. Mr. Capshaw doesn't want anything to happen to you while you're his guests here."

"Please tell Mr. Capshaw that we really appreciate

his concern, but we'd like to just kind of be quiet tourists," Jordan said. "At least until we get passports and have some idea of when we might be able to go back to the US. You can stay as close as you want, Tim, but we're going to move around Asunción by ourselves. You said we're not prisoners, right?"

Tim was clearly uncomfortable having Jordan and Christy on the loose, but Jordan had left him no choice. He took Christy's arm, and they began walking together in the general direction of the buildings they saw off to the east of their cottage.

Earlier, they'd carefully examined the clothes they'd been provided. Seeing and feeling no obvious listening devices sewn into anything they were wearing, Jordan believed if they could simply walk by themselves, especially in a bustling downtown environment, he could quietly brief Christy on some plans he'd formulated overnight.

Chapter 12

The file Skeeter had provided Ronnie with on Nelson Calder went way beyond interesting. He'd graduated summa cum laude with a BA in Statistics from DePauw University in Greencastle, Indiana, at age nineteen. Young Nelson had migrated to New York City and worked on a master's in mathematics at NYU. Near the end of his second year, two civilians attached to the Pentagon paid him a visit. They'd recruited him to work for the Defense Intelligence Agency as an analyst. His job was to take apart coded messages intercepted by air force and army security outposts and decipher their words and, if possible, their meaning.

After two years at the Pentagon, Nelson was assigned to Wright Patterson Air Force Base in Dayton, Ohio. It housed the headquarters of the United States Air Force's Electronic Security Command. He'd functioned as a senior-level analyst and as an interface between military and civilian intelligence services until nine years ago. That's when he quit the DIA and moved back to Greencastle to work a hundred-acre farm.

Along the way, he'd picked up a wife, Leslie, and their union had produced a daughter, Christy. He'd decided to farm mushrooms and built a very nice agricultural business for himself and his family. After high school, Christy left for college at IU and then law school at Harvard. When she graduated, she moved to Chicago, which put her close, but not too close to her parents. After she passed the Illinois bar exam, she joined a public interest law firm with offices in Chicago and Springfield. Her work had involved defending undocumented immigrants facing deportation and women claiming discrimination and abuse in the workplace. She'd also teamed on two First Amendment cases.

When Leslie died on the operating table, Christy left her practice and joined the Peace Corps. Jordan, still Nelson Calder at that time, sold his farm, rented a big RV, and traveled around the country for a year and a half. He visited Christy in Africa, and then, after she told him she'd been reassigned to Asunción in Paraguay, he waited two weeks before letting her know he planned to pay her a visit there. Soon after, she disappeared.

Two months later, for all intents and purposes, Nelson Calder vanished, and Jordan Censell had emerged on the scene.

Ronnie already knew the Jordan part of the story. The Dommerich part—the part that had sent Hallie cursing and pacing—he'd read later, before working it through with her.

Ronnie exhaled and shook his head. This was a very smart guy who had orchestrated his own vanishing act to pursue learning whatever had happened to his daughter.

. . .

In his office in Minneapolis, Michael Capshaw received twice-daily updates on goings on in Paraguay. He was displeased with Dommerich's contracted security apparatus. The agents apparently weren't sophisticated enough to maintain a much closer handle on Jordan Censell and his troublemaking daughter. But the reports seemed to indicate that they'd both warmed to the idea of keeping themselves happy and busy in South America. He'd be happy as soon as the EPA and FDA finished their damned due diligence on Dommerich's two new products.

He'd managed, through a well-compensated contact in the US State Department, to obtain a replacement passport for Christy Calder but he couldn't get one for Jordan Censell because, he was somewhat surprised to learn, Jordan Censell had never been issued a passport in his name.

Capshaw had a photo of Jordan taken when he was brought to Minneapolis. He'd had what he believed was all the information necessary for State to create a passport in the name of Jordan Censell, but his contact was squeamish about simply issuing a passport without anything resembling appropriate documentation. Frustrated by yet more bureaucracy, Capshaw resourced $100,000 from his departmental slush fund to cover all the palms needing grease. All of this for a passport in the name of Jordan Censell, with the man's dour face on the first page, and an arrival stamp into Paraguay affixed in the appropriate spot. At least, Michael told himself, it wasn't his own money.

• • •

Hallie punched a single number into her phone.

"Berkowitz 1110," said a pleasant, high-register female voice. Hallie smiled.

"Secure transmission, please. Garard 11235."

A pause, then, "11235 secure. When the hell am I going to see you?" Emily asked.

"You know, bitch, they have planes that actually fly into Orlando," Hallie said. "Lots of 'em! And, they have a gazillion hotel rooms here. And a whole lot of fun stuff for a couple of hot chicks to do!" She hesitated. "I miss you, too."

"I really want you to come back soon," Emily said. "Ready to roll?"

"Yep."

"We. Are. Rolling."

"FBI Special Agent Hallie Garard, voiceprint identification 11235. Interagency Task Force, action file, delta hyphen Nancy hyphen Charlie, Orlando 32812."

Hallie dated the call and made a comprehensive report of everything that had transpired over the preceding forty-eight hours to update her SAIC in Washington.

• • •

Ronnie sat alongside Joe Hill in his publisher's office. Tobe Hillenmyer said, "You know you have my confidence, Ronnie, but I also must pay attention to Joe's concerns. How credible is the information you've uncovered so far?"

"This is way out of our lane, Levitt," Joe said. He called all his reporters by their last name. "We have the guy, Censell, right? He's local, but everything else that's going on seems to be all over hell and creation. I trust you and I trust your instincts, but . . . I guess I'm concerned about how much we'll have to put out to get a story that may not resonate that much with our readers here in Central Florida."

Ronnie knew Joe was sincere. He also knew he had Tobe's backing, thanks to the Pulitzer and because of her history of supporting risky propositions with potentially high upside. He closed the door to Tobe's office and walked over to her whiteboard. First, he wrote "local guy" and put a box around it. Then, off to the right, he wrote "blank page" and put another box around it with a line connecting the two.

"The guy who wakes me up every Saturday morning with his damn lawn mower," he said, pointing to the "local guy" box, "was created out of thin air a little over a year ago." He pointed at the "blank page" box. Off to the left, he wrote the words, "onetime DIA analyst." Beneath the "local guy" box, he wrote "Dommerich Worldwide."

He told them, "One of the largest pharmaceutical and pest control product companies in the world is at the center of everything." Then, he wrote "FBI Interagency Task Force" on one side of "Dommerich Worldwide" and "*Orlando Chronicle*" on the other, both with arrows aimed at "Dommerich."

"In addition to ours, there's a concurrent FBI investigation involving two other government agencies. Tobe and Joe looked at each other. Then they turned their focus back on Ronnie. "I'm not sure exactly how all of this is going to play out, but Jennie and I apparently live in a house located literally at ground zero of everything that's going on. I've got an agent from the FBI living two houses away from me. The feds put her there. They've been on this for about seven months. Next door to me, I've got a freelance pharmaceutical rep and her husband, a finance guy. They've told me, off the record, of course, that Dommerich is playing fast and loose with both the FDA and EPA approval processes, and possibly aren't exactly transparent within global financial markets."

"Sheesh!" was Joe Hill's response. Tobe opened a drawer in her desk and removed a bottle of Glenlivet and three glasses. She poured respectable shots for herself and Joe Hill. Ronnie waved her off.

"I'd rather eat my calories, Tobe, but thanks anyway."

"This all started when your wife saw your neighbor taken away by two guys in a black SUV?" she asked. Ronnie shook his head.

"No, not really. It started earlier that morning when he asked me to take care of his dog if, later in the day, anything strange happened involving him. I guess, depending on a couple of minor variables, if I hadn't gone to work on Saturday morning, if Jennie hadn't collected our trash can when she did, we would have missed the whole damn thing."

Joe Hill smiled. "Divine providence, right, Levitt?"

Ronnie smiled. "Call it whatever you want, boss. This is what we have."

"What do you need from us?" Tobe asked.

• • •

Jordan and Christy meandered through a few tree-lined residential streets on the outskirts of Asunción's city center. Christy brought Jordan up to speed on her ten months in captivity. He wanted her to get through everything, so they turned corners and strolled slowly, allowing Tim and Mack to slow-roll behind them as if they didn't know they were being followed.

"It really was kind of strange," Christy said. "I guess I've seen too many movies about rebel encampments or guerrilla staging areas, if that's where I was being kept."

"What do you mean?" Jordan asked.

"I don't know, Dad," she said. "Except for not being able to leave—although, to be honest, I never tested it—it's like I told you. The worst part of being there was the boredom, having nothing to do. Every now and then someone would bring books or magazines, but they were all in Spanish. No television, no work . . . They didn't make me *do* anything. Occasionally a couple of the women who worked there invited me to come to the river to help with laundry or to help in the kitchen. Invited, not demanded."

"Did they ever question you or anything like that?"

"The day I got there, the guy who appeared to be in charge, Colonel Negron, asked me why I thought I'd been brought there. He spoke English very well, but until this morning, that was pretty much the last real interaction I had with him."

"How did you answer his question?"

"I told him I had no clue," she said. "He smiled and nodded, thanked me, and had me escorted to my holding place."

"Seems like an odd kind of confinement," Jordan said.

She threw her head back at the SUV tailing them. "Do they have any idea you've been here before?"

"Not that I know of, and certainly not from me," he said. "I'm not sure any of that matters, though. I remember a little bit about the place, but I was so focused on you, I don't really remember anything likely to help us."

Ahead, the boulevard widened. There was some traffic, and they began noticing shops on both sides of what a street sign proclaimed was Avenida Eusebio Ayala. There was a small plaza with a handful of shops. Jordan nudged Christy in the direction of a coffee shop.

"Mickey and Goofy back there are going to try to follow us inside," he said to her. "Before they get out, walk over, knock on their window and ask them how they like their coffee."

"What will you be doing?"

"For now, some quick reconnaissance," he said. "I have a hunch, and if I'm right, we'll need to keep them from coming inside for a few minutes."

Jordan entered Café Perfecto and came back outside a moment later. He nodded at Christy. Just as Tim opened the passenger side door of the SUV, Christy walked up to him with a big smile on her face.

"What can we get for you guys?" she asked. "How do you like your perfect cup of coffee?"

"We'll just come inside and get our own," Mack said.

"There's no need, guys," she said. "We're going to come outside with ours as well. I think my dad went in first to use the bathroom. He told me to order for all of us. What can I get you?"

They looked questions at one another. Mack shrugged his shoulders. "I take mine black," he said. "If they have anything that looks like a donut, that'd be great." Tim wanted the same, but with two sweeteners and whatever they used to lighten it. Christy took a moment to repeat their orders, gifted them with another big smile, turned, and walked inside Café Perfecto.

Less than five minutes later, the four of them were enjoying, if not perfect, a very good cup of coffee and a range of pastries Christy had purchased. Jordan drove the conversation. "How long have you guys been in Asunción?"

"Actually, we got in late, night before last, not long before you arrived, just early enough to pick up your daughter."

"Where was she being held?"

"I couldn't tell you where; we needed a local driver, just like from the airport."

"How long a ride from the house where we're staying?"

Tim shook his head. "Hard to tell, most of it was in pretty heavy jungle."

"But with decent roads, right?" Jordan asked.

Mack was visibly uncomfortable with Jordan's questions. "Look, Mr.—"

"Jordan," he said. "Just call me Jordan."

The four of them were standing in a small space behind the black SUV, in the parking area of the busy shopping center. People were coming, going, walking by, and driving by. Some were laughing. Others were stone-faced. Some took note of them. Others ignored them. For all the onlookers knew, the four of them could have been plotting the overthrow of the government. Nobody gave them more than a passing glance. Except perhaps for the fact that they were all Anglos, the locals didn't appear to be interested in any of them.

"Jordan," Mack said, "our instructions are simple. We don't have a lot of information about who you two are, why you're here, or anything like that. There are six of us, we work twelve-hour shifts, and we are not to let either of you out of our sight."

"So," Jordan said, "we are . . . like . . . prisoners?"

It was Tim's turn. "No, no, not at all, obviously not," he said. "It's totally about your safety. There are rebel forces actively trying to overthrow the Paraguayan government. They could come into town at any time, and if you're in the wrong place . . ."

Jordan turned to Christy. "Like when you were picked up, right? Was that some rebel group?"

Christy didn't know how to respond to Jordan's question, so she told the truth.

"I was downtown when I got picked up. Over by the Palacio de los López, near the bay," she said. "They put a hood over my head and placed me in the back seat of their car, so I didn't see who took me. I don't even know what they were driving."

"That's what I mean," Tim said. "Shit like that . . . sorry, ma'am—stuff like that happens here all the time."

"But you ended up in some camp outside the city, right?" Jordan asked.

"I suppose that's who they were," she said.

Jordan pivoted. "You guys work for Dommerich?"

"No," Mack said. "We work for GSA . . . Global Security Associates. Dommerich is one of the companies who contracts with us. That all happens above our level."

Jordan looked at his wrist. "Ah, still no watch. Weren't you guys going to get my stuff from the plane?"

Mack looked Jordan in the eyes. "That's right, sir, I did say that yesterday, didn't I? Unfortunately, the plane left early this morning, and I never got out there in time to retrieve it. I'm very sorry. Let me reach out to—"

"No worries, Mack," Jordan said. He looked around. "We'd like to continue meandering, if that's okay with you." He turned to Christy. "Come on, baby, let's see what sights there are here in Asunción." They began walking up the street they were on.

"Why don't you let us drive you around?" Tim called after them.

Jordan turned to face them. "No need," he said, smiling. "Neither of us knows where we're going, right?"

Jordan and Christy quick-walked a couple of blocks, with the SUV following behind, until they came to a one-way street. "Come on, kiddo," he said. "Let's mess with these guys and see how short a leash we're really on." They turned onto the one-way street going against the traffic. Halfway up the block, Jordan looked back. For the moment, at least, no one was following them.

Chapter 13

Tuesday

Ronnie drove the Prius into his garage, turned off the ignition, and exited the car. When he turned around, Hallie was standing about eight inches away from him. "Jeez, Hallie, where did you materialize from?" he asked, nearly bumping into her.

"Over there," she said, gesturing in the direction of her house. "We need to catch up. Come on, let's go talk to Nurse Jackie."

"Wait, what?" Ronnie asked. "Weren't we going to keep the others out of this?"

"Nope," she said. "We were, but now we're not. Ken and Barbie are already inside. Let's do this."

"Ken and—We're reading Stacy and Doug in? Should I call Alberto and Mikey? And why don't they get *Big Bang* nicknames?"

She looked at him and shook her head. "Nooooo, Sheldon, let's keep Wolowitz and the Indian guy out of things, at least for now. If I need to, I'll figure out code names for them later."

Ronnie brought her up to date on what he'd already learned from Stacy and Doug regarding possible criminal activity and financial vulnerabilities. But he couldn't help himself from playing her game.

"Does everyone in your world have an alternate personality from *Big Bang*? Shouldn't Jennie be . . . Penny?"

"Well, Professor Cooper, that's a problem. You see if she's Penny and I'm Leonard . . ."

"Okay, I see what you did there."

Hallie nodded.

Maybe, he thought, *Jennie is right about her*. He entered the house and Hallie followed close behind.

Stacy couldn't wait. "I knew there was something strange about you, Hallie," she said. "Is Hallie even your name?"

Hallie shared her FBI credentials with everyone in the room.

"What are we getting ourselves into, Ronnie?" Doug asked. "I don't want to put my securities licenses in jeopardy here."

"Everyone, please, just take a deep breath," Hallie said. "First, nobody's losing any licenses, jobs, or livelihoods. That said, what we have here is a potentially huge crime, maybe a whole bunch of crimes, being perpetrated by a large global company that has a whole lot of juice with a couple of major federal agencies, as well as on Capitol Hill."

"Maybe we should just start from the beginning," Ronnie said. Hallie gestured for Ronnie to move into the center ring of the small circus taking place in his living room.

Jennie asked for drink orders and headed for the kitchen to get three beers, tea for herself, and a Diet Coke for Stacy. "I know the beginning," she said. "Bring Doug and Stacy up to speed."

Ronnie walked Doug through the earliest stages, impressed with Stacy for not talking to Doug too much about their first foray into Jordan's home. Everything after that was news for Stacy as well, including finding Jordan's flash drive and, later, his computer. Ronnie didn't mention Skeeter's existence or his work; he didn't want Hallie to go completely batshit. At least not yet anyway. He passed off Skeeter's contributions as his own research. Jennie returned and handed each of them their beverage of choice.

"I've gotten clearance from my supervising special agent to let you all in on what we're doing"—Hallie pointed to Stacy and Doug—"with the strict proviso that all we hope to obtain from you two doesn't tip off anyone involved with the target of the investigation. That target is Dommerich Worldwide. Penny . . . er, Jennie, has Ronnie kept you looped in on everything so far?" Hallie asked.

"Yes, Leonard, he has," Jennie said, smiling. Ronnie felt his cheeks burning.

"Sorry, you two," Hallie said to Doug and Stacy. "We haven't come up with *Big Bang* nicknames for you yet."

They looked at each other. "What's *Big Bang*?" Doug asked.

"How do you not—" Ronnie said. Hallie waved him off.

"Never mind that," Hallie said.

Hallie asked Stacy and Doug to see what they could provide in the way of more than just rumor or gossip involving shady testing practices or financial shenanigans on Dommerich's part.

Ronnie said, "Do you want—"

"We have some things we need to discuss," Hallie said. "Doug, Stacy, thank you both very much. Let's talk . . . What's today?"

"Tuesday," Jennie said.

"Let's meet again either this weekend or on Monday. I'm not sure if I'll need to fly up to meet with my people. I'll keep in touch." Hallie clearly wanted everyone from the Susie Q Court contingent to understand who was in charge of things.

After Stacy and Doug left, insecure with the knowledge that they were part of a federal investigation, Ronnie and Jennie sat together on the sofa in their living room. Hallie paced a bit. "This is not generally how we do these kinds of things," she said. "We don't typically involve citizens in investigative activities."

Ronnie waved that off. "Of course you do, Hallie,"

he said. "Same as I do at the paper. If we're lucky, we have sources, and we use them to get information we wouldn't ordinarily be able to get. It's part and parcel of doing both our jobs. Of course, yours involves badges and guns and other coercive components. The rest of us just have to use the tools at our disposal to find out what we need to know."

"I know," she said, "but they're . . . they're not investigators like you and me. They're civilians, and we have to make sure they know what they're getting themselves into."

Ronnie knew where she was going. "I know Stacy comes off a little . . . What's the right word?"

"Blonde?" Hallie asked.

"Not fair, Hallie," Jennie said. "She's a college graduate, and she knows what she knows very well. Yes, she may not be as world-wise as you two, but don't make the mistake of underestimating her."

"Fair enough," Hallie said. "You know her way better than I do. What about him?"

"He's a shark," Ronnie said. "The only concern might be him worrying about her."

Ronnie's mobile buzzed. "It's Stacy," he said. "Hey, Stacy. What's up?" He listened for a minute. "Don't arouse any suspicions." He listened a minute more. "Okay, Stacey, thanks." He hung up.

"She called her contact at work and told him she was available if they had anything rolling out," he said. "He volunteered they'd been alerted that Dommerich had two possible approvals coming in the next week or so. One pharmaceutical, one on their pest management side."

"Uh-huh," Hallie said.

"Yeah," Ronnie said. His phone buzzed again. He looked at it. It was an email. "What is this? I don't know any Jorge Acevedo. Oh . . . *oh!*"

"What?" Hallie and Jennie asked at the same time.

"Subject line. It says 'Ola, neighbor. Greetings from . . . Paraguay'!"

· · ·

Jordan and Christy walked up the Avenue Venezuela for three blocks.

"I know you have no idea where we're going, Dad," she said, "but parts of this city are considered dangerous, and when I got here, we were instructed to avoid those areas."

"This place is way bigger than I remember," he said. "I need to be able to speak freely with you for a couple of minutes before Frick and Frack find us and make us go back to the house."

"Why?" she asked him. "What's up?"

They stopped walking. "Let's get back to that main street we were on. I think I saw a market. *Mercado*, right?"

"Still a quick study, Dad," she said. They walked back the way they came and found the Avenue Simon Bolivar again.

"I managed to get an email sent to my neighbor, the newspaper reporter, Ronnie Levitt," he said.

Christy looked at him. "How did you do that?"

"Old school," he said. "There were a half dozen kids on computers in the coffee shop. While you were entertaining Tim and Mack, I dropped a twenty in front of one of them and told him to get himself a cup of coffee."

"What exactly do you think is going on here, Dad? I mean, they got me out of that camp; they brought you here; we're together . . ."

"Which makes us easier to manage . . . or to control," he said. "Our guards may not think we're prisoners, but if we happened to, say, mosey on over in the direction of the American Embassy, you'd see how quickly we'd be contained."

Christy nodded. "Okay, I see what you're saying. What did you tell your friend?"

"Where we are, that we're together, and that we probably only have a few days max to get out of here and get home, or we might be in trouble," he said. "I also told him to check out Dommerich, Michael Capshaw, SaniScal, and Veracozen." He stopped walking and turned to her. "All of this has been to find you and bring you home, baby. Let's get back to that street or avenue where the coffee shop is. I don't want them thinking we're running. Not yet anyway."

Seconds after they turned back onto the Avenida Eusebio Ayala, the black SUV pulled alongside them.

"Come on Mr. Censell, ma'am," Mack said through the window. "Let's go back to where you're staying."

Jordan looked at Christy. They both shrugged and walked toward their ride. "I've got a better idea," he said. "Let's find someplace to grab a bite." He pulled out a big wad of Paraguayan currency. "My treat!" *Michael Capshaw's treat, actually.*

. . .

Michael Capshaw felt a bit more confident about how things were playing out. The security contractor in Paraguay reported nothing of concern. Even the brief side trip they'd taken out of sight and earshot of the guards seemed to warrant no concern on his part. His focus was totally aimed at the EPA and the FDA.

Experience told him the agencies were powerless to do anything but approve both products. Dommerich's scientists and lobbyists along with colleagues from other multinational companies competing in the drug and pesticide segments helped write the rules and regulations governing the approval processes for new products. Dommerich's testing organizations were beholden to the company. After all, Dommerich was paying for the studies and, without having to say it, for the outcomes. The wheels of so-called oversight in the public's interest turned based on how much was provided by those who would profit from sale of these products. It wasn't a question of if the products would be approved, only when.

Obtaining FDA approval for SaniScal should have, in Michael's view, been a slam dunk. With the advent of impressive new testing technology, a willing pool of human test subjects, and some investment in the well-being of a couple of key FDA functionaries, SaniScal should have been approved for rollout several months ago. A single death of an eleven-year-old test subject, a boy from Oregon who, it turned out, had a serious underlying medical condition, had knocked the process off the rails.

The product was already in wide distribution, with few issues reported, in Germany, France, the UK, and Australia. Internal Dommerich ROI and profitability targets either were being met or were within reach in those markets.

The USA, though, typically accounted for both revenue and profit numbers three, four, or five times those of European and other marketplaces around the world. Michael Capshaw's personal compensation and his own standing within the company were dependent on a successful rollout in North America.

Among his peers inside the company, he was, and wanted always to be, the biggest dog in the pack. Capshaw punched a memorized number into one of the six mobile phones he kept under lock and key in his office. Quickly, he was on the line with Jack Winter, one of his bureaucrat retainers in Washington.

"There's no holdup, Michael," Winter said. Winter was the Food and Drug Administration's clinical director ultimately responsible for releasing SaniScal from the purgatory of the federal government's stifling bureaucratic process machine. Once released, it would find its way to the shelves overseen by pharmacists ready to dispense the promising new shampoo into the hands and onto the heads of Americans anxious to rid themselves of the scourge of dandruff.

"Oregon was a setback, as you know, but in the past six months, only a handful of significantly lesser reaction issues have surfaced. Nothing, in my estimation, for you to concern yourself over."

"Those words are reassuring, Jack," Capshaw said, "but we need a green light and a clear highway, and we need it sooner rather than later."

Jack Winter was a well-established resource for Dommerich inside the FDA. His daughter was receiving an unofficial Dommerich scholarship to attend college at Wellesley. "How's Monica doing in Boston?"

Winter cleared his throat. "She's good, Michael. Thank you for asking."

"It would be a shame if she couldn't, I don't know, finish her undergrad up there. Is she still on track for a degree in biology?"

Winter hesitated for a moment before answering. "Let me check the status, Michael. There's no reason this shouldn't have happened by now, unless—"

"Unless is not a word that gives me confidence, Jack," Capshaw said.

"Michael, I'm certainly trying to avoid bringing

Congress into this conversation, but I'm not in control when things become political."

No doubt a reference to Jordan Censell's recent persistent and annoying outreach to FDA and EPA political appointees as well as the congressional offices of senators and representatives seated on committees tasked with oversight of the two agencies.

"I understand, Jack," Michael Capshaw said. "If you would, please make a short visit to your colleagues upstairs and see what you can find out. I promise, I'll be grateful for anything you can do to speed things along. Have a good day, Jack, and please send my and Dommerich's best to Monica."

Chapter 14

"Paraguay?" Hallie asked, sitting cross-legged on the living room carpet. "What the bleep is a Paraguay?"

Ronnie laughed out loud at her. "Small, landlocked country in the south-central part of South America," he said. "Bordered by Brazil, Bolivia, and Argentina. Bolivia is the other landlocked nation in South America. Anything else I can tell you?"

"I'm in the FBI, asshat," she said. "I could arrest you. Or shoot you."

"Maybe I could just read the email to you?"

"Good idea, Bernstein," she said.

"Well, finally you got the ethnic part right. Okay, here goes: 'First, both I and my daughter are fine, mostly. We're in Asunción, Paraguay. I'm pretty sure people associated with Dommerich had her held somewhere in the jungle near here for almost a year. Focus your attention there and on a sleazy creep/executive name of Michael Capshaw. Christy's a public interest lawyer currently doing Peace Corps work. She started pushing back on Dommerich activities in Mali last year and got shipped off to Paraguay. Soon after arriving she was at some rally and got snatched. She was taken somewhere in the jungle and kept prisoner there until yesterday. I was flown to Minneapolis on Saturday for a meet with Capshaw. Now I'm here, with her. I think they're trying to keep us out of the way until two products, SaniScal and Veracozen, get FDA and EPA approval. I may not be able to reach out in this manner again. Got lucky in a coffee shop in Asunción. Do what you do, Ronnie. Say hey to Jennie and the FBI chick.'" He turned to her. "There's a smiley face emoji."

"Well, he is former DIA," Hallie said. "Here I thought I'd been undercover."

"You had me fooled," Ronnie said. "I thought you were just a professional smartass."

"Who wants some lunch?" Jennie asked and headed for the kitchen.

Ronnie reread the Professor's email. "I need to make a couple of calls," he said.

"Yeah," she said, standing in a single fluid motion. "Let's hook back up here in half an hour. And tell Jennie thanks, I'd love some lunch."

• • •

"Skeeter," he said, answering Ronnie's call before the phone even rang.

"How do you do that?" Ronnie asked.

"Do what?"

"Answer the phone before it rings."

"Stupid question," he said. "You want what I got, or you want to tell me what you need?"

"Tell me what you learned," Ronnie said.

"Dommerich's a real piece of shit company," he said. "Bugs and drugs. Stock's flat, nothing new or exciting for maybe two years, and a piss-poor record of long-term success with several of its products."

Ronnie asked, "Can you investigate two upcoming products, SaniScal and Veracozen?"

"Already did," Skeeter said. "Hang on."

Skeeter came back on the line. "Sorry, I hate getting stuck in traffic."

"Where are you?"

"Not relevant. Honey gets stressed when we stop moving. Truck's got some transmission stuff going on."

"Okay, did you learn anything about a guy, Michael Capshaw?"

"I saw his name. You want a deep dive?"

"Twenty thousand fathoms, please."

Skeeter disconnected. Ronnie shook his head and realized he didn't get what Skeeter had on the two products. He dialed Joe Hill's number.

"Your quarter," Hill said.

Ronnie filled him in on Jordan's email.

"Hmmm. So . . . What? You want to go to South America?"

"No, no, not yet, anyway," Ronnie said. "I do want to go to Minneapolis. I need an ID package from corporate. Business cards, bio, you know, the works."

"Yep. Tomorrow, midafternoon work for you?"

Boy, that was easy. He didn't even ask why. "Perfect. Thanks, Joe."

Ronnie didn't want to tip his hand when he first approached Michael Capshaw. A reporter from Orlando would arouse suspicion that his visit had something to do with Jordan's disappearance. Ronnie would use a different approach. He'd present himself as a corporate-based journalist headquartered at One World Trade Center in New York's financial district, a feature writer doing a snapshot-in-time story about the current state of the pharmaceutical marketplace for the business sections of Capital Media Group's eighteen dailies and thirty business weeklies throughout America.

Once the corporate package was completed, he'd have business cards, a snazzy pocket folder with his current head shot, a corporate biography, including information outlining CMG's status, ticker symbol, and filler sufficient to establish his national bona fides. He'd reach out to Capshaw as soon as his backstory was in place.

• • •

Instead of checking in with her handler, Hallie reached out to a trusted contact she'd cultivated at the Central Intelligence Agency.

"Hey, Guillermo, what's shaking?"

"Hallie Garard. You called me," Willie Vasquez said.

"Right, no foreplay," she said. "You got a few minutes?"

"What do you need?"

"Paraguay."

There was momentary silence on the line. "I've heard of it," he said. "Where'd that come from?"

"We're tracking a couple of folks down there," she said. "How stable is it?"

"Let me call you back from a different phone." He hung up. Two minutes later her phone buzzed.

"Hey, it's me."

"So?"

"It's a bowl of nuts," he said. "We're in and out of there, supporting larger, ongoing operations in Brazil, Argentina, and Chile. Government seems semi-stable but there are a few groups trying to disturb the status quo."

"You ever get down there?"

"No, well, not in a while, but we have interests in the region. Something I need to know?"

"Truth, Willie, I don't know. We have a couple of people we're trying to keep an eye on down there." She took a minute to bring him up to speed on what she'd learned from Ronnie's mysterious source about Jordan and Christy.

"They in trouble?" he asked.

"Could be but, honestly, I don't know. You familiar with a pharmaceutical company, Dommerich?"

"Sure," he said. "They're big."

"Any idea what their interest would be in Paraguay?"

"Forest? Jungle? Don't they make pesticides also?"

"Yeah, they do."

"They might be looking for source material for active ingredients in pesticides or pharmaceuticals, I guess. Several of the big drug and pest control producers do that down there, also over in Africa. I'll check, see what I can find out."

"That would be great," she said. "You in Miami?"

"Keep in touch, Hallie Garard."

"Will do. Thanks, Willie V."

• • •

Jordan and Christy were quiet on the ride back to their Asunción crash pad. They actually enjoyed their dinner with Tim and Mack. Jordan put them at ease with a bonhomie the security guys didn't seem accustomed to.

At 9:00 p.m. local time, Craig and James relieved Tim and Mack. Jordan and Christy retired to their living room to catch some satellite television. They kept the sound up so they could whisper to one another without much chance of being overheard. They made sure they talked in the open often enough to keep the guards satisfied.

Over the two days they'd been in residence, Jordan had found several locations in the house he believed were likely to include listening devices. They were everywhere, in the living room, kitchen, and both bedrooms. He couldn't be certain about the courtyard behind the house or the bathrooms, but he assumed they were similarly wired.

They talked mostly about Leslie, her death, how much they both missed her, and about Jordan's road trip around the USA. Christy filled him in on her experiences in Chicago defending undocumented Latin Americans from sudden deportation. She mentioned more than once how much she missed living in Chicago.

He pulled her in for a hug. "If the email landed," he whispered, "things could take off quickly. I know the FBI is already involved, along with a hotshot investigative reporter. I've already made noise at the EPA and FDA. The next move by Dommerich will tell the tale. We need to be ready for anything." She nodded.

He looked into his daughter's eyes. He saw intelligence, strength, and resolve.

"I love you, Dad."

"Double, baby."

• • •

WEDNESDAY

Michael Capshaw arrived in New York for a day and a half of meetings with market analysts, financial media, and SEC regulators. His purpose was to tease SaniScal and Veracozen, to try and stimulate some upward movement for Dommerich's stock, and to set the table for the next quarterly report. He met with Nathan

Becker at the hotel. Becker was in town to attend industry functions and, Capshaw knew, to entertain investors and network with fellow C-suite types. He'd probably also pick up a bauble or two for his wife.

"If I understand you correctly, Michael, we should be good to go with Veracozen by the end of this week, but there are still some hurdles for us to overcome with SaniScal. Have I got that right?" Becker asked.

"You do, sir," Capshaw said. "As you know, the unfortunate occurrence in Oregon triggered a mandatory ninety-day delay in SaniScal's approval. My sense, after talking with a friend at the FDA, is that they're simply being cautious."

"Caution is fine, Michael, but I'm responsible for the performance of Dommerich Worldwide's most important business unit." Capshaw believed himself superior to his CEO on several levels, but Becker took every opportunity to remind Capshaw who was in charge. "We have hard objectives to meet. And I need to know you're doing everything possible to facilitate FDA approval for SaniScal. Please keep me appraised of anything I need to know."

"Absolutely, sir," Capshaw said. "As soon as I know something, you'll know it."

• • •

Capshaw was on his way to a lunch meeting on Wall Street when Nancy Kuo called on his official corporate mobile phone. "Yes, Nancy."

"A Ronald Levitt with Capital Media Group called. They own—"

"I know who they are, Nancy," Capshaw interrupted. "What does Mr. Levitt want?"

"He'd like to meet with you in Minneapolis when you return."

"See what you can find out about him and call me back."

"Yes, sir."

. . .

Ronnie got the call from Capshaw's executive assistant agreeing to host him at Dommerich's North American headquarters in Minneapolis.

"Mr. Capshaw would be happy to send one of our jets to New York to pick you up, Mr. Levitt," Nancy said.

"Please pass along my gratitude for the offer, Ms. Kuo," Ronnie said. "I'm not in New York as we speak. Plus, I'm not permitted to accept Dommerich's generosity. Journalistic ethics and all that."

"Mr. Capshaw will be here through the weekend," she said. "After that, he's scheduled to be away on business himself. Can you give me an idea of when you might be able to get to Minneapolis?"

"How's tomorrow afternoon, say 3:30 p.m.?" Ronnie asked.

"I've got you down," she said. "Are we permitted at least to pick you up at the airport?"

"That would be fine, Ms. Kuo," Ronnie said. Per her request, he faxed her the bio page from his new corporate ID package.

He'd asked Tobe Hillenmyer's own executive assistant, an officious but efficient twit named Charles, if he would please handle his travel arrangements. He sent texts with the flight information to Hallie and, separately, to Jennie. He'd spend Thursday night in Minneapolis at a Hilton near MSP before catching a morning flight on United back to Orlando.

Chapter 15

"Skeeter."

"I'm out of town for a day and a half," Ronnie told him.

"Why tell me? I'm not your mother."

Sometimes, despite his capabilities, Skeeter Bates could behave like a monumental pain in the ass.

"Well, that solves that mystery," Ronnie deadpanned. "If you need to talk or to send me something, use the backup cell and email address. Okay?"

"Okay." He was gone.

Ronnie's phone rang. "Levitt."

"Ronnie? It's Stacy, from next door." She, on the other hand, was adorable.

"You're the only Stacy I know, Stacy," he said.

"Oh, well, okay," she said. "Listen, I've been thinking about stuff . . . this stuff with him, across the street. I need to tell you a couple of things. About, you know, that . . . company."

"Okay."

"Can I come over? Or can you come over here?" she asked.

"Of course, Stacy," he said. "Which works better for you?"

"Can you come here?"

"Be right there."

• • •

Ronnie saw Stacy was agitated the moment she opened her front door. She brought Ronnie into the kitchen. They sat on stools at the kitchen counter. She'd already poured glasses of water, separated by a small bowl of salted peanuts and M&M's, and a couple of paper napkins. No matter what she happened to be wearing, Stacy Peterson looked like she'd just stepped off a magazine page. She was in crisply ironed white shorts, a coral-colored, sleeveless blouse, and just enough makeup. She wore coordinating flip-flops on her feet and coral-colored toenail polish to match her fingers. Ronnie was hopelessly in love with his wife, but he had to wonder if Stacy rolled out of bed in the morning looking that good.

"Doug and I talked it over last night, and we decided I should tell you everything I know about Dommerich that might have anything to do with what's going on with . . . What did we decide his name is?" she asked.

Ronnie didn't want to add to Stacy's angst with more information about Jordan's identity than was necessary. "Jordan," he said. "Jordan Censell. What's going on, Stacy?"

"I don't know what you and Hallie are doing about all this, but Doug and I thought the more you know, the better chance you'll have of dealing with these . . . people," she said. "What I know comes from other people, mostly, so you may have to get, what do you call it . . . collaboration?"

"Corroboration," Ronnie said. "We can do that, Stacy. I'm not recording anything. This, for now, is just a conversation between neighbors and friends. If it would make you more comfortable, I won't even take notes."

"No, of course you can take notes, and yes, corroboration was the word I was looking for. Anyway, early last year Dommerich released a new product. It wasn't pharmaceutical so other people repped it, but it was called Fulaxifon, and it was used for household pest control." She hesitated. "Wait a second." She quick-walked over to a kitchen alcove and picked up a sheet of paper.

"What's . . . ?"

"I want to make sure I get this right, Ronnie," she said. "You know, when I call on physicians, I mostly work from a prepared presentation. Otherwise, words fly out of my head, and I have no idea where they go or what I should or shouldn't say. Anyway," she referred to what appeared to Ronnie to be a full page of typed text, "somehow this product got EPA approval even though Dommerich had to settle a drinking water contamination problem out of court. Doug thinks they probably paid people off. Anyway, I don't know if Fulaxifon is currently on the market or if it's been pulled, but a guy I know from my company confirmed about the payoff."

Ronnie scribbled a few notes. "Can you give me the guy's name? The one who told you about it?"

"Let me ask him first if it's okay. But there's more," she said. She put the paper down.

"Okay."

"I personally repped two Dommerich drugs two years ago," she said. "One was called Laxoza. It was for pain, specifically arthritis pain. The other was . . ." she turned the paper back over, "it was called Quapakacen, and it was supposed to help the body release more insulin for patients with diabetes."

Ronnie began to reflect on what Jennie had told Hallie, about Stacy possibly not being as world-wise as some others might be. She indeed did know what she knew very, very well.

"Supposed to?" he asked.

She began fidgeting with the piece of paper and with her diamond engagement ring and wedding ring.

"Can this be off the record, Ronnie?"

"Right now, Stacy, everything is off the record until I get it corroborated . . . by someone other than you," he said.

"It's just, we know, the people who do what I do, we sometimes know stuff that regular people, the general public, doesn't know, wouldn't have any way of knowing. You know what I'm saying?" she asked.

Ronnie couldn't help but see how scared his neighbor, his friend was. "Stacy," Ronnie said, "Hallie is working on a case involving the EPA and the FDA. I'm trying to find out what happened to our neighbor, Jordan. We are both just really feeling our way around, and"—he reached out and took her hands in his—"nothing you tell me is going to suddenly end up in the newspaper without you knowing what it is and when it's going to happen. I promise."

"Doug said I should tell you this, so I'm going to tell you," she said. "Those two drugs never, ever came to market. We were—there must have been twenty of us up in Atlanta—we were trained, given a six-month contract, and less than three weeks into prerelease marketing, our contracts were paid off in full, and they told us to go home."

"Prerelease marketing?" Ronnie asked.

"That's where we visit our docs, tell them what's coming, get them all excited, so when the drug finally drops—that means after it's approved and then released—they'll prescribe it and give away our samples," she said. "We never even got to give the docs our samples, Ronnie. They paid us and that was that. Neither of those drugs ever made it to market. Easiest money I ever made."

Ronnie gulped down his water. "I don't understand, Stacy. If they caught something before it was released or before you distributed any samples, is that a problem?"

She nodded and smiled at him. "I know," she said. "Seems like it shouldn't be a problem, right?" Ronnie shrugged his shoulders and waited. "Both of those drugs were released in Europe, South America, and South Asia, you know, India, Indonesia, places like that," she said. "Far as I know, they're still being distributed and prescribed there. Just not here."

Ronnie sat, stunned. "Stacy . . ."

"Three years ago, another drug," she referred to her paper, "Choralizine, a powerful antidepressant, got pulled, but only after it had been on the market and had been prescribed for almost six months."

"I have to ask—"

"Ronnie, Dommerich—all the major pharmaceutical companies—have to do years of tests and clinical trials in order to get approval from the FDA. It's a very long, very expensive process," she said. "They tell that to us all the time, how expensive it is to bring a drug to market." She moved into their living room and sat down on a beautiful pale-green upholstered Queen Anne chair. She signaled for him to join her.

"I have no way of knowing how many prescriptions were written, how many patients took the drug, how many had adverse reactions, even how many may have died because they used a drug I repped," she said. Ronnie saw tears welling up in her eyes. "I don't recall any other company I've repped, any other product

I've helped take to market, where even though they stopped pushing the drug here, they kept it on the market in other places." She was shaking, close to tears. "I know it may sound stupid, Ronnie," she said, "but I feel like I've been an accessory to whatever these awful people did."

Ronnie needed to talk to Hallie, and he needed to get ready for Minneapolis in the morning. "Stacy, first, you had no more to do with anything bad that happened to anyone because of one of Dommerich's drugs than the salesman at the auto dealership does if a car he sells has a safety problem he knew nothing about. Second, if I can get any of this corroborated, and I'm pretty sure I can, it's starting to seem like Dommerich has a pattern of behavior demonstrating complete disregard for either the efficacy or the safety of its products. And third, I'm heading to Minneapolis tomorrow. I have a meeting scheduled with an executive at Dommerich. It's nothing to do with anything you've told me. I just want to get a sense of the company. I need to know you're going to be all right if I have to leave."

She smiled at him. "I'm okay, Ronnie. I really wanted to get this off my chest and give you, I don't know, ammunition, in case any of it can be useful to you. You go ahead; I'm fine."

The Levitt's and the Petersons had been neighbors for almost four years on Susie Q Court. This was the first time Ronnie had ever hugged Stacy.

"Thanks, Stacy," he said. "This is pretty impressive stuff you've shared with me." He turned to leave.

"Who are you meeting with at Dommerich?" she asked him.

"His name is Capshaw, Michael Capshaw."

"Ugh," she said, and made the gesture for causing herself to vomit.

"You know him?"

"Ronnie, believe it or not, I get hit on a lot in this job," she said.

"Oh, Stacy, I had no idea," he said, smiling. "You're such a beast. I mean, who'd want to do anything like that?"

She rolled her eyes. "He was at a training session they held last year," she said. "Our CEO made a big thing about him being there. After one of the sessions, he came on to me. 'Let's go get a drink, maybe dinner,' yada, yada. He was so creepy. I called Doug that night and told him I'd rather sell real estate than put up with people like him."

"Anything else you can tell me about him, other than his excellent taste in women?" Ronnie asked.

She laughed. "Really, it was just that. I blew him off, and he just moved on to another girl. A first-class dick."

"Got it, Stacy . . . I promise, I won't mention your name. But seriously, thanks so much for sharing this with me. I can't be sure yet, but I have a sense, at some point, it's all really going to matter."

Chapter 16

Thursday

"Don't tip him off to the fact that he's on everyone's radar, Sheldon," Hallie said before Ronnie left for the airport. "My investigation is some pretty serious shit."

"Yeah," he said, "and our neighbor and his daughter are in some serious shit as well, Leonard. I'm hoping I can just get a sense of the guy, the company, you know, maybe poke the bear just a little.

"How are you gonna approach him?"

"The plan is to put him at ease by making the story about this moment in time in the pharmaceutical industry," he said. "I'll tell him he's one of several executives I'm talking to about the overall health of the sector, what challenges the industry is facing, what's new at Dommerich . . . that kind of stuff. I sent him a corporate bio so he'd have a sense about me, but nothing about where I work."

"You going to poke the bear with anything Stacy told you?" she asked.

"Depends," Ronnie said. "The minute I bring up anything like that, the whole tenor of the conversation changes. I have to be prepared to get ushered out of his office, get yelled at by my management, that sort of stuff."

"You concerned?"

He looked at her, a small, half-smile on his face. "I'm about as concerned about hurting his feelings as you'd be."

"Hey," she said. I'm a very sensitive person."

"Yeah," he said, "you and Jack Reacher."

"Who's that?"

"Never mind," he said. "I'll give you a call if I need encouragement."

· · ·

Jordan and Christy enjoyed another good breakfast in the quiet of the kitchen inside their Asunción cottage.

"What's on the docket for today, Father?" she asked.

He made a show of looking around at the ceiling. "I don't know about you, but I've heard there's a pretty good art museum here in Asunción," he said. "You think maybe our friends would drop us off, then pick us up a couple hours later?"

"Yeah! If I remember right," she said, "it's down near the bay. I guess we could ask them. Or we could just walk. You know, after ten months in the jungle, I like idea of just walking around."

"Well," he said, standing up and collecting their dishes, "why don't you go ask them, and I'll get these things cleaned up."

Christy walked outside and encountered the third team of security guards, Steve and Raul.

"Good morning, gentlemen," she said. "Do you guys like fine art? My dad and I would like to visit the National Museum of Art today. Feel free to come along or take us and pick us up in a couple hours. What do you think?"

It quickly became clear neither Steve nor Raul had any real interest in fine art. Raul told Christy they'd be happy to drop them off at the museum, find a place to have breakfast, and pick them up later.

They arrived at the National Museum of Art just before 8:00 a.m. "We'll be back at ten," Steve said. "If there is somewhere else you'd like to visit, we'll be happy to drive you."

"I didn't know you were such an art aficionado, Dad," Christy said as they slow-walked the halls of the museum.

"I can take it or leave it," Jordan said. "Testing the waters for a couple of things. You think they're really going to go find something to eat, or are they going to park close by to make sure we don't go off by ourselves again?" Christy shrugged her shoulders.

"I don't know," she said. "I'm not quite as paranoid as you, so . . ."

"Why not? Aren't you even a little paranoid?" he asked. "You're the one who was yanked off the street, blindfolded, and deposited in some rebel camp in the jungle for almost a year. You're not even a little bit thinking these may not be the nicest guys in the world?"

Christy stopped and stared at a lovely Madonna and child by a Paraguayan artist she'd never heard of.

"I guess it's a matter of perspective, Dad," she said. "I understand what confinement feels like. I'm not feeling confined right now. Men with guns watched me every waking moment, probably when I slept, too. This doesn't feel like that."

He smiled at her. "You're definitely the Goody Two-shoes in this clan, baby," he said. "And I am definitely not."

She scanned the museum gallery. At the moment, a dozen or so children were in tow of a single chaperone. The woman was trying and failing to wrangle the group of yammering seven- and eight-year-olds.

"Why are we here, Dad?"

"If I'm not mistaken, we are a decent but not too distant walk, if we walked briskly but without calling too much attention to ourselves, from the US Embassy," he said. "Now, not today, maybe not even tomorrow, but perhaps in two or three more days, if we can gain the trust of every shift of watchers, we can make a run for American soil and get ourselves the hell out of here." She nodded her head. "And that, my darling daughter, is what we're doing here."

"So that's our endgame? The embassy?" she asked.

"Unless you have another better idea, baby."

She didn't.

• • •

Ronnie landed at Minneapolis–St. Paul International Airport eleven minutes before his scheduled arrival time. He carried a backpack with a single change of clothes, along with a brown messenger bag containing his computer, a digital recorder, and notes he'd made during the flight. Michael Capshaw's assistant told him to look for a limo driver carrying a sign with his name on it. There were three drivers waiting for passengers in an open area once they'd cleared security. He found the one with "Mr. R. Levitt" printed on it.

The Lincoln Town Car covered the drive from MSP to Dommerich North America corporate head-quarters in the Nicollet Mall complex in downtown Minneapolis in just short of forty minutes. The driver opened the street side passenger door. "Just check in at the security desk, Mr. Levitt," he said.

"Thanks," Ronnie said. He stood for a moment taking in his surroundings. He had a reservation at an Embassy Suites hotel near the airport and for a flight to Orlando leaving Friday morning. He hoped he could finish with Michael Capshaw by 6:00 p.m., which would give him sufficient time to collect his thoughts and notes, have a bite of dinner, and get a good night's sleep.

He walked into the lobby of the high-rise and found the security desk. He showed his Capital Media Group photo ID, was presented with a visitor badge, and was asked to take a seat. While he waited, he removed a second digital recording device from his bag, turned it on, and placed it in the breast pocket of his jacket. Within a minute, a tall, slim Asian woman approached. She wore a tight, bright-green sleeveless dress, ending midthigh, and a pair of black stiletto heels.

"Good afternoon, Mr. Levitt. I'm Nancy, we spoke on the telephone," she said in perfect Midwestern English. She extended her right hand. "Mr. Capshaw is anxious to meet you. Please, follow me."

They walked to a bank of elevators, and she ran her badge over a keypad. Moments later they arrived at the twenty-seventh floor. The elevator opened and Nancy stepped out to her right.

"Mr. Levitt, a pleasure! Michael Capshaw." He extended his hand, which Ronnie shook and quickly let go of.

"Hi, Mr. Capshaw. Thanks for fitting me in. I know how busy you must be."

Capshaw wore a blue-and-white microdot Zegna shirt with a red-and-pink Hermès Twillbi silk tie. His suit pants, dark blue with white pinstripes, broke perfectly at the tops of black Ferragamo loafers. Ronnie thought, *Dude has more invested in what he's wearing today than I have in my car.* He followed Capshaw past Nancy's curved gatekeeper desk into his office, a suite befitting a man of such importance. The floor-to-ceiling glass wall faced northeast, providing a view of downtown Minneapolis, and beyond, the Mississippi River. Past the river, Ronnie could make out a portion of what he suspected was downtown St. Paul. The room, in both appearance and temperature, was quite cold.

"Wow! What a view," Ronnie said, paying off Capshaw's obvious attempt to impress his guests.

"I know," Capshaw said, smiling. "It never gets old. Let's sit over here, where we can both enjoy it." He directed Ronnie to a beveled glass conference table with white leather captain's chairs. A crystal pitcher filled with water, an ice bucket, a tray of sliced roll-up sandwiches, a stainless-steel tray filled with peeled and deveined shrimp, and a matching small shell-shaped bowl containing cocktail sauce all made for a welcoming and most appetizing impression.

Ronnie felt a moment of sartorial insecurity; he almost never wore a suit, seldom put on a jacket and tie, and was accustomed to showing up for an interview in jeans, an Izod or Dockers golf shirt, and a pair of Sperry Topsiders, often without socks. On this day, he wore an old herringbone jacket, a pair of gray slacks, and a white dress shirt with the sleeves buttoned at the cuffs. He doubted everything he wore cost as much as Capshaw's suspenders.

He opened his messenger bag and removed a reporter's notebook and a second Sony digital voice recorder. "Do you mind?" he asked.

"Not at all. If it becomes a problem, I'll let you know," Capshaw said, smiling. Ronnie wondered if the guy had done any research on him.

"Before we get started, I'm curious. Would you tell me just a little about your Pulitzer Prize?" he asked. "How does that process work?" Ronnie smiled, recalling the Pulitzer's mention in his bio. He'd been asked variations of this question so often he had a well-practiced response.

"Oh, well, thanks for asking. It was thoroughly unexpected, really. It began as a relatively ordinary kind of story about a county government's process for approving real estate developments. The system turned out to be remarkably corrupt. Ultimately, the stories led to changes in how business got done in the county, but, really, I was the most surprised guy in the newsroom when we got the notification," he said. "I guess the good thing about it turned out to be the job I have now."

Capshaw had his hands together in front of him, almost as if he were praying. "I'm sure you're being modest, Mr. Levitt. Anyway, congratulations. I have to deal with reporters—journalists, in your case—all the time, but I'm pretty sure you're the first Pulitzer winner I've ever met."

Ronnie had no intention of becoming best friends with Michael Capshaw, but he felt it might benefit things if he were to ingratiate himself, just a little bit, with the man. "I've met a few others over the years," Ronnie said. "We all kind of have the same notion of how luck really plays a very large part in who wins a prize and who gets passed over."

Capshaw, took a two-pronged cocktail fork, speared a shrimp, dipped it into the cocktail sauce, and took a bite. He had blinding white teeth. He dabbed a napkin at the corners of his mouth. "How does it work?" he asked, seeming genuinely interested.

"You have time?" Ronnie asked.

"Absolutely."

"In my category, local investigative reporting, there's a seven-member jury selected to judge the entries. That's where the luck comes into play. If the jury tasked with considering the nominations contains a few former investigative journalists from small or midmarket dailies, a story such as mine has a better chance of resonating than if most of the jurors come from major-market papers. I guess, when you boil it down, I just got a sympathetic jury."

"Hmmm," Michael Capshaw said, smiling. "A sympathetic jury. I'll wager the people you reported on—the targets of your investigation—wished they'd had a sympathetic jury."

Ronnie couldn't help himself. "Honestly, Mr. Capshaw, the seven of them could have had their brothers and sisters on the jury, and they still would have been convicted. They were so arrogant and so flagrantly deceitful. They dismissed the checks and balances built into the development approval process as if those rules didn't apply to them. I'm pretty sure they were going to be found guilty the minute they were placed in handcuffs."

"Please, Mr. Levitt, may I call you Ronnie?"

"Sure. But I'll still call you Mr. Capshaw, okay?"

He smiled. "Okay. Please enjoy some refreshments. How can I be of service to you?"

Chapter 17

Ronnie spent the next hour asking benign questions about the state of the pharmaceutical industry in America. He expressed interest in learning the kinds of successes the industry, and Dommerich in particular, had experienced of late, and the challenges both were being asked to confront. He touched on the pesticide side of the industry and was interested to learn that, in addition to Dommerich, several large-scale pharmaceutical companies also operated in the pest-, termite-, and rodent-control space.

"As you probably know, Ronnie," Capshaw said, "I'm not a scientist. I know just enough of the science to be dangerous. Here at Dommerich, we employ or contract with literally thousands of brilliant scientific minds all over the world. During preliminary research into the efficacy of a particular active ingredient for, say, a drug to help reduce cholesterol or even an over-the-counter pain reliever, our scientists invariably discover that a particular product, in perhaps a different dosage or in combination with secondary ingredients, will have qualities or applications that support additional investment in research to determine if there's potential for a pest or termite control product."

"That's really interesting," Ronnie said. It was time to gently open a different line of questioning.

"I've spoken to a few of your colleagues in the pharmaceutical industry, Mr. Capshaw," Ronnie said. "I was fascinated to learn even a little bit about how the approval process works, how costly it is, and how much time it takes to get a product through the rigorous review process performed by the FDA or the EPA. Could you talk a little about that? I have to believe the public doesn't really have much of a sense about the level of investment companies such as Dommerich make just to bring a product to market."

Capshaw showed no hesitation. "That's very perceptive, Ronnie. You ask good questions."

"Just so there's no misunderstanding, I don't know if any of this applies to the story I'm writing for Capital Media about the state of the industry, Mr. Capshaw. I'm just . . . interested, curious, you might say. Do you mind helping educate me?"

Michael Capshaw willingly walked through the door Ronnie had unlocked. For almost twenty uninterrupted minutes he expounded on the myriad frustrations Dommerich and other similarly situated companies experienced every day dealing with government bureaucracies in the US and around the world. While he generously allowed it was the same with many of Dommerich's colleagues and competitors, he expressed doubt that products submitted by American-owned companies were subjected to the same exhaustive level of scrutiny as those submitted by foreign-owned corporations. He talked, Ronnie thought, without any filter about all the formulation checks and balances, the patents, proprietary formulas, and active and inactive ingredient experiments. Then he talked about tests on animals, trials on humans, the reams of paperwork, lawyers, marketing and advertising content, and even the labeling and the packaging.

"There's an enormous, front-loaded investment, Ronnie," he said. "And the more impactful a product is or even might be, the more complex and in-depth the process becomes."

"And you, you're personally involved in all of that, right?" Ronnie asked.

"It's literally the essence of my job. At the end of the day, after the scientists, the R&D people, the compliance and regulation people, the lawyers, the finance guys . . . once they're done producing the pill, the potion, or, in the case of our pest- and termite-control space, the poison, my job is to get the product into the marketplace. And then I'll hopefully watch it succeed, obtain a return on all that investment, produce a profit for Dommerich, and, of course, generate value for our shareholders."

Ronnie noted Capshaw had totally ignored any

mention of whether the product helped consumers or what kind of disruption the accumulation of source material for active ingredients created around the world.

"Sounds like you have an enormous responsibility," Ronnie said. He took a plate, placed a few shrimp and a couple of slices of what looked like a ham and Swiss cheese roll-up on it, and began to nibble.

Capshaw was clearly enjoying himself. Ronnie fed his ego, asked the kinds of questions he believed Capshaw would feel beyond competent to address. He was tossing softballs and watching the batter knock them off the outfield wall.

"It is an enormous responsibility, Ronnie, but trust me, it has its rewards," he said.

Ronnie hesitated for a moment. He wanted to give his next pitch the attention it deserved.

"I'm trying to figure out how to ask this next question," Ronnie said.

"Just ask," Capshaw said, leaning back in his chair.

"Okay. What happens if you go through that long, arduous, immensely expensive, and complex process, and the product either fails to do what you'd hoped it would do or, worse, has negative effects? That happens, right?" Ronnie put a that-has-to-suck expression on his face.

Capshaw stared at him. He put his hand in front of his mouth, a gesture Ronnie had learned years earlier signaled the interviewee really didn't want to utter the words planted firmly on the tip of his tongue. Finally, Capshaw leaned forward, nodded his head, and pointed a finger.

"This is one of the reasons some of the products we and others in our space produce end up costing a great deal more to deliver to people who need them than either we or they would like," Capshaw said. "There are points in a product's prerelease process at which we stop to determine whether the product will do what we want it to do, will fill a hole we believe exists in the marketplace, or will compete favorably with similarly situated products already available." Capshaw paused. "Ronnie, what does this have to do with the state of the industry and Dommerich's place in that landscape?"

Ronnie was ready. "It may not, Mr. Capshaw. As I said, some of these questions are more a matter of my own innate curiosity . . . I guess you could say my education about how this all works." It was time to poke the bear. "Let me ask you this. A couple years ago, Dommerich had a product in its pharmaceutical space called Choralizine. I believe it was—"

Capshaw exploded out of his seat. "Where in the hell did you come up with that? What are you really up to here?"

Ronnie put his hands up. "Whoa! I'm just trying to understand what happens when a product you've taken to market . . . I'm not trying—"

"The hell you're not!" Capshaw said. "I don't have anything more to say to you, Mr. Pulitzer winner. In fact—"

"It's clear I've upset you, Mr. Capshaw. I'm very sorry. It was not my intention." Ronnie stood up, began packing his bag and stepped in front of the table where they'd been enjoying each other's company until a moment earlier. "Thank you for your time."

Ronnie walked toward the door, but Capshaw wasn't done with him.

"I'd like the tape out of your recorder, Mr. Levitt," Capshaw said. "This interview went far afield of where you indicated, and I have no intention—"

"First of all, it's not a tape, it's digital, and second, it's automatically saved onto my cloud account. Mr. Capshaw, you extended an invitation for me to visit with you; you spent almost two hours talking amiably with me and only lost your temper when I mentioned a product Dommerich produced that failed to meet expectations. You didn't say anything incriminating, in fact, you didn't say anything at all about Choralizine."

"Where did you even hear the name Choralizine?" Capshaw asked.

"I can't reveal a source, Mr. Capshaw, but you need to understand something. In my line of work, the one thing we never, ever want to happen is for something factually incorrect or inaccurate to get into print. It could be something very minor, a misspelled name, for example, or it could be something bad, like attributing something to someone who never said what was quoted."

Ronnie could see the wheels turning in Capshaw's brain. Jennie always told him he owed a substantial portion of his success to an outstanding ability to get people to confide in him and to trust him. He hoped he could reestablish the sense of well-being necessary, at least for now, to keep Michael Capshaw out of enemy territory and talking.

"It was not, is not, will not be, my intention to write anything inaccurate or untrue about you or about Dommerich," Ronnie said. "I guess I can tell you this. One of our researchers suggested I ask you about Choralizine. That's it! The only thing I know for sure is that Dommerich recalled it, and I want to understand how that process works, what it means in the scheme of things. I told you twice, at least, that a lot of what we talked about today has nothing to do with the specific story I'm writing. It's just stuff I want to understand. I'm curious by nature. It's like how you asked me right off the bat about the Pulitzer. It's got nothing to do with why I'm here or why you're talking with me."

Capshaw walked to the table and collected Ronnie's digital recorder.

"I think I need to keep this until your story is published."

Ronnie made a show of exasperation. "Okay. That's a problem, Mr. Capshaw," he said. "Everything we spoke about before . . . everything is on that recorder. I guess I could rely on my memory . . ."

Capshaw smiled like the cat who just swallowed the canary. "I thought it's all on the cloud."

"Yeah, I'm sorry I said that. I didn't have time . . ."

"Look, Ronnie, I'm sorry I got upset and I'm sorry you saw it. That particular chapter in our company's long and storied history is something we wish we could have avoided. The truth is it should have never happened."

"What did happen?" Ronnie asked, showing what he hoped Michael Capshaw saw as genuine concern.

Capshaw thought for a moment. He took in a deep breath and exhaled. "It wasn't so much an issue with the product," he said. "It was an issue with the product's labeling. Somehow, Choralizine got labeled for advanced depression in individuals over sixty years of age. It should not have been so indicated. It happened after the approval process had been exhausted, and the person at the FDA who let it get through is no longer there."

"So, it wasn't Dommerich's issue? It was an FDA snafu?"

"Well, I wish I could say that, but no, not entirely. Someone on our team drafted the label's indications language. Look, Ronnie, I really . . . I don't want to go there."

There was a lull in the action. Ronnie knew to keep his mouth shut. Capshaw was trying to dial it back. "In any case," he said, "I think we're probably done here. Again, I'm sorry I lost my temper."

"And I'm sorry something I said triggered it. Are we good?"

"If there's anything else I can tell you that doesn't involve some unfortunate history, please feel free to reach out," he said, offering Ronnie his hand.

Ronnie shook his hand. They said their goodbyes. Ronnie walked out, passed Nancy Kuo's empty desk, and called for the down elevator. He hoped her badge was only necessary to access the upper floors and not to leave. The wait seemed long. Capshaw never left his office.

On the way down, Ronnie accessed his Uber app and entered a request for a ride to his hotel. He sent a text to Skeeter: *Choralizine. VERY deep dive!* He removed the second recorder he'd brought from his jacket pocket, turned it off, and slipped it inside his messenger bag.

Ten minutes later, his Uber arrived and took him to the Embassy Suites near the airport. The bear, indeed, had been poked.

• • •

Michael Capshaw opened a credenza door behind the table where he'd been sitting with Ronnie Levitt. He removed a bottle of thirty-year-old single-malt Scotch, poured himself three fingers in a crystal glass and started popping shrimp like they were cashews.

He picked up his office phone and punched in four digits.

"Guzman," the voice at the other end said.

"Nick, I need you to check someone out for me," Capshaw said. "A full workup. Name is Ronald Levitt." He spelled the last name. "He's with Capital Media Group."

"Consider it done, sir."

• • •

Hallie Garard studied the cheese-filled tortellini drowning in a garlic pesto sauce at the end of her fork.

"This is absolutely the best damn piece of pasta I've eaten since I took this assignment, Willie," she said. "Look at this!"

"Watching you eat is one of the great pleasures of my life, Hallie," Guillermo Vasquez said. "Now, will you put it in your mouth, savor it, swallow it, and tell me what the hell we're doing here? Please?"

Hallie had enjoyed the company of her best girl, Emily, the night before. This, she was certain, accounted for her heightened awareness of the pleasures of the palate. It was 2:45 p.m. and she'd already had an early breakfast, a late-morning brunch, and now a late lunch at Alexandria's la Madeleine on King Street. She was only in DC for one more night, so she took the opportunity to pick Willie's brain about the politics and intrigue in Paraguay.

"You told me, I think your exact words were, 'a

few groups' are trying to shake things up down there. Could you tell me a little bit more . . . Maybe be a bit more specific?" He stared at her plate of tortellini. She pushed it across the table. "Use your own fork." He did.

"I checked with a couple of people. Mostly, it's nothing. The only question mark of any interest, at least for us, is a group calling itself the Republican Front," he said. "Their leader is a former top field commander in the Paraguayan military, Roberto Negron. Col. Roberto Negron."

"Interesting, why?"

"We have a couple of people inside," he said. "Look, this isn't gonna bite me in the ass, is it Hallie?"

"I don't even know who you are," she said. "Why are you sitting at my table and eating my food?"

"Okay. These are very well-armed, very well-fed, mostly clean guys."

"Why is that odd?"

"Most of these Latin American 'insurgent groups,'" he said, using air quotes, "are pretty ragtag. A few guns, some cans of Beanee Weenees. Mostly they do some snatch-and-grab stuff, kidnapping for ransom idiot Americans hiking in the jungle. They live off the proceeds for a while. They pose no real threat to the government."

"But not Negron's Republicans?"

"It's weird," he said. "There are maybe three hundred of them, living in relative comfort about sixty miles across the border, inside Bolivia, technically, but deep in the jungle. They have trucks, beds. If I didn't know who they were, I'd think they were an army company doing field training."

"Are they causing any trouble for the government?"

"Nothing that we can tell," he said. "Now, to hear the government, they're the reincarnation of Che's guerrillas. 'We must remain vigilant in the face of anarchy,' you know, that kind of bullshit."

"Hmmm," she said, taking the remains of her lunch back. "No hit and run shit in Asunción?"

"Maybe twice last year a small group came into town and tore up a supermarket or something, but nothing worth anything. Like I said, it's weird."

"Okay," she said. "This has been instructive, maybe, I think. I don't know. Thanks, Willie."

"Thanks for lunch, kid. You heading back to O-Town?"

"Tomorrow. You?"

"Same. You know it's always a party on South Beach. Or maybe we should take in some jai alai some time. We could hook up in Ft. Pierce. You in?"

"Panamanians with baskets throwing around a wooden ball? I don't think so. My Dad always told me not to gamble on anything that can talk."

"What does that even mean? Jockeys don't talk?"

"They may talk, but the horses don't." She left two twenties on the table. "See you soon, buddy."

Chapter 18

Mack answered his phone with, "Hey, Mr. Capshaw."

"Things quiet down there?" It would be nearly dinnertime. Tim should be on duty, too.

"Boring, sir. They haven't made an appearance yet today."

"Any more trips to town?"

"Sure," he said. "We take them, drop them where they want to sightsee or whatever, maybe we have lunch, bring them back. Any idea how long we need to keep them under watch?"

"Until I tell you otherwise." Capshaw disconnected the call and then punched in another number.

"*Buenos días*, Señor Capshaw. How are things in Minnesota?"

"*Muy bueno*, Colonel. How are things on your end?"

"We are getting close to making our push to put an end to the corrupt regime occupying my beloved country, Señor Capshaw." This was Negron's stock answer when talking to all gringos. Capshaw knew the colonel hated them all, but he knew which ones were useful.

"I may require a little more of your hospitality for some troublesome Americans soiling your beautiful slice of heaven, Colonel," Capshaw said. "Might you be amenable to such a task?"

"As always, Señor Capshaw," he said. "We welcome the opportunity to partner with a great international business such as Dommerich, so long as the . . . incentives are appropriate."

"Nothing to worry about on that end, Colonel," Capshaw said. "With your permission, I'll be in touch again soon."

"*Adios, mi amigo*," Negron said.

"*Adios*, Colonel." Capshaw hung up the phone. There was a light knock at his door. "Come!"

Nancy walked in with a blue folder and placed it on his desk directly in front of him. "From Nick Guzman," she said. She turned and slowly walked to the door, giving him a better view than the one behind him that had so impressed his visitor the day before.

A typed label on the file folder read, "Levitt, Ronald. Capital Media Group." Capshaw opened the file and began reading. After approximately three minutes, Michael Capshaw threw the file across the room. "That goddam lying motherfucker."

• • •

FRIDAY

Back in Orlando, Ronnie updated Joe Hill and Tobe Hillenmyer. After he finished, he got on the phone to CMG's *Washington Standard*. Entering the serious "poking of the bear" phase of this particular investigative project, he briefed Melanie Goldenberg and Sam Brunetti, seasoned reporters who covered EPA and FDA matters respectively for the *Standard*, on what he knew, mostly from Jordan's notes, about Veracozen and SaniScal. His goal was to get the names of the functionaries at the agencies tasked with determining if these two Dommerich products deserved approval. Once that happened, he would begin writing the story that he, his editor, and his publisher believed would kick-start the process of dismantling the impeccably dressed Michael Capshaw and, when all was said and done, perhaps even Dommerich Worldwide.

Ronnie was polishing the language necessary to ignite the fuse under Capshaw's Brioni-suited ass when his phone pinged a message from Skeeter. He clicked on the attachment and was rewarded with an unexpected treasure trove. There were emails, internal Dommerich memos, copies of confidential legal files, and a file Ronnie believed might constitute a smoking gun. He pored over a spreadsheet containing the names of people who had either died or had been damaged by Choralizine. It included the amounts the company had paid out to avoid public disclosure of what happened. There were 162 names on the list.

Also contained in the product of Skeeter Bates's foray into the dark digital domain of Dommerich North America was a short note directing Ronnie to check a series of texts between Michael Capshaw and a Colonel Roberto Negron, commanding officer of something called the RFPI. Ronnie punched in Hallie Garard's number.

"What's shakin', Sheldon?" she asked.

"Whole lot of shakin' goin' on, Leonard," he said. "Where are you?"

"Uh, two doors down?"

"I'm at the paper," he said. "Any chance you could come over here? I've got a bunch of stuff to download and—"

"Oh, I love when you talk download, baby. I have some goodies as well. Out the door and on my way."

• • •

Michael Capshaw disconnected from his call alerting Colonel Negron to expect not one, but two packages later in the day, and that, per their ongoing agreement, two hundred thousand dollars had been wired to the numbered Cayman Islands account holding the funds of the Republican Front for Paraguayan Independence.

He'd earlier wrapped the second of two calls, the first to the EPA, the other to the FDA, and learned both SaniScal and Veracozen had been provisionally approved by both for release. Final approval would come in ten business days from the EPA and in fourteen days from the FDA. Provisional approval by the FDA signaled it was okay to prepare marketing materials and labeling information and to begin training field operations personnel, everything except actual production and release of products to physicians, hospitals, and pharmacies. He thought he might explode with the anticipation of success. He felt so good, he allowed Nathan Becker to give the good news to the folks in Munich.

A potentially shitty day had turned into apple pie à la mode for Michael and for Dommerich, and he wasn't about to let a couple of pains in the ass slow down what was going to be a highly successful quarter for Dommerich. He dialed his team in Asunción.

• • •

As Jordan and Christy turned the corner onto the Avenue Mariscal López, Tim and Mack were fewer than twenty feet behind. Jordan had a phone in his pocket that he'd picked up when they were out from under their minders. He planned to call Ronnie as soon as they were safely ensconced inside the compound of the US embassy. Christy was pointing ahead to the gates when the Suburban pulled in front of them, and Mack jumped from the front seat.

"Sir," he said, "please don't make me show my

weapon. You and your daughter need to get into the vehicle. Now."

Jordan smiled. "I think it would be a great idea for you to show your weapon, Mack, right here in front of those marines, in fact." Jordan began walking forward when Tim, who'd circled behind the two of them, announced his intentions.

"Sir, I have my gun pointed directly at your daughter," he said. "Our orders are to take you back to the house. We were told explicitly that if you don't cooperate, we are to terminate both of you."

Jordan quickly considered his situation. Behind those gates, he and Christy were safe. Out here, on the street in Asunción, clearly not so much. Were he alone, he might gamble. But no way would he put his daughter's life in jeopardy.

"This we will do, sir," Mack said. "Please, for everyone's sake, don't do anything we'll all regret."

Jordan and Christy looked at each other. He nodded. She did the same. They walked to the SUV. When Jordan got into the back seat, he reached into his pocket and removed the phone. While Christy was put in next to him and Tim and Mack returned to their seats, Jordan punched in Ronnie's mobile number. He put the phone between the two of them and alerted her with his eyes to what he was doing.

"Just follow my lead," he whispered to her. Tim turned the Suburban around and headed in the direction of the house.

"You didn't really think we were going to just let you walk into the embassy, did you, sir?" Tim asked, looking into his rearview mirror.

"Actually, Tim, I don't know why you don't let us go to the embassy," Jordan said. "After all, we're not prisoners here in Paraguay, are we?"

"We're just soldiers, sir," Mack said. "We follow orders. Sometimes, that means doing things we'd rather not be doing."

After a couple of turns away from where the house was located, Christy said, "You're not taking us home, are you, Tim?"

"I'm sorry, ma'am," he said. "Just following orders."

"Uh, huh, just like the Germans in World War II, right boys? Just following orders?" Jordan said. "You're no better than those assholes you work for. When this is done, unless you kill us—" Tim slammed on the brakes of the SUV. Jordan stopped talking mid-sentence.

"Are you letting us out?" Christy asked.

Tim and Mack got out of the Suburban and opened the back doors. They placed hoods over both Christy's and Jordan's heads. They seemed not to have spotted the phone between the two prisoners.

"I'm sorry, sir. Sorry, ma'am," Mack said.

"You're taking us back there?" Christy shouted. "You're the assholes who took me off the street last year, aren't you?"

"We weren't here last year, ma'am."

"Maybe not you two," Jordan said, "but Dommerich sure was."

• • •

In the newsroom at the *Orlando Chronicle*, Ronnie muted his phone. "Can we get a trace on this call? We need to find out where they're being taken."

"Give me a minute," Hallie said. "Numbers, numbers, I need numbers!" She dialed out on her own phone, went through her authentication process with her contact in Washington and gave Ronnie's cell number to the operator.

"They're somewhere in Paraguay, Tommy," she said. "I don't know how he's still transmitting, but we need to know where they are once they get wherever it is they're being taken. Can you identify the number he's calling from?"

She listened for a few moments. Hallie and Ronnie hadn't finished sharing what they'd learned on their respective trips, but he was impressed with how quickly she took charge and how effectively she employed the resources of the FBI.

"The RFPI," Ronnie said.

"The Republican Front for Paraguayan Independence." Hallie said. They high fived. The rest of the newsroom, including Joe Hill and Tobe Hillenmyer, looked as if they were witnessing an extraterrestrial landing.

• • •

Col. Negron instructed two of his soldiers, one male, and one female, to prepare accommodations for two guests for an unknown period of time. "I believe one is the same young woman we recently released," he said. "If I understand correctly, the other is the young woman's father. I see no reason they can't stay together in one of the cabins near the river."

When the two soldiers left, Negron walked onto the screened porch of his headquarters and signaled for his *numero dos*, Major Arturo Colon. Colon was seated on a bench under a nearby tree, reading.

"What are you reading, Major?"

"I am rereading *One Hundred Years of Solitude*, sir. So, Colonel, did I hear correctly? We are back in the hospitality business?"

"*Si*, Arturo," Negron said. "A party of two, this time."

"Are they paying the prevailing rate for their room and board?"

"Our guests are going to be very comfortable here at the Republican Front Resort and Spa, my friend," the colonel said. "These stupid idiot Americanos! What would we do without them?"

"Indeed, Colonel," Colon said. "They make our struggle very . . . rewarding."

"Yes, they do. Come in," Negron said. "I have fresh coffee."

Chapter 19

Hallie and Ronnie were cloistered in Joe Hill's office reviewing the status of what Ronnie now knew was a major, maybe national, maybe international story.

"If we're able to put Capshaw and this Colonel Negron together," she said, "and if we're able to put Christy Censell, or Calder, or whatever her name is, captive in some Paraguayan rebel stronghold, I mean, holy shit, Sheldon."

"Sheldon?" Joe Hill asked.

"Don't ask," Ronnie said. "Not important. What is important, at least to me, is first, getting these two people home safely, and second, shining some light on how at least one major international organization conducts its business in this grotesquely profitable, highly competitive space."

"I hate speculation, Levitt," Joe Hill said, "but let's blue sky this for just a minute. What, exactly, do we know?"

"Leonard?" Ronnie said.

"Okay," Hallie said. "We now know for sure that Jordan was taken, first to Minneapolis, where he must have met with Michael Capshaw at Dommerich North America's home office, and then to Paraguay, where he was, I guess, reunited with his daughter, Christy."

"And," Ronnie said, "we know Dommerich is close to obtaining approval on two new products . . ." He consulted his notebook. "SaniScal, a prescription dandruff shampoo, on the pharmaceutical side and Veracozen, a new pest-control thing."

"We also know," Hallie said, "that Christy spent time in Africa with the Peace Corps in Mali but was transferred to Paraguay after she was involved in some kind of dustup about how Dommerich was keeping a number of villages from getting access to drinking water because they needed to harvest some plant, which, if I remember right, would be used in the production of SaniScal."

Joe Hill liked to pace when attempting to come to terms with how strong a story is or might be. For a moment, Hallie and Ronnie kept quiet while Joe ruminated.

"Okay," he said. "Now, let's talk about what might be."

Ronnie recounted his kerfuffle with Capshaw regarding his mention of Choralizine. "For a moment, he came completely unhinged, and I thought I'd end up on a plane to who the hell knows where," he said.

"I reeled him back in, but he was still hesitant to talk about it."

"What is it?" Hallie asked.

"No idea," Ronnie said, "except I learned it was recalled by Dommerich after, according to Capshaw, it was discovered that the drug had been mislabeled. Now, the thing that's interesting is that I came into possession, don't ask me how, of a spreadsheet indicating Dommerich paid off 162 people for claims rather than going to trial and attempting to blame the FDA for the screw-up."

"Why wouldn't they take their chances in court?" Joe asked.

Hallie nodded. "Because they wanted to avoid discovery," she said. Ronnie looked at her. "Yeah, yeah, Sheldon, I'm a lawyer. A lot of us feebs are lawyers but not the scumbag kind. That's where the Bureau does a lot of their recruiting, at law schools."

"Let's get back to that later," Joe said. "How did the Bureau get wind of all this?"

"It was our neighbor, Mr. Censell, er, Calder, who first brought things to the attention of the FDA and the EPA," Hallie said. "He was looking for his daughter and was persistently rattling cages within the federal bureaucracy and in Congress. He learned he couldn't get help from either the Peace Corps or the State Department. Boy, talk about a stifling bureaucracy. State couldn't find its own ass with both hands and a flashlight. Anyway, after he contacted the EPA and the FDA, the ball bounced into our court. When two or more federal agencies are involved in what is or might become a complicated law enforcement or criminal issue, as opposed to some relatively minor civil thing, it gets kicked over to the Bureau. Our task force takes over in order to help avoid potentially conflicting priorities. I've been working this particular issue for more than seven months."

Joe nodded and sat back in his chair. "So, based on that phone call you received, and you had traced, what should we assume?"

They both started talking at once, but these were Ronnie's people, so Hallie ceded the floor. "Well, the call was traced to Asunción, which is the capital of Paraguay," he said. "That's as close as the Bureau was able to get, right?"

Hallie nodded. "The last thing we were able to hear, I guess it was Christy, saying, 'You're not taking us back to the house, are you, Tim?' Is that right?"

"That's what I heard," Ronnie said.

"And you both independently got information about this so-called rebel group?" Joe asked.

"The Republican Front for Paraguayan Independence," Ronnie said.

"And what do we know about them?"

"My contact at the Agency indicates there's something squirrelly there," Hallie said. "Wait! You didn't hear me say 'Agency,' right? *Right?* You didn't hear that . . . word. That word. You didn't hear that."

Joe and Ronnie shrugged their shoulders and shook their heads. "What word?" Joe asked. "I didn't hear any word. Did you hear any word?"

Ronnie laughed. "You mean . . . oh, that word. No, no, I didn't hear that word."

"You know I've got a gun, right? Okay, they haven't gone after the government or the president or anything like that for, I guess around three years. They formed right after the current president was"—she made air quotes—"elected."

"Is he a problem? The current president?"

"No," she said, "just your standard garden-variety greedy, corrupt 'elected' South American president."

"I'd love it if we could learn more about the Republican Front," Joe said. "Any thoughts on how we might do that without having to send my reporter into a South American jungle?"

Hallie and Ronnie both nodded. "I know a guy," Hallie said.

Ronnie nodded. "Yeah," Ronnie said, smiling at her, "I know a guy, too." They both turned and grinned at Joe Hill. For the first time since Ronnie had brought this story to his editor, Joe Hill grinned back.

• • •

Thanks to the euphoria he was feeling resulting from the provisional approvals of SaniScal and Veracozen, Michael Capshaw moved what he now knew about

Ronnie Levitt to a file in the lowest drawer of his brain. Nick Guzman, Dommerich's in-house technology whiz, had let Capshaw know Ronnie's bio was left available on the *Orlando Chronicle*'s website. An accident, he was sure. He lived in Orlando. A simple DMV search placed Ronald Levitt's vehicle registration address on Susie Q Court, the same street Jordan Censell had been picked up from when he'd wormed his way too far into Dommerich's business.

When the final approvals arrived from the FDA and EPA, and after both products were successfully rolled out, Capshaw would entertain some thoughts about what to do about Mr. Ronnie Levitt and, perhaps, his family.

"Nancy," Capshaw called to his assistant, "tell flight ops I need the jet for a quick down and back to South America, either later tonight or first thing tomorrow morning. And call President Acosta in Asunción. Tell him I would be very grateful for an hour of his time," Capshaw looked at his Rolex, "tomorrow afternoon."

• • •

Two hours after they were picked up outside the US Embassy in Asunción, Jordan and Christy found themselves seated in the comfortable but well-guarded headquarters cabin in the camp of Colonel Roberto Negron's Republican Front for Paraguayan Independence.

"I suppose the two of you have done something necessitating you being accommodated at our humble camp," Negron said.

Jordan and Christy looked at one another. "No," Jordan said, "not that I can think of." He looked at Christy. "Did you do anything wrong?"

She shook her head. "Nope, can't think of anything special I did." She looked at Negron and smiled. "Did you miss me?"

He smiled back. Then he started laughing. His phone rang.

"Negron," he said. He stiffened. He listened for a minute. "*Si . . . gracias.*" He hung up the phone. He looked off to his right, pursed his lips, and then turned his attention back to his guests. "This gets, how do you say, curiouser and curiouser." Negron signaled for one of his guards. "Would you take Mr. and . . . Miss—these two people here, to their cabin? Excuse me. I must attend to some business. Would you be so kind as to join me for dinner later?"

"Sure," Jordan said.

"Why not?" Christy said.

The guard took them to a cabin overlooking a narrow creek. Their jungle accommodations came with two bedrooms, a bathroom, and a small sitting area.

"I think it's fair to say we've both seen worse," Christy said. "Look!" She pointed to two matching overnight bags, one outside each bedroom. "Tim and

Mack even brought the stuff your friend had them buy for us. How sweet."

Jordan nodded. "There is something very strange about this place and that guy," he said.

"I know," Christy said.

"Did he ever invite you to dinner?"

"No," she said. "I told you. I saw him once when I arrived and then once more before they came and got me. He asked me the same question about what I did then, too."

"Curiouser and curiouser indeed," Jordan said. He'd noticed a bench on the porch when they came in. He opened the door. A guard was there. Jordan pointed to the bench. The guard nodded his head. Jordan and Christy sat on the porch and watched as absolutely nothing else happened for nearly three hours until the guard's radio crackled.

"You should get cleaned up for dinner with the colonel and the major," he said.

• • •

Hallie was back inside her house on Susie Q Court when she noticed, not for the first time but in greater relief, how similar her living conditions were to those of Jordan Censell. In her case, everything was in the living room, except she used the kitchen and a downstairs bathroom and none of the bedrooms, all three of which were on the second floor of the house. Lady had set up her own accommodations in the kitchen, on the same dog bed she'd come to know and love while domiciled with her lord and master across the cul-de-sac. Hallie punched a number into her phone.

"Hey, cutie," Willie Vasquez said. "I like that we keep meeting like this."

"You like torturing yourself, too, right?" she asked, smiling.

"A guy can always hope. What can I do for you?"

"A meeting," she said. "On the books."

"Oooh," he said. "You sure?"

"Yeah. We can do it on a secure channel. I need something from the Company. Gotta be straight up legal, though, buddy."

"Can you give me a hint? You know how much they love working with the Bureau."

"Sure. It's about that southern hemisphere thing we're working. Should be a day at the beach for a plugged-in dude like you."

"Call you tomorrow?"

"Nope. You've got two hours. Pins and needles, handsome."

• • •

"Hello," a soft unknown voice said.

"Uh, Honey?" Ronnie asked.

"Uh-huh."

"Skeeter available?" There was a pause.

"You know, Levitt, your timing really stinks."

"Sorry. Thought you were out of commission from the waist down."

"You are one dense mother—ah, what do you want?"

"The Republican Front for Paraguayan Independence; as much as possible, as soon as possible. Have fun!"

"I was, asshole!" Skeeter yelled and hung up.

• • •

Saturday

The Dommerich Gulfstream G-5 left Minneapolis at 7:00 p.m. on Friday and arrived a dozen hours later on Saturday morning in Asunción, following a quick refueling stop in Miami. Nancy had told Capshaw that President Javier Acosta could squeeze him in for an hour at 2:45 p.m. local time. Tim and Mack picked him up at Silvio Pettirossi International Airport. He had them take him to the presidential palace, where he'd meet with the president of Paraguay.

They filled him in on recent events. "They were on their way to the embassy, Mr. Capshaw," Mack said. "There's no doubt that's where they were going."

"We picked them up when they were less than five minutes away," Tim said. "You called right after we'd dropped them in the city. They said they were going sightseeing. We were with them the whole time. We cleaned all their stuff out of the house and took it to Negron's camp."

"I think you two got a little careless with them," Capshaw said.

"The entire time they were here, what, four days? They were almost never out of our sight," Mack said. "You told us not to make them feel like prisoners. We gave them some room. Until yesterday, it was fine."

"Keep in touch with Negron," Capshaw said. "Make sure he doesn't get careless. Soon as I finish some business here, I'll need to get right back to the airport."

"Copy that, sir." Tim said.

Chapter 20

Ronnie and Hallie were seated cross-legged on the floor in Ronnie's living room. They were lost in their own thoughts, tossing a wadded-up piece of paper back and forth.

Ronnie's phone rang. Skeeter.

"Hey," Ronnie said.

"One of Dommerich's jets touched down in Asunción, Paraguay, about an hour ago. You know these assholes have a whole fleet of jets? Since Desert Storm, I have to pay nearly a grand a month on fucking pharmaceuticals and they get to fly around like fucking movie stars. Scumbags." He hung up.

Ronnie looked at the phone. "Somebody needs a hug," he said.

"Who?" Hallie asked, smiling.

"Somebody. A Dommerich jet landed in Asunción an hour ago. I wonder who's on the passenger manifest. I wonder what business he has down there. I wonder if Mr. Crapshaw is going to visit our neighbor."

"You are a man filled with wonder," she said. "Guess that puts off my plan for a day or two. Oh, by the way, how the hell do you know that? Oh, right. Don't ask."

"Plan? What plan?" Ronnie asked.

"I was going to pay him a visit. You know, informally. You got any plans?"

Ronnie walked into the kitchen and came back with two Heinekens. "I do," he said, handing Hallie a bottle of beer. "Need a glass?"

She took a pull from the bottle. "Share," she said.

He sat on the sofa. "I'm going to get on the horn to the FDA and EPA. I'm going to ask for whoever is responsible for approving things like SaniScal and Veracozen. Gonna keep asking for supervisors until I get sent to the mouthpieces for the commissioner of the FDA and the administrator of the EPA."

"Okay. Rattling cages?"

"It's what I do, Leonard. My raison d'être!"

She joined him on the sofa. "Any concern about maybe tipping your hand too soon?" she asked.

"I was in Capshaw's office a couple days ago," Ronnie said. "Almost got thrown out his window for asking a benign question about a Dommerich drug that got recalled years ago. I'm guessing by now he knows who I am, where I work, probably where I live. Nope. I am not concerned."

"What's your approach to these agencies going to be? Only asking because they're like, you know, my clients in this whole business," she said.

"I want to find out how far along they are in the approval process. I'd like to plant seeds with them, tell them there may be something peculiar going on in Minneapolis, and that they may want to take a breath before putting these products into the American marketplace," he said. "If I think it's appropriate, I'll tell them I'm writing a piece on Choralizine, the antidepressant drug they had to recall. Mostly, I want to push them into contacting Capshaw to tell him some snotty reporter is nosing around in his business."

"Pretty badass, Sheldon. Just make sure you watch your six."

"I don't think I need to, Leonard," he said. "I've got a smartass—excuse me, I mean badass—FBI agent, with a gun, watching my six."

· · ·

A young woman knocked at the screen door of the cabin where Jordan and Christy were busying themselves putting their clothes and toiletries into nightstand drawers. Were it not for the manner in which they were collected and conveyed by Dommerich's henchmen, this might have seemed like a field trip or some version of a Boy Scout summer camp.

"Señor, señorita, you come please?"

She was small, perhaps five feet tall, wearing loose-fitting jeans, a red T-shirt, and a pair of dark brown sandals. She kept turning around as they followed, making sure they were still walking behind her. She stopped at a small cabin near Col. Negron's headquarters and gestured for them to go inside. "Enjoy, please," she said, and left.

When they walked up the three steps and through the screen door, they were met by a different man dressed in military fatigues and a peaked cap. "Good evening," he said. "I'm Major Arturo Colon, Colonel Negron's adjutant. And you are . . ."

They introduced themselves as Jordan Censell and Christy Calder. Christy told him she was Jordan's daughter. Major Colon nodded and gestured to a pair of matching throne-like rattan chairs.

Colonel Negron walked in with a tray holding a bottle of whiskey, four glasses, a bucket of ice, and what looked to Jordan like a bowl of nuts. The colonel poured four generous portions of the amber liquid on the rocks. Jordan didn't recognize the label.

"I hope you are able to enjoy a good single-malt Scotch," Negron said.

Although neither Jordan nor Christy drank Scotch, they nodded and accepted the base commandant's hospitality.

"Colonel," Jordan said, "as you mentioned earlier, this whole thing here is getting curiouser and curiouser." He gestured and looked all around. "Can you tell us what this place is?"

The two officers looked at one another. Negron nodded his head.

"This is the headquarters of the Republican Front

for Paraguayan Independence," Maj. Colon said. "Col. Negron is our commander. I am his . . . I guess you could say I'm his number two. We are currently, technically, not inside the borders of Paraguay. When you were brought here, your driver crossed an unmarked boundary between Paraguay and Bolivia. However, the Bolivian government, such as it is, doesn't care that we are camped here. For all intents and purposes, this part of the jungle is a kind of no-man's-land."

"Don't get too caught up in these minor logistics, Mr. Censell, Miss Calder," Negron said. "Please consider yourselves our guests. You are not in any danger unless you do something silly, and neither of you look like silly people."

"I have to say, Colonel," Christy said, "I'm envious of how well you both speak English. Somehow, I didn't expect . . ."

Negron laughed. "You didn't expect some group of renegades living in the jungle to be led by someone who went to UCLA, and then got a master's in political science at Stanford. Why would you?"

"I, myself," said Colon, "graduated from the University of Texas before getting my master's in international relations at the University of Chicago."

"Please," Negron said, "we've invited you to share a meal with us so we can get to know each other. There will be plenty of time for, how do you say, pulling back the curtain. I hope you both like New York strip steaks, rice and red beans, and some delicious Argentinian melon." The girl who'd escorted them materialized from a room behind the one they were seated in.

"Now, a very important question. How do you prefer your steaks? Medium rare? Medium?"

• • •

Michael Capshaw was somewhere over the Caribbean when he shut his laptop, rubbed his eyes, and pressed the call button for his flight attendant.

"Yes, sir?" she asked.

"Can I get a sandwich or some soup or something, Julie?" he asked.

"What would you like sir? We stocked your preferences before we left Minneapolis. We have some potato and Vidalia onion soup. I can whip you up a western omelet. What's your pleasure?"

Capshaw asked for a ham and Swiss cheese on rye and a cup of the soup. While waiting for his meal, he reviewed his upcoming meeting with Paraguayan president Javier Acosta.

As he'd expected, the person he viewed as the tin-pot dictator of a banana republic wanted a sizably larger bribe before committing to allow Dommerich to denude a large swath of jungle between Asunción and the border with Argentina, so Dommerich could harvest as much Verawood as it needed. Five million US dollars was beyond Capshaw's spending authority, so he had needed to run it by Becker, who perhaps consulted Soldinger in Munich. He had been supplied with the secret numbered account Acosta held at a bank in Panama. He dozed off for the remainder of his time in the air.

. . .

Monday

Ronnie spent the afternoon on the phone annoying as many people as he possibly could in two federal regulatory agencies. He began his queries in a benign fashion. Once connected to whomever he could get on the phone, typically a functionary within the public information office, he would proceed as if he were adrift in an ocean of ignorance and beg for a lifeline from someone obviously far more versed in the bureaucratic maze of a huge government department. Blessed with a soothing voice, Ronnie felt the smile of dame fortune wash over him when he found himself talking to Wendy Cole in the communications department at the FDA.

"Hi, Mr. Levitt. How can I help you today?"

"I have to be honest, Ms. Cole. I don't know if anyone can help me with this. I'm woefully ignorant of how things work at the FDA so let me begin by apologizing if I'm at all wasting your time."

"How can I help you, Mr. Levitt? Who are you with?" *A tad officious*, Ronnie thought.

"I'm so sorry," Ronnie said. "I'm Ronald Levitt with Capital Media Group. We have—"

"I know who Capital Media Group is, Mr. Levitt."

"I'm sorry. Okay. I'm following the progress of a product . . . I believe the name of it is . . . SaniScal? Does that sound right?"

The silence on the other end was punctuated by the sound of keys on a keyboard being tapped at a furious speed. "I'm not showing—How is that spelled?"

"I have it written here as capital S-a-n-i- capital S-c-a-l. I'm always fascinated by the names of these products. I wonder if the companies keep a Scrabble set around so they can come up with a catchy, memorable name," Ronnie said. "Can you tell me—"

"Can I ask, Mr. Levitt, what is CMG's interest in SaniScal?"

Ronnie felt the always satisfying pull of a fish taking the bait.

"Oh, yeah, sure, Ms. Cole. By the way, please call me Ronnie. I've been in contact with someone at Dommerich North America for an article we're doing on what it takes for something to be approved in the pharmaceutical space. They told me it's been in the process with the FDA for way longer than they thought it should have been for a . . ." Ronnie paused and shuffled a couple of pieces of paper, "dandruff shampoo." He started to laugh.

"Well, first of all, Mr. Levitt, Ronnie," she said, "there's nothing funny about the approval process at the FDA. Our mission involves protecting the public.

The process takes as long as it needs to take for us to be able to assure the American people that they're using safe and effective products."

"Oh, I'm so sorry, Ms. Cole, I mean no disrespect. I'm way out on a limb here. Normally I write about other things. The intricacies of scientific investigation are way out of my wheelhouse. Has the process taken longer than it should?"

"No, not at all," she said, almost too quickly. "In fact, the latest status update indicates SaniScal has been granted provisional approval." She went on to explain that provisional approval is typically followed by final approval within as little as two weeks.

"Oh, that's great," he said. "Thanks so much, Ms. Cole. I think that's all . . ." It was time to bait the next hook. "Actually, you know, while I was researching this submittal, I discovered a few years ago Dommerich had to recall a product after final FDA approval had already been granted. Can you explain to me what happened in that instance? What is the FDA's role when a company recalls a drug you've already approved?"

More key tapping ensued. "Can you tell me the name of the product? I don't see anything here in our data base about—"

"Choralizine. That's C-H-O-R-A-L-I—"

"One moment, please, Mr. Levitt." Ronnie walked into his kitchen, collected a jug of Arnold Palmer from his refrigerator, and poured himself a glass. He suspected he'd be on hold perhaps for the rest of his natural life.

It took almost ten minutes for the response Ronnie had suspected would come his way to arrive. "Mr. Levitt?" Male voice. Ms. Wendy Cole, it seemed, had been relieved of the responsibility for this particularly annoying call.

"Yes."

"This is Dick Berlin. I'm director of communications for the FDA."

"Hi, Dick, my name is Ronnie Levitt. I'm a senior correspondent with Capital Media. Is there a problem with my inquiry regarding the status of SaniScal?"

"No, no problem at all, Mr. Levitt, not with SaniScal."

"Okay, then," Ronnie said. This is the guy Ronnie wanted to irritate. "I was talking with Wendy Cole—she's good, by the way—and I just wanted to know what happens when a product approved by the FDA suddenly gets recalled by a company, in this case, Dommerich North America. What does the FDA do in a case like that? Is getting that information a problem?"

Had they been in the same room, Ronnie was pretty sure he would have seen Dick Berlin expel so much air he'd have shot to the ceiling like a deflated balloon.

"Can I ask how you know about that?"

"Why?" Ronnie asked. "Is that secret information?"

"Well, I'm sure Dommerich isn't advertising it."

"You know I can't reveal a source, Dick," Ronnie

said. "But we don't have to talk about Choralizine per se. In general, does the FDA, I don't know the proper terminology, but does the FDA flag a company that has had a problem like that for any, you know . . . extra scrutiny the next time they submit something for FDA approval?"

"Ronnie," Dick Berlin said, now talking to his new best friend, "are we okay to go on background?"

"Sure, Dick."

"I've been at the FDA for seventeen years. I never heard of anything like that happening before, and I've never seen anything like that since Choralizine."

"Okay," Ronnie said. "Back on the record, Dick. Hypothetically, does the FDA in any way and in any circumstance keep a more focused eye on a company with which it has experienced anything untoward in the approval process?"

He waited while the FDA's chief communications officer pondered how to best get himself out of the way of a question as loaded as the one Ronnie had just put forth.

"For the record?"

"Yep."

"Every product submitted to the FDA receives the same exhaustive level of close review and examination before we put our stamp of approval on it. Does that answer your question, Ronnie?"

"Thank you very much, sir. And please thank Ms. Cole for me."

Ronnie didn't have the heart to tell the man there was no article being drafted. But he knew, or at least suspected, that Dick Berlin would, at the very least, reach out to people inside the FDA's labyrinthine product review structure and tip them off that something might just be amiss with Dommerich's application for final FDA approval of SaniScal.

He dialed Hallie's number to give her a heads-up about his conversation.

Chapter 21

Jordan and his daughter enjoyed a lovely dinner, complete with more Scotch for the soldiers and some delicious Chilean Cabernet Sauvignon for him and Christy. Col. Negron offered cigars from Cuba. Colon accepted but Jordan demurred.

"You know, Colonel," he said, as the four of them sat on facing rattan loveseats in the protection of a screened patio behind Negron's private dining room, "this has to be the most comfortable imprisonment a person could ever ask for."

Negron smiled. "I know," he said. "You must have at least one or two questions. Please, ask."

"What exactly is our status, Colonel," Christy asked, "and, is mine different now than it was a week ago?"

Major Colon said, "You must know, Miss Calder, that we have no intention of causing harm to either you or your father."

"On some level, I do, Major, and I'm comforted by that knowledge, but that being the case, why are we here? And why was I your 'guest' for nearly a year? What exactly is going on?"

"Some things we can explain to you and some things will become clearer after both of you are released and back home in the United States," Col. Negron said. "Simply put, 'what exactly is going on,' is very complicated. And there are many different players, and there are numerous layers and moving parts. I'm not attempting to be obtuse, but this is a true statement."

"So, what can you explain?" Jordan asked.

Col. Negron leaned in and lowered his voice. "Things are not exactly as they seem, Mr. Censell. Everyone associated with this . . . exercise in theatrics you have been subjected to has an agenda. You, sir, have an agenda: you wish to bring your daughter home safely. Mr. Capshaw and his employers have an agenda. Paraguay's president, Javier Acosta, has an agenda. And, if we're to be honest with one another, Major Colon and I also have an agenda. Sadly, at least for now, I may not be able to be precise regarding how long it will take for everything to play out and for things to become clear, but I can tell you that under almost no circumstance are you at all unsafe. I promise, both of you will return home, probably in as soon as a few days or, at most, a week."

Jordan sat back and digested what he thought constituted the dessert course they had been served.

"We are aware," Major Colon said, also in a conspiratorial voice, "of things happening up north, which will determine whether you'll be home sooner or a little later. We don't wish to burden you with information that really doesn't concern you. Three things must happen, and they must happen in a particular order, for everything to work out as it is supposed to work out."

"You both know that you're speaking in squares and circles and are not really telling us anything, right?" Jordan asked.

Negron laughed. "Of course, we know, Mr. Censell. We are, if nothing else, educated men. What we are trying to do is put you and your daughter at ease. Everything that is happening here and up north in the United States was precipitated by Miss Calder's Peace Corps transfer from Africa to South America." The Colonel hesitated for a moment. "Again, in the spirit of complete honesty, it was the single biggest blunder made by Mr. Capshaw in pursuit of his avaricious goals. Had he facilitated your transfer virtually anyplace else in the world, he would have gotten everything he wanted, we would have never encountered one another, and you'd have been free to pursue good works, which is what I assume you and your fellow Peace Corps volunteers wanted to do in the first place."

"Capshaw facilitated Christy's transfer?" Jordan asked.

"Of course!" Colon said. "You could very easily have upset his plans in . . ." he looked at Negron.

"Mali, Arturo," he said.

"In Mali. Had the UN or the central government

in Mali discovered what he was up to over there, he'd have been in a world of trouble," Colon said.

"I thought the Mali government knew Dommerich was blocking access to water for all of those villages in the south," Christy said.

Negron shook his head. "No, no, no. He was bribing the provincial overlords in the south, in Bougoula. They—the people at Dommerich—were not paying appropriate attention or tribute to their masters in Bamako. It is our understanding that Mali's central government in Bamako knew nothing of what Dommerich was up to."

"The fix was in, Christy," Jordan said. "He gets rid of you before you can get to Bamako, and he has clear sailing. This is how things work in places like that."

"This is how things work in places like this as well, Mr. Censell," Colon said.

Jordan was stunned at the casualness with which Major Colon referred to the corruption rampant in Paraguay. "Are you telling me—

"Let me be clear, Mr. Censell," Negron interrupted. "Bribery and corruption are the way of the world. Surely you know this from your own time as a cog in the wheel of America's intelligence apparatus."

Jordan stood up. "How in the hell do you know—"

Negron put up his hand. "All I'm telling you, sir, miss, is that corruption is a way of life on this continent, even in more progressive or westernized nations like Brazil and Argentina. And, of course, you in

America know all about Chile, am I correct? We like to think we are not quite as bad as some of those others, but these are the rules under which the game here is played."

"I just don't understand how you know so much about us, about me," said Jordan.

"Please sit, Mr. Censell, excuse me, Mr. Calder," Negron said, smiling benignly. "We're telling you what we can tell you. You and Miss Calder will understand everything as it all unfolds."

The woman who'd taken care of their meal appeared at the doorway to the patio carrying a tray filled with wonderfully aromatic desserts. She placed the tray on the coffee table separating the two loveseats. Negron rattled off some quick Spanish instructions and the girl left.

"This is a traditional Paraguayan dessert. It's called budín de pan here. You call it bread pudding. It's heavenly. Lupita will bring coffee in a moment," he said.

Jordan was impatient. "Colonel, let me ask it again: How do you know all of this? How did you know about Christy's time in Mali and what happened over there? How do you know my real name and where I used to work?"

Negron sat back and took a long pull on his cigar. "You know," he said, "it is, from my experience—and I apologize if this offends you—a uniquely American kind of thing, this constant asking of the same questions over and over again and expecting different answers. Some things I am comfortable telling you now. Other things must come when it is the right moment. I promise you, for maybe the fifth time and, hopefully, Mr. Calder, for the last time, if everything is permitted to play out the way it should, everyone will get everything they want, except for those *jaguarembos* at Dommerich and especially Mr. Michael Capshaw."

"What does jaguar . . ." Christy asked. Negron smiled and started shaking his head.

"You don't want to know," Colon said. "Trust me."

• • •

TUESDAY

Special Agent Hallie Garard had, in her investigative repertoire, a persona for almost every occasion. Based on Ronnie Levitt's report of his visit to Minneapolis, she decided on one that was a bit slutty on the outside but arrow-direct in her approach. *Yeah*, she thought, *more like a tactical fucking nuclear weapon.*

She got more than her fair share of looks on Monday morning, from both men and women, at the airport in Orlando and then on the Delta A300 to MSP via Chicago O'Hare. She would arrive a little before two and was on Capshaw's calendar for 3:00 p.m.

"How's that book?" the guy in the aisle seat next to her asked. He was all right. He only interrupted her peace after he stopped tapping on his keyboard.

She looked at the cover, as if to remind herself of what she was reading.

"I like Scott Turow," she said. "Takes a more literary approach to a legal procedural."

"I saw the movie," he said. "Harrison Ford."

"Yeah," she said, closing the book. "I'm not much on movies. You can't do justice to a complex story in two hours. Plus, you miss a lot of the fun details."

He nodded his head. "You getting off at O'Hare?"

"No," she said. He nodded.

"I'm Frank."

"Yep, I can see that," she said, returning to her book.

• • •

Hallie told the turbaned Sikh cabbie she needed to be downtown by three. This he translated to mean "Step on it." He did, both on the gas and on the brakes. They arrived at Dommerich's building at 2:55 p.m. He nodded like a bobblehead doll and provided Hallie with a broad, toothy smile. She smiled back, dropped two twenties in his pass through, and bolted from the taxi. She took a couple deep breaths, calmed her nerves and her digestive system, and walked into the building housing Dommerich North America's headquarters.

Nancy Kuo was waiting for her in the lobby. The two women took the measure of each other. "Ms. Garard?" Nancy asked.

Hallie's only reason for visiting Michael Capshaw

was to further provoke him. Seeing Nancy Kuo was an unexpected side benefit. "Special Agent Garard," Hallie replied. "How does he keep his hands off of you?"

Nancy smiled. "Why on earth would he? Please, Special Agent, follow me."

"Gladly." Hallie said, then whispered, "Almost anywhere."

Capshaw was waiting by the elevator. "Ms. Garard," he said.

"Special Agent Garard," she said, choosing not to accept his offered hand.

"Please," he said, unruffled, and gestured for her to enter his office. The view was spectacular, and the office reeked of minimalism and money. His desk was a glass table, no drawers, and steel legs digging into lush white carpet. There were two white leather captain's chairs in front of the desk. Capshaw walked to one and offered Hallie the other.

"God," she said. "Do you hang meat in this place? It's freezing in here."

"It's how I prefer it," he said.

"Who'd you kill to get this office?" She asked, removing her jacket, and placing her briefcase on the floor next to her chair.

"No one you'd know, Special Agent Garard," he said, staring at her.

She sat in the chair he offered and crossed her legs, hiking up her short gray skirt. Black three-inch heels and a white blouse with the top three buttons undone completed her look. "That's good, Mr. Capshaw," she said, leaning in, "because I do carry a set of handcuffs in my bag."

He laughed. "This is all very entertaining, but why is someone from the FBI in my office flirting with me?"

It was her turn to laugh. "Is that what you think I'm doing?"

He said nothing. He stood and walked toward the other side of the room, in the direction of a glass-topped table surrounded by six chairs. He opened the credenza behind the table and took out a bottle of what looked like Scotch whiskey.

"Can I offer you a drink, Special Agent Garard?"

"Sure, you can offer, but no, thanks. I'm working," she said. "But, by all means, help yourself Michael. May I call you Michael, Michael?"

"Absolutely. May I call you . . . ?"

"No, you may not," she said. "Are we going to do more of this silly banter or are you at all interested in knowing why I'm here in the North Star State?"

He was dressed impeccably. Gray slacks, black Versace loafers with a useless but lovely silver buckle, a pink cotton Armani shirt, and a dark blue Roberto Cavalli tie covered with small pink squares. Hallie suspected somewhere between this office and his comely assistant's desk hung a dark blue or black wool blazer with polished brass, perhaps even gold-plated, buttons. *Guy probably jerks off while looking at his closet.*

He poured himself a drink and brought the glass

back to where they were seated. He placed the drink on a leather coaster on his desk.

"You know, Michael, I'm sorry. Do you have anything like tea, maybe?"

"Of course," he said. He went to his desk, buzzed Nancy, and told her to bring Hallie a cup of tea. "Cream? Sugar?" he asked.

"Actually, no, I take it straight." She smiled.

Nancy quickly arrived with the tea. Hallie looked up at her. "Thanks, so much." She could tell Capshaw was getting just a little antsy.

"Now, please," he said. "Why are you here? And don't FBI agents typically travel in pairs?"

"Typically, yes, but I'm not your typical special agent, Mr. Capshaw."

"Are you sure you're not flirting with me, Ms. Garard?"

"Not on your best or my worst day," she said. "Okay, here's the deal. I'm running point on an investigation into criminal complaints lodged with two federal agencies of substantial wrongdoing on the part of Dommerich North America and specifically you." She smiled and batted her eyes. "How's that for flirting?"

If Hallie were scoring herself as if in a boxing match, she'd have given her opening round an eight. Capshaw dropped all pretense of cordiality.

"What kind of wrongdoing? What agencies? What are you talking about?"

"Okay, here's how this works. I ask, you answer. By the way, how's Dommerich doing with its two latest pending approvals with the FDA and the EPA? San-iScal? Veracozen?" She waited a moment. "I'm sorry, am I speaking a foreign language here?"

He hesitated, then stood, and walked to the door.

"That, Special Agent Garard, is none of your or the FBI's damn business," he said. "Now, this can go one of three ways. You can leave and we can part . . . friends. You can leave and we don't part friends. Or you can just leave." He opened the door.

She stayed where she was seated and pointed to the white leather captain's chair he'd vacated. "Sit down, Mr. Capshaw. I'm not finished, and I think you're going to want to hear what I have to tell you." She stood up. "Now, sit the fuck down! Please."

He stuck his head out the door to the office and said something to Nancy. She poured his drink into her teacup and placed the glass into her bag. Hopefully she would be able to keep him sufficiently off balance so he wouldn't notice. He returned and sat down.

"My corporate counsel is on her way. Until she arrives, I've nothing more to say to you, Ms. Garard."

"Here's the thing, Michael," she said. "Once we start getting lawyers involved, the whole tenor of things changes. And by the way, she's not going to do you much good. What I'm investigating involves a range of criminal felonies, not contract or civil or corporate bullshit."

"Both Veracozen and SaniScal have received pre-liminary approval, Ms. Garard," he said. "Both should receive final approval by the end of next week. If you'd have checked with—"

"Oh, Michael." She rewarded him with a wide smile and sighed. "It's always painful when you're sure you're the smartest guy in the room, and then the smartest guy shows up," she said, looking at her watch. "I'm not 100 percent sure, but I believe a call to your retainer will reveal SaniScal is still mired in the muck at the FDA. You asked earlier—"

A knock sounded softly, and Nancy opened the door. "She just left for Munich, sir. Shall I try—" He shook his head and waved her away.

"You asked earlier," Hallie said, "if FBI agents travel in pairs. My partner, I'm certain, has finished his call to the EPA regarding Veracozen. Those people, I'm told, are quite skittish when it comes to approving something with the potential of causing a major international incident."

"Ms. Garard—Hallie—as much as I'd love to continue this visit," he said, standing again, "I'm not sure we can accomplish anything without Dommerich's counsel in attendance." He started again for the door. This time, Hallie stood and walked a few paces behind him.

"Let's see . . . bribery, corruption, falsification of test results, and those are just the low-hanging domestic charges, Mr. Capshaw," she said. "The international issues—Paraguay, Mali—well, those are not in my purview. Well, not yet anyway." She walked by him.

"Goodbye, Michael. It won't be paranoia if you find yourself thinking you're being watched. Have a good day." She smiled at Nancy as she approached her desk. She stopped, reached into her bag, retrieved a business card, and handed it to Nancy. She smiled again and mouthed the words "call me."

Chapter 22

Hallie decided to swap out the ticket she'd held for a flight on Wednesday-morning and instead took an immediately available one from Minneapolis to Atlanta, with a connecting flight at 11:15 p.m. into Orlando. She called Ronnie from ATL to update him on her visit. He filled her in on his second conversation with Dick Berlin at the FDA.

"Berlin told me they're going to take another look at the Veracozen application," he said.

"Good," she said. "It doesn't mean they won't move forward, but at least it will show this sleaze we mean business. This Capshaw creep is so slimy he could dive into a swimming pool and not get wet."

"I know. I've been in the man's company. Also, I got some very interesting intel from a source about this Republican Front group. Believe it or not, we might have an opportunity there."

"What kind of intel?" she asked. "What kind of opportunity?"

"We should talk about that in person, Hallie," he said. They agreed to connect the following morning. Her next call was to Willie Vasquez.

"Where you at, hottie?" he asked.

"It's Hallie, Willie, and I'm waiting for a plane in Atlanta."

"Yep, been there, done that," he said. "What's up?"

"I had a thought," she said.

"And you called me? I'm encouraged."

"You're not encouraged. You're an idiot. I need to talk to you more about this Republican Front for Paraguayan Independence. I'm waiting on what promises to be some interesting intelligence regarding this supposed rebel insurgent group. Did you set up that official meeting?"

"Yeah, I did," he said. "Just tell me when and how you wanna do it."

"Tomorrow, secure video, meaning you call me, maybe 2:00 p.m.?"

"Done. See ya."

• • •

WEDNESDAY

Hallie was awakened by a call from the FBI's technical assistance team. They'd isolated a spot in the jungle approximately sixty miles from Asunción where they last picked up a signal from the burner satellite phone they'd traced before it returned to a residential street just outside the Paraguayan capital.

"One of our analysts believes it's a camp possibly occupied by some rebel insurgent group."

• • •

Ronnie was at his desk at the paper when Hallie reached out. She told him what she'd been up to, about the call from tech assist, and about her meeting with Capshaw.

"He didn't know what hit him," she said. "I just held all my shit up to his nose and invited him to take a good, long whiff. By now he probably suspects the FDA and the EPA might no longer be his BFFs. What's up with you?"

"Writing," he said. "The way I'm looking at it, and I think my people are on board, soon as we know the two agencies have pulled or at least suspended provisional approval on SaniScal and Veracozen, we have the first part of the story ready to go. By digging up Choralizine and everything that's involved there, you should be able to get DOJ to issue subpoenas. When those papers hit the street, dominoes will start to fall fast all over the place."

• • •

"There's my girl," Willie Vasquez said when Hallie's face appeared on his screen. "You're looking good, G-man."

"I know. Eat your heart out, Guillermo."

"What you got for me?"

"You guys feel up to rescuing a couple of Americans who we are, I don't know, 72.5 percent sure are being held in a camp about sixty miles from Asunción, Paraguay?"

"Wow, 72.5 percent?" Willie said, smiling. "That's like almost maybe, Hallie."

"Didn't you tell me you had some people inside that Republican Front group?"

Willie was trying to keep the smile on his face. "Did I tell you that? I guess if I told you that, well, then it must be true."

"I'm serious, man," she said. She held up a picture. "It's this guy. As I might have mentioned, his name used to be Nelson Calder but now he goes by Jordan Censell; I'm not sure why he changed his name. He and his daughter, Christy Calder, well, we're pretty much certain, are being held by this Republican Front group."

"Did you tell me *you* had some intel about this group?"

"Are we alone?" she asked.

"Just you and me, baby. But we are on the record here."

"Yeah, here too. There's been a lot of back and forth between this group and the presidential palace in Asunción," she said. "There's also been traffic between the head guy of this group, a Colonel Roberto

Negron, and person or persons housed at a pretty impressive complex in Langley, Virginia. Would you know anything about that, Guillermo?" She leaned in so her face covered almost the entire screen, her eyes boring into his.

"That's some real interesting intel you got there, Ms. Special Agent Hallie Garard," he said, his smile returning. "Where did you get—"

"Gotcha, Willie," she said, smiling. "I want those two people brought home. Are you in any position to make that happen? Huh?"

"I'll be in touch real soon, baby," he said and disconnected.

• • •

"Damn it! Damn it! Damn it!" Willie said. "How the fuck did the Bureau stumble onto this?"

"Don't ask me," said Chuck Massey, Willie's control supervisor who'd been sitting behind the computer while Willie and Hallie were talking. "Be good if you could find out, though. What do you want to do?"

Willie paced around the SCIF, a secure room at Langley.

"We have to keep them at bay," Massey said, "at least until Negron and Colon make their move on Acosta."

"Yeah," Willie said. "I'm gonna go down there. I'll take Charlie Cook with me."

"What's the plan?

"Soon as I have one, you'll be the first to know, Chuck."

• • •

Ronnie was in the middle of crafting his story for the Sunday edition of the *Orlando Chronicle* when his phone pinged.

Can you talk? It was a text from Skeeter.

Of course, he texted back. His phone rang. "What's up?" he asked.

"You're gonna be mad."

Things were happening bobsled-run fast. Both Hallie and Ronnie had multiple balls in the air. They were almost certain that Jordan and Christy were, at the behest of Michael Capshaw, in the custody of the Republican Front for Paraguayan Independence, and that they were in the Paraguayan jungle, or maybe the Bolivian jungle, not far from Asunción.

If, in fact, the FDA and EPA were reconsidering final approval on SaniScal and Veracozen with any urgency, Capshaw might just be getting ready to run. Now this, with Skeeter. "Why am I going to be mad, Skeeter?"

"I might have stumbled across some very delicate stuff, totally by accident, of course."

"Let me let you in on something, buddy," Ronnie said. "My biggest problem may be continuing to hide your existence so I don't have to go to jail. If you have something you need to get off your chest . . ."

"Hypothetically," Skeeter said, "would it be of interest to your investigation, which I totally support by the way, and I want to make sure you know that . . ."

"Skeeter?"

"Five million dollars may have found its way into an account, in a bank, in Panama. Panama City, actually. Said account is, for the moment, controlled by the current, massively corrupt president of Paraguay."

"And the five million dollars came from?"

"An electronic transfer of funds from an IP address located in a bank next door to a building located in, of all places, Munich. That's in Germany, Levitt."

Ronnie scribbled two quick notes on the last empty page in his Dommerich notebook.

"Yes, I'm aware of that. Thanks. And why, exactly, would this knowledge make me unhappy?"

"It's not that," Skeeter said.

Ronnie released an exasperated sigh. "Are you jerking my chain, dude?"

"I would never do such a thing. There's been phone traffic between a cellular number currently located at a building on the Nicollet Mall in Minneapolis and a satellite phone located in the jungle near the capital city, Asunción, Paraguay."

"And?"

"The satellite phone was part of a shipment received over a year ago . . . drum roll . . . by the Paraguayan military." There was laughter coming through Ronnie's phone. "Had you worried, right?" Skeeter asked.

"You are such a—"

"Try not to call when I'm getting my jiggy on, man."

"How the fuck am I supposed to know—" Skeeter laughed and disconnected the call.

Ronnie smiled, shook his head, and looked down at his notes. *Okay*, he thought, *Dommerich sends five million to an account being held in the name of the Paraguayan president. There's been telephone traffic between someone at Dommerich and the Republican Front. And the Republican Front used a satellite phone owned by the Paraguayan military.*

Ronnie had learned a long time ago never to question Skeeter's results. He also knew the information Skeeter shared would never make it into a courtroom. Still, he needed to get with Hallie and see if the FBI had what they needed to bring Jordan and Christy home and to prosecute Michael Capshaw and other Dommerich executives, which would get the *Orlando Chronicle* to green-light Ronnie's story into print.

He called Hallie.

Chapter 23

"I'm afraid you and I need to meet, Colonel Negron," Willie Vasquez said. "Our relationship has become known to some people outside our otherwise very tight circle. Also, things are happening very quickly, and I don't want either of us to lose the opportunity we have to finish what we both want to get done."

"You obviously know things which are still unknown to me, Mr. Vasquez," the colonel said. "Are you coming to Paraguay?"

"I'm on my way, sir," Willie said.

"Then, by all means, we will meet. Where and when do you propose?"

"I'm in the air, heading your way, sir. I'm traveling with Charlotte Cook, a colleague of mine whom I trust with my life."

"You know where we are. I will leave instructions at the security post. When will we see you and Ms. Cook?"

Willie looked at his watch. He'd been airborne for four hours. "It should be in time for dinner, Colonel."

"Dinner it will be. Safe travels, Señor Vasquez." They disconnected.

Willie sent a text to Hallie Garard: *Operation Censell Calder Return underway.*

• • •

Kimmie Levitt answered the doorbell. "You got a dog!" she said.

Hallie smiled. "I'm watching her for someone. Are you parents at home?"

"My dad is," she said. "Dad! Hallie's here. She's got a dog!"

Ronnie came through the kitchen to the front door.

"Let's take a walk," Hallie said. "Lady has business to do on Alberto's lawn."

"Jennie's not here, and—"

"Don't worry," she said. It's just around the cul-de-sac. You'll be okay, right Kimmie?"

"I'm watching TV," she said. "Can she stay?"

"Not this time, sweetie," Hallie said. "She needs to poop, and I don't want her doo doo to mess up your mom's beautiful, super clean house."

"Okay, bye," Kimmie said.

"You think people will talk about us walking Lady together around Susie Q Court?" Hallie asked with a sly grin.

"We can only hope," Ronnie said. "You're a piece of work, Hallie."

"My late mother's exact words, on more than one occasion, Sheldon."

"See? Until just now I thought you might have been created in a beaker in some chem lab somewhere, not born, you know, like the rest of us."

She smiled at him. "You'd have liked her," she said, "my mother."

"I'm sure I would," he said. What's up?"

She told him a friend from the Company was on his way to Paraguay to rescue Jordan and Christy. He stopped walking. They were in front of Mikey's house. He looked her in the eyes.

"I called him," she said. "May have told him a little of what you told me your fucking source gave you. You know, I'm going to need to know about this source of yours, Sheldon. Or, you know, I could just tap your phone."

"And I told you that's not going to happen, Leonard." They walked in silence for a few steps. Lady really wanted to go potty, but Hallie wanted her to take her dump in Alberto's front yard. "And, just so you know, my source is in possession of maybe a hundred burner phones purchased all over North America. He changes his contact device weekly, at least." They walked in silence. Ronnie wondered what his neighbors on Susie Q Court would think about everything that was happening right now. He stopped walking again. "You didn't tell your friend at Langley about the five million, did you?"

She began to act like a junior high school girl, rolling her eyes, smiling, turning around, her version of playing coy.

"Jesus, Hallie."

"I might have let it slip. I can't be sure."

"Okay, here's my take on things," he said. "This Republican Front group is just that, a front. I'm pretty sure they're talking to the government in Asunción . . ."

"Why do you think that?" Hallie asked.

"Because the phone was part of a shipment made to the Paraguayan military," he said.

"I won't ask how you know that." She sneered.

"That's good," he said.

"And, for good measure, they're talking to the C. I. fucking A.," she said. "And now my friend and his partner are headed down there because I let him know what I know."

"Hmmm," he said. "Shit's getting real, Hallie."

"I have a feeling, just a feeling, mind you, Sheldon, that whoever is running the Republican Front has his eye on President Acosta's job," she said.

"And, if Acosta goes down for taking a big bribe from Dommerich so they can mow down a huge part of jungle for some drug or some pesticide—"

"Okay, wait," she said. "So, what's the CIA's interest? Don't answer that. That's a rhetorical question. With spooks, you just never fucking know."

As soon as they got to Alberto's lawn, Hallie bent down. She started rubbing behind Lady's ears and telling her to be a good girl. Within seconds, Lady made a deposit directly in front of Alberto's prized Robellini palm.

"She's such a good girl!" Hallie said.

"He's going to blow up your house, Hallie."

"He's going to shit bricks when he finds out I'm a fed," she said.

"I think the CIA is interested in getting rid of one corrupt regime and putting in a maybe slightly less corrupt government they can work with," Ronnie said. "Isn't that their typical game?"

"I'm telling you, man, it's smoke-and-mirror world over there at Langley," she said. "What's next?"

. . .

Capshaw's phone rang at 7:00 a.m. Thursday morning, central daylight time.

"Hello," he said, groggily, "Capshaw."

"Michael," said Nathan Becker. "My office, exactly thirty minutes." He hung up.

"Fuck! It's . . . What time is it? What does he want?"

Nancy rolled over and curled up with her pillow. "Only one way to find out, Michael," she said.

. . .

Michael walked into his boss's office carrying a cup from the Starbucks on the lobby level of the building. "Took your own sweet time, Michael," Becker said.

"I walked, Nathan," he said. "What's so pressing it couldn't wait?"

"You really don't know?"

"I really don't know, Nathan, and I'm really not happy—"

"I don't give a single small shit if you're happy or not, Michael. I'm not happy, Michael. I'm not happy and Gunther's not going to be happy when I talk to him as soon as you and I are done here."

Capshaw sat down and assumed the suppliant posture he turned on whenever his boss was in a snit. "I'm sorry, Nathan. Please, what happened?"

"You see, Michael, this is a big part of our ongoing problem," Becker said. "You're supposed to be reporting to me, not the other way around. Jack Winter from the FDA called *me* at home. Provisional approval on SaniScal has been rescinded."

Capshaw's jaw went slack. "What? When? Why?"

"He told me, and I quote, 'Media and the FBI are making inquiries.' The FBI, Michael. The FBI! Your portfolio with Dommerich includes you knowing about shit like this before I do and before it creates a problem."

"Fuck." Capshaw said, standing up. "Let me get on this, Nathan. I've spoken to the FBI. I've talked to—"

Becker stood up and shouted, "You what? You what, Michael? You talked to the FBI, and you didn't put me into the center of that loop? Are you stupid? Are you blind? Can't you read what it says on that door out there? It says president and chief executive officer. Did it not even occur to you that the president and CEO of Dommerich North America should know his SVP of external affairs *talked* with the F. B. fucking I.? My god, Michael."

"Nathan, I'm on this, I promise. Let me . . . I'm on this," Capshaw said. He left before the dragon behind the desk could breathe any more fire at him.

• • •

Down in his office three floors below, Michael Capshaw sat alone, a glass of Scotch in front of him. He tried to work through which one of his potentially career-ending problems was greatest; the media inquiry when Choralizine came up, the visit by the bitch from the FBI, or the fact that provisional approval on SaniScal had been rescinded. SaniScal. That was money. Big, serious fucking money.

He tried Jack Winter's mobile but was sent to voice-mail. He left a message. "Jack, it's Michael . . . Capshaw at Dommerich. I'm sorry to bother you. Please call me as soon as you get this message. It's important. You know the number."

He left another message on the mobile of his guy at the EPA. He dialed the number on Hallie Garard's card. No answer. Not even voicemail. He didn't bother with Ronnie Levitt from CMG. He tried to reach his crew chief in Mali to suspend operations. No answer.

He called Nancy's mobile. It went straight to voicemail. That really bothered him.

. . .

Willie Vasquez and Charlie Cook had slept on the plane and were fresh and cleaned up when they arrived at the camp of the Republican Front for Paraguayan Independence. They cleared security as soon as the armed guard at the gate saw their credentials.

"Mr. Vasquez, Ms. Cook, so good to see you, my friends," Colonel Negron said. "I hope you're hungry. We have a lavish dinner for you." Major Colon was all smiles.

"Thank you, Colonel, Major," Willie said. "I hope all is well here and that you're both ready to assume your rightful places in the presidential palace in Asunción."

"Are we close?" Colon asked.

"We are," Willie said. "I have news for you. I believe your ascension to the presidency is imminent."

"Has that 'trigger event' you've talked about finally occurred?" Negron asked. Willie didn't answer but his smile said all that needed saying. "Come, come," Negron said. "Let's talk over dinner."

"One quick thing, Colonel," Charlie Cook said.

"Yes, Ms. Cook?"

"Are your two American guests okay?"

"They are fine," Negron said. "And they seem like fine people, as well. Perhaps you'd like to meet them?"

"Let's wait until after we've spoken, Colonel," Willie said.

• • •

Willie Vasquez confirmed to Colonel Roberto Negron that an event had occurred, enabling change at the top in Paraguay. The colonel and his adjutant met the news with excitement and enthusiasm.

"We are both ready to return to our homes, to our families, and to our destinies," Col. Negron said. "I hope we can keep it . . . bloodless?"

"I think there's a way you can, Colonel," Charlie said, "if President Acosta is at all pragmatic . . ."

"You are thinking we let him keep the money," Maj. Colon said.

"He gets to keep his life, and he gets to keep *their* money," Willie said. "It's dirty money, anyway. And, it really doesn't have anything to do with our goals."

"There's something . . . I don't know . . . distasteful about letting a corrupt leader benefit from his treachery and abuse," Colonel Negron said. The camp cook stepped from the kitchen and nodded at him. "Ah, dinner is ready!"

They devoured a meal of braised Argentine beef, steamed locally grown vegetables, red Chilean wine, and Breyers ice cream. After dinner, Willie and Charlie both accepted Negron's offer of Cuban cigars.

"I pray this is not offensive, but there's something

very . . . alluring about a woman smoking a cigar, Ms. Cook," Colon said. She smiled.

"What's good for the goose, Major," she said.

"Indeed," Col. Negron said.

"I know it's not a perfect situation, Colonel," Willie said. "But I can assure you, with the removal of President Acosta and concurrent reassignment of the seated American ambassador, things will be ripe for progress and substantial US investment here in Paraguay."

"May I visit with your American guests now, Colonel?" Charlie Cook asked.

"Major, would you be so kind?"

"Come with me, please," Major Colon said. They walked to the cabin where Christy and Jordan were enjoying their own dinner.

Once inside the cabin, Charlie nodded at Major Colon, indicating she'd like some private time with her countrymen. Jordan began to stand but Charlie motioned him to stay seated.

"Please, finish your dinner," she said. "I'm Charlie Cook with an agency of the United States government. Within the next two, three days, max, my partner and I will be taking you home. I've been instructed to inform you both that Ronnie Levitt and FBI Special Agent Hallie Garard send their regards." Jordan laughed out loud.

"Hah! I knew it! I told you she was a fed," he said to Christy.

Charlie explained the process they'd undertaken to ensure everything happened exactly in the manner and on the timeline it had to. There were questions, of course, but the two agreed to a structured wheel of events in which they were small but important cogs.

"Get a good night's sleep," Charlie said. "Once this switch flips, things are going to move at breakneck speed."

Chapter 24

Hallie went nuts on Guillermo Vasquez when he called her from the hot zone. "I just don't fucking understand why you couldn't read me in on this, Willie," she said. "Someday, this bullshit between the Bureau and the Agency needs to stop. I thought—hell, we all thought—after 9/11, we'd do better, but you guys are always keeping shit secret that shouldn't be and doesn't need to be a secret."

He knew she was right, but those kinds of decisions needed to happen at a much higher pay grade than theirs. "I know this is an emotional response, Hallie," he said. "And to be honest, you're right, we should be able to work better together, but our side of this operation has been in place for nearly two years. You guys are way late to this party, man. And remember, you called me. Once you did that, everything changed. If this whole business with Dommerich hadn't happened, I have no idea how long it would have been for our operation to conclude."

"Don't mansplain me, Willie," she said. "I'm no virgin here. I've been clocking time on this for, shit, seven months now."

"Really? You've been sullied?"

"Hey, fuck you, asshole," she said.

They both took a breath. Then they discussed the Agency's relationship with the Republican Front. She asked him how long a leash the Agency had Negron and Colon.

"Frankly, I'm not sure who is holding the leash and who is wearing it," he said. "These are very smart guys, Hallie, American-educated in top schools. That said, they've kept their word with us all along the way. They've managed things with Acosta's regime; I don't think he suspects what's really going to happen. They've played the hell out of Dommerich and this Capshaw clown. And they've taken good care of our people. All in all, I think they're okay."

"Let's hope so. Listen," she said, "in case you haven't completely figured this part out yet, there's a third leg to this stool."

"Yeah," he said, "your reporter friend."

"Yeah, my reporter friend is responsible for a whole lot of really useful intelligence, for both of us."

"He is, and I'm going to have a conversation with him when all of this is done. I don't know where he gets some of the stuff he comes up with, but I gotta say—"

"He'll go to jail before revealing his source," she said.

"In any event, I have no control whatsoever over his timetable, and he's got to be close to running with at least some of what he's uncovered. I made him promise not to name either of us, but inside our jobs, people are going to put stuff together."

"Once it's all out there and done, it shouldn't be a problem, right?" he asked.

"It shouldn't, but who knows? By the way, we're so worried about our own asses, how are our people? What do they know?"

"Charlie debriefed them last night," he said. "They're good. They're smart and they both have history with Uncle Sam, so they know how stuff works. They shouldn't present any problems. They just want to go home."

She told him they'd talk again as soon as she learned Ronnie's timeline for getting his story into print.

• • •

The first installment of Ronnie Levitt's story would run almost three thousand words. Joe Hill and his top copyeditor attempted to shave where they could, but the story was dense. Ronnie had learned early in his career to render unto editors that which fell under their purview. In the end, it was his byline. He'd argued to protect the identities and, if possible, the affiliations of Hallie Garard and Willie Vasquez, and he wrote in such a manner as to maximize Dommerich's systemic evil and minimize any foolhardiness on the part of his neighbor and his neighbor's daughter. He'd been careful not to mention or make even obscure reference to Skeeter's role, or for that matter, his very existence.

The story highlighted Dommerich's five-million-dollar payoff to President Acosta in Paraguay; several hundreds of thousands of dollars in payoffs to warlords and criminal gangs in southern Mali; and Capshaw's machinations involving, first, Christy Calder, and then her father.

Skeeter had uncovered a pattern of dangerous corruption at three testing facilities, all of which had presented only affirmative findings on products dating back to the earliest days of Michael Capshaw's tenure in the position he currently held. In addition, Skeeter had found instances, beyond those associated with Choralizine, of payoffs to individuals to ward off costly lawsuits and bad publicity for the company. This revealed Dommerich's disdain for either product safety or efficacy. *Profits over anything and everything,* Ronnie had written, *should be the company's slogan.*

Once the story ran in the *Orlando Chronicle*, it would, within a day, be picked up first by Capital Media Group's other dailies, its business journal division, its broadcast and cable news operations, and its online sites. After that, it would go out into the entire global media machine.

Doubtless, heads would roll quickly in both Minneapolis and Munich in an effort to bolster the company's share price and to save whatever might survive of Dommerich's brand and corporate legacy. Both efforts, Ronnie believed, would be fool's errands.

• • •

Ronnie had left the newsroom and was in the lobby when his phone buzzed. It revealed an unknown caller. "Ronnie Levitt," he answered into a scratchy, static-filled line.

"My name is Willie Vasquez, Mr. Levitt. We have a short, cute mutual friend in the FBI."

"Okay," Ronnie said.

"I'm calling from Paraguay, Mr. Levitt."

"Okay."

"I'm going to have to work for this, right?"

"I don't even know who you are or what *this* is, Mr. Vasquez."

"How soon can you get your story into print, Mr. Levitt?"

Ronnie looked skyward. He didn't have to ask who Willie Vasquez was or how he knew there was a big story coming. He exhaled.

"We're planning on Sunday's edition. Largest circulation."

"Events on the ground here might render parts of your story old news by that time, Mr. Levitt," he said. "Can you move the release up?"

Ronnie didn't really care when the story ran. Tobe Hillenmyer was pushing for Sunday, but he was pretty sure she could be convinced to move it up. "Can you tell me how Mr. Censell and his daughter are?" Ronnie asked.

Willie hesitated. His priority was the regime change in Paraguay. "They're fine. The sooner you hit the send button the sooner they get home, Mr. Levitt."

"I'll call you right back."

He jumped onto the up escalator. The newsroom was to his left. The executive offices were on the right. He turned right.

"I need to see Tobe," he said to her gatekeeper.

He pushed a button, opening the door to the executive suite. Tobe was on her couch reading copy, nodding her head.

"This is really good stuff, Ronnie," she said. "You might get another one of those . . . things you don't like to talk about." Ronnie mostly ignored Pulitzer talk.

"I just got off the phone with Paraguay. They need us to release ASAP. Shit's going down fast down there."

"Who?"

He shook his head.

"Will we get whatever happens first?"

He nodded. "That's been the deal from the beginning."

She picked up her desk phone and pushed a button. "We need to redo page one." She listened for a few seconds. "Yes," was all she said, and hung up.

"We're good for tomorrow's edition. This is good stuff, Ronnie. Very good."

He nodded his thanks and pulled out his phone.

He punched in the number Willie Vasquez had given him. It took several seconds.

"Go ahead," Willie said.

"Tomorrow morning," Ronnie said. He listened for almost a minute. "Will you be there? Okay. We can talk then."

Ronnie hung up. He turned to his publisher. "Our two Americans will be setting down at Executive Airport tomorrow night," he said. "It will be too late for Thursday's edition, but we'll have a bunch more for Friday. Or, if you want, two separate stories on Sunday."

• • •

At 10:00 p.m. Paraguayan time on Thursday night, Col. Negron, Major Colon, Willie Vasquez, and Charlie Cook drove to downtown Asunción and were quickly waved through the gates at the presidential palace. Col. Negron explained the lay of the land to President Javier Acosta, who was in his bedroom in his underwear, a young prostitute still in his bed. "A private plane is fueled and ready at the international airport. You and up to five others of your choosing will be flown to Panama City, Panama, dropped off, and from that moment forward, left on your own."

By dawn, a battalion of soldiers from the Paraguayan Army under Major Colon, took over the presidential palace and established a temporary custodianship led by Col. Negron. The soldiers had, for nearly three years, been assigned by President Acosta to occupy a camp in the jungle. They were there so Acosta could loot the national treasury with impunity, having continuously stoked fears in the country's population of imminent attack from a band of so-called rebel insurgents. Col. Negron planned his first publicly stated order of business to be a commitment to national and local elections six months in the future "to put into place a true constitutional democratic republic established in the image of our very good friends and neighbors to the north."

• • •

FRIDAY

At 6:30 a.m. Michael Capshaw was awakened by an urgent call from Nick Guzman. He directed his company's SVP of external affairs to a front-page article that had been published overnight on the digital edition of the *Orlando Chronicle*.

Capshaw tossed the phone aside. "Why is he waking me up for this shit?" he said, rubbing sleep from his eyes.

Nancy was dressed, makeup on. "This is why," she said. She handed him his phone. "Call me later, Michael," she said, "when you decide what you're going to do." She let herself out the door of his downtown Minneapolis condominium.

Capshaw sat on his bed and scrolled through the

article on the front page of the *Orlando Chronicle*. He cringed when he saw the headline and the byline.

"Lies, Bribes, and Kidnapping: An International Drug Giant Denudes African Deserts and South American Jungles in the Name of Obscene Profits"

By Ronald Levitt

A young volunteer with the Peace Corps, whose passion for doing good work could not be contained, may, in the end, be credited with bringing down a corrupt South American regime and a huge and influential multinational corporation.

Dommerich North America, headquartered in Minneapolis, is a subsidiary of Dommerich Worldwide, an enormous global pharmaceutical and pesticide manufacturer. The *Orlando Chronicle* has uncovered incontrovertible evidence that the company paid bribes in the US to functionaries in the Food and Drug Administration and the Environmental Protection Agency to overlook

inconsistencies in product testing and to facilitate approval for
two new products, a prescription
dandruff shampoo and a pesticide.

Dommerich North America's Sr.
Vice President for External Affairs, Michael Capshaw, bribed a
Peace Corps official in order to
have a volunteer based in Mali in
sub-Saharan Africa reassigned. Her
activities threatened the company's plans to disrupt a drinking
water project so they could harvest a plant providing source
material for a yet-to-be-approved
prescription dandruff shampoo,
SaniScal.

The young Peace Corps volunteer,
Christy Calder, 27, was reassigned
to Paraguay. Three weeks after she
arrived, Ms. Calder was kidnapped
while watching a demonstration by
Asunción locals protesting Dommerich's plans to denude almost
20,000 acres of pristine jungle
so the company could harvest bark
from a rare tree to be used in a
new pesticide, Veracozen.

There was a great deal more to the article. Capshaw dropped his phone and stared out his bedroom window into the darkness of the early Minneapolis morning. He called out for Nancy but remembered she had left.

"Call me later when you decide what you're going to do." He walked into his kitchen and turned on his Keurig coffeemaker.

• • •

At 7:00 p.m. Friday evening, Paraguayan time, Jordan Censell, Christy Calder, Charlie Cook, and Willie Vasquez boarded a CIA jet bound for Miami, Florida. Following a nearly five-hour debrief and a few hours of sleep, Jordan and Christy boarded the same jet and, at 1:45 p.m. the following afternoon, landed at Orlando Executive Airport.

Ronnie and Jennie Levitt, along with Hallie Garard and a Basenji named Lady, met the plane. Following greetings, introductions, and hugs, Jordan told Hallie he'd made her as a fed a week after she moved into the house the FBI had purchased on Susie Q Court.

"Well, *Nelson*," she said, smiling, "I guess now knowing you were a DIA spook yourself, it's not surprising. It takes one to know one."

The *Orlando Chronicle* secured a two-bedroom suite at the Grand Bohemian in downtown Orlando, mostly for Jordan and Christy to decompress and ease back into life in the United States. Ronnie wanted some one-on-one time with Christy so she could fill in blanks about her experiences in Mali and Paraguay. It would help complete the second installment of his story about Dommerich's treacherous activities on two continents.

Hallie Garard had one more task requiring her attention. Later Friday evening, she dropped Lady off at a nearby boarding facility and caught the last flight from Orlando to Minneapolis, where she looked forward to personally handcuffing Michael Capshaw and bringing him to justice.

Chapter 25

Michael Capshaw knew of four different ways to leave his condominium building. Warned by Hallie Garard days earlier that he would be under surveillance, he decided to use the most convoluted and least likely method available to him. If the feds had all the possible exits covered, so be it.

He'd been prepared to beat a hasty retreat ever since the ugliness in Mali almost a year and a half earlier. He collected his Michael Antonucci identity package from a locked box stored in a closet and checked one last time to make sure the passport, credit card, and driver's license were all up to date. He returned the documents to the manila envelope, folded it, and placed it in the inside pocket of the blue Isaia blazer he'd chosen for his trip.

Despite the fact he was going far, far away, and despite the fact he almost certainly would not be returning to Minneapolis, or the United States for that matter, he'd be traveling light. The only things he'd carry on board with him included his computer bag and a single tote with three changes of clothing and whatever cash he could get his hands on. When he got to where he was going, he'd figure out the rest of his future.

He took the elevator down from his condo to the second floor of the building. The coffee shop had been open since 5:30 a.m. He walked in, picked up a large cup of black coffee, and exited through the shop's back door. The back door opened onto the fourth floor of a parking garage, which also connected to a building on the opposite side of the four-building complex.

He passed on the BMW 7 Series he'd received from Gunther Soldinger two years ago as a bonus for outstanding revenue performance. Nancy favored the restored cocoa-colored 1969 Jaguar XK-E when they were able to get away for weekend trips together. Since he suspected the feds were probably watching his condo, his office, and his BMW, he decided to take the Jag, pick up Nancy, and get out of town.

His escape plan was audacious. The key to success, of course, relied first on getting to Chicago, and then getting onto the first leg of his flight. He pulled out his phone and punched in Nancy's number. It went straight to voicemail.

"Call me ASAP." He thought about adding something about leaving town but didn't, just in case the FBI was listening in. "It's important," was all he said. He slid his bags behind his seat, climbed in, and cranked the goosed-up engine.

. . .

When Hallie woke up Saturday morning in Minneapolis, she noticed a pair of missed calls on her phone from the same number in the 612-area code. *The only two people in Minneapolis who have this number are Michael Capshaw and his comely assistant.* She dialed the number.

"Hello, Ms. Garard." It was the assistant.

"It's Nancy, right?"

"Yes, Nancy Kuo."

"Hold a second, please." Hallie climbed into a cab at the airport and recited the address of Michael Capshaw's office.

"Is there something I can do for you?"

"Are you looking for Michael?"

"Do you know where he is?" There was a momentary silence on the line. "Ms. Kuo?"

"Yes."

"Do you know—"

"I don't know where he is, but I believe I know where he's going."

Hallie nodded silently. "I'm actually on the ground in Minneapolis, Ms. Kuo. Can you tell me where he's going?"

"Will you meet me somewhere?"

"Of course." She told Hallie to meet her at a sushi place inside the Mall of America. Hallie told the driver to forget downtown and gave the new destination. He wasn't thrilled.

Ten minutes later he dropped her at one of the mall entrances. "How big is this place?"

"Biggest in the world, lady," the driver said, a bit more thrilled at the twenty-dollar tip she gave him. She started to ask him if he knew where she might find a decent sushi place inside, but he waved as he sped away. She walked inside.

"Holy . . ." she said. *This place is fucking huge*, she thought. She found a kiosk map of the place and checked to see where she was. Then she found the listing of food and drink establishments. "Two sushi restaurants?" she asked herself out loud. Her phone rang.

"You didn't say there was more than one sushi restaurant in this place."

"I know. I'm sorry. It's really big. You've never been here?"

"Amazing, I know. Where are you?"

She told Hallie where she was. Hallie started walking and punched in the number of the Minneapolis field office and asked for a couple of agents and a ride.

"Where inside the mall should we meet you?"

"I've got no idea. Call me when you get here. I'm going to be dining on bait."

Eight minutes later, Hallie was eating sushi Nancy had selected for them.

Even dressed down, Hallie thought Nancy looked spectacular. She wore a Twins baseball cap, a maroon University of Minnesota sweat suit trimmed in gold, and a pair of black high-end Reeboks.

"Man, do you ever look just . . . ragged?" Hallie asked her. Nancy ignored the compliment. Her hands were shaking.

"He's expecting me to come with him," Nancy said. "I don't want to go where I think he's going. Really, I don't want to go anywhere with him. This has all been fun, and he bought me a condo here in Bloomington, but . . . I don't know. He does some scary things, and I don't want . . ."

Hallie put her hands over Nancy's. "Don't think about him. Think about you. A guy like this? Trust me, Nancy, I wouldn't be within a thousand miles of this place if I didn't have to take Michael Capshaw down."

"Do you know that Capshaw isn't even his real name?" Nancy asked.

Hallie went cold. "His name is not Michael Capshaw?"

"His name is Michael, but . . . it's something Italian, I think. He told it to me once, a long time ago."

"He told you Michael Capshaw isn't his real name?" Hallie asked again. *This guy's not even remotely in the top thousand smartest guys in the room*, she thought.

While they finished their sushi, Nancy told Hallie

she thought Michael was planning to go someplace in the Pacific. She wasn't sure of the name. "He wants to live on some small island somewhere," she said.

At least, Hallie thought, *we can get agents to cover the airports.* Her phone rang. "We're on the upper level," she said. "A sushi place. It's on the South Avenue, I think." Nancy nodded. Hallie gave her agents the name of the restaurant.

"I'm having a couple of agents meet me here," she said. "It's nothing about you, unless—"

Nancy stood. "I'm going to leave," she said. "I've probably told you too much already." She turned to leave, then turned back. "One more thing. Don't look for his BMW. That's his company car. He hates it. Look for his Jaguar. It's brown, an old sports car. It's really a very nice car." She gave Hallie a sad smile. "Bye." She walked away. Then she began to jog, right there in the Mall of America. Hallie watched her until she was out of sight. Her phone rang.

"Call me." Nancy said and disconnected. *Yeah, no, I don't think so,* Hallie thought. *Not like that.* She thought about Emily. She sighed. "Damn!"

• • •

On I-94 outside Minneapolis, headed toward Chicago's O'Hare Airport, Michael punched the single digit for Nancy again and again but was sent to voicemail each time. "I tried," he said the final time. "This could have been fun. Say nothing! Say nothing, Nancy. If anyone asks, you know nothing." He was surprised. He felt a small sense of loss. But he was sure she wouldn't say anything.

• • •

Christy Calder told Ronnie about the time an American had visited their encampment in Mali. Ronnie described Capshaw. Christy just nodded her head.

"Seriously?" Ronnie said, stunned.

"Yeah, I'm pretty sure that's him," she said. "He came over to see if he could convince us to relocate our water project so his company could enjoy unrestricted access to a large area where some shrub they were interested in grew in abundance. These Dommerich people had gall, I'll give them that."

"So, these two members of your team told Capshaw it wouldn't work, why it wouldn't work, and that's when he tried to bribe them?" Ronnie asked.

Christy nodded. "I was right there," she said. "Alan and Sheila were really nice about it. Even suggested there might be other places where the plant they were interested in grew in greater abundance. He offered them $100,000 each! The guy's head must have been made of cement. He knew we were with the Peace Corps. If we'd been about money, would we have signed up as Peace Corps volunteers so we could live some life of luxury in sub-Saharan Africa? I was a lawyer, for God's sake."

"Tell Ronnie what you told me," Jordan said. "I guess

there's no way to be absolutely sure, but the timing of things seems just a little too coincidental."

"How long did this all take place after you came home?" Ronnie asked Jordan.

"I left in April, this was near the end of June," Jordan said.

"There were lots of social problems in that region," Christy said, "but the real danger, when there was any, came in the form of what would probably be called gangs by people living in the States."

"What kinds of social problems?" Ronnie asked. "I want to offer some flavor of what life is like in that part of West Africa."

"Different places, different problems," she said. "Homosexuality is a crime in several countries—not Mali, but for sure in other places. In some places, women are subject to genital mutilation. Boko Haram was active there, operating out in the open. These were very bad people.

"Virtually every government in that part of the world is corrupt to some degree. They'll sell anything to anyone if they can make money for their own personal or political ends. Not everyone and not everywhere, but if you focus on that aspect of life over there, on what's wrong, you can come away with the idea that it's not a very safe place, but really, these days, is there any truly safe place?"

"Not like over there, honey," Jordan said.

"I know, Dad," she said. "Don't worry, I'm not going back. I'm done with all that."

"I have to ask, Christy," Ronnie said. "Can you tell me what happened to your friends?"

She bit her lip, then swallowed hard. "After Capshaw failed to either convince or bribe them, he left," she said. "A few days later, one of those gangs I mentioned—young, angry, armed to the teeth—came through where we were surveying a stretch of desert between the Niger River and Koulikoro. They made a lot of noise. This was, let's just say, not uncommon, but it didn't happen all the time. We wrote it off and went about our work."

"What did they do?" Ronnie asked.

"Fired weapons in the air, screamed and yelled at us, especially at the women, pointed fingers . . . intimidation tactics, I think, probably designed to get us to leave. But then, a few days later, a larger group came through and set fire to a few of our buildings. When Alan and Sheila came out of their room—Did I mention they were a couple?—the group stopped what they were doing. Then, and I saw this, they shot Alan and took Sheila." She stopped talking for a moment. "They just took her. Four days later, they came back, dumped her body right in the middle of our camp." She stopped again to take a drink of water. "Less than a week later, I was on a plane to Asunción. That move was not of my doing or with my blessing."

"It was a blessing to me," Jordan said, putting his arm around her.

• • •

Hallie called Ronnie and filled him in on her visit with Nancy. He blew her mind with Christy's recounting of Michael Capshaw's visit to Mali.

"So," he said. "Might you be able to hang a murder charge on Capshaw?"

"Doubt it," she said. "Conspiracy at best, even if we could find out who did it and get them to testify in . . . where? Bumfuck, Mali? But it tells us a few things."

"Tells us he's a bigger piece of dung than we already thought," Ronnie said. "Tells us he's much more dangerous than we already thought. Tells us—"

"Tells us he's probably making his run right now as we're sitting here chatting about how big a douche he is," she said. "Jordan and Christy good?"

"Yeah," he said. "Exhausted, of course, but I'm guessing Jennie and Stacy are going to be taking Christy shopping, fixing up the house, that sort of stuff."

"Oh, shit," she said, "I forgot to tell you. Lady is in a boarding place over on Pershing, near South Goldenrod Road. Can you . . . ?"

"Yeah, sure, consider it done," he said. "What's next for you?"

"According to Nancy," she said, "he's driving some penis car, an old Jag."

"XK-E?"

"What is it with men and penis cars?" she asked. "Yeah, brown, if you can imagine. Who drives a brown penis car?"

He laughed. "You'll understand if you see it."

"Obviously, he knows we have MSP covered. We have to figure out where he's going now."

. . .

"Skeeter."

"Levitt."

"I know. What?"

"If I wanted to get lost somewhere, like an island in the Pacific . . ."

Skeeter didn't answer right away. Then, "Vanuatu."

"And may the force be with you as well."

"Cute, but that's the point. Nobody knows about this place. Vanuatu. Island. Islands, actually, several islands. Tax haven. Lax banking system. No treaty."

"Tre—No extradition treaty?"

"Yep. Nice place if you want hot weather, warm water, scuba diving, maybe to disappear. Not much else there."

"Where is it?"

"Not far from Australia, New Zealand, Fiji."

"Okay, buddy, thanks."

"By the way," Skeeter said, "whoever's going there—you know, some Dommerich executive, for example—unless they took the long way, you know, flying to the east, they would almost definitely stop on the West Coast or in Honolulu, either to change planes or to refuel. Just sayin' man."

"Thanks, Skeeter."

Ronnie dialed Hallie. "Look into a place called Vanuatu," he said.

"Vanna what? Vanna White?"

"Van-oo-ah-too," he said. He spelled it for her. "I'm told people go there either to scuba dive or to get lost."

"So, which one do you think our boy is doing?"

"Capshaw's looking for a place to get lost that doesn't have an extradition treaty with the US," he said. "And he's looking for a place with, let's just call it, uncomplicated banking laws."

"Bet the fucker's been stashing cash there," she said.

"Bet you're right, Special Agent Garard," he said.

"Bet he's going to Chicago, first," she said.

Ronnie nodded. "Easier to get someplace like that from O'Hare than from MSP."

"TTYL, dude."

"Yep."

Chapter 26

Michael stopped at a Mobil station off I-90 near La Crosse, Wisconsin. While the pump was doing its thing, he tried—for the last time, he told himself—to reach Nancy.

"Hello, Michael," she said.

"I thought you'd be leaving with me."

She sighed. "No," she said, stretching the word out. "Your dream isn't my dream. Frankly, I'm not all that crazy about Minneapolis, or Bloomington, either."

"Where are you?"

"Right now, I'm at work," she said. "Acting normal. It's . . . quiet, actually."

"I'm not surprised." *Levitt's article, the FBI chick's visit. Probably lots of hunkering down going on.*

"Where are you?" she asked.

"On my way to gone, Nancy," he said. "You can still—"

"That woman? From the FBI? The agent? She came to see me."

"When?"

"Few hours ago. I met her at the mall. I didn't say anything because I don't know where you are or what you're doing, right?"

"Right," he said.

"Oh, and you should know," she said, "Nathan has been arrested."

Michael was quiet for a moment. Then, "Really? And I care about that, why?"

"Take care of yourself, Michael."

"I always do, Nancy," he said. She hung up. "Time to move on," he whispered.

He paid cash for the gas, bought a packaged sandwich and a fountain drink, and set out for Chicago O'Hare. He had four more hours of driving ahead of him.

. . .

One of Hallie's people found the Jag. Or, at least, she identified the one Michael Capshaw was most likely driving, probably to Chicago. There were not a lot of absolutes in a case like this with a guy like this.

There was a small handful of vintage Jaguar XK-Es registered in Minnesota. Two were registered in the Twin Cities area. The one they decided was the one Capshaw was driving was registered to a Michael Antonucci. It was brown.

They'd pulled a DMV picture of Mr. Antonucci.

He bears a striking resemblance to the occupant of that big, cold office, Hallie thought.

"Bazinga!" Hallie said. She was running around the Minneapolis field office like a manic Chihuahua. "We need airline reservations from any airport within driving distance of Minneapolis, most likely O'Hare, to Vanuatu in the middle of the Pacific Ocean. When's it leaving? Where is it stopping? Is someone named either Capshaw or Antonucci holding a ticket?"

Two agents were contacting gas stations on I-90 and I-94 between Minneapolis and Chicago, asking about a brown vintage Jaguar sports car. It was the longest of long shots, but she knew this was the stuff of investigative work. It was the way cases were broken.

"I hate that I'm just sitting here," she said to the SAIC of the field office, a twenty-seven-year veteran agent named Will Cushing.

"If you want, we can fly you to O'Hare, but the guy might be going to Milwaukee, St. Louis, or Des Moines, maybe even somewhere up in Canada. When we know he's going to this Vanuatu place, we can find out where flights between all those places and their stops for plane changes, refueling—"

"Refueling! Listen, Will, can we get agents from Chicago to descend on O'Hare and check out westbound flights that could possibly . . ." She noticed Cushing losing interest.

"Think for a second, Garard," he said. "Let's work

this methodically. First, let's check reservations to Vanuatu." He yelled to the room for someone to find out what airport serves the island archipelago. "Typically, people make airline reservations from point of departure to the ultimate destination. The individual legs of the reservation show up automatically. Maybe the guy is going to stop in LA for a few days before going on. Maybe Honolulu."

"Maybe, maybe, maybe . . . I know, Will," she said. "I want this son of a bitch. Now that I know he may have had a couple of Peace Corps volunteers whacked over some fucking dandruff shampoo . . ."

"I know, Hallie. But let's be smart. Smarter than him, okay?"

Someone in the room shouted, "He gassed up an hour ago in La Crosse, Wisconsin! I got pictures!"

What the agent had came from a security camera inside the convenience store. It was Capshaw. He was buying a sandwich and a drink. The car was barely visible behind a pump, but it was him. Hallie smiled.

"Fucker's on his way to O'Hare."

• • •

Ronnie and Jennie had Christy and Jordan over for dinner. Christy said she couldn't stop laughing when she first saw how her father had been living. "It's about the same size as those cells we had in Mali," she said. She turned to her father. "I guess you liked having everything in one place."

"Cells?" Jennie asked.

"Over in Mali, we were housed in cells in an old jail. At least we weren't locked in."

Jennie brought out Lady to be reunited with her owner.

Nuzzling the Basenji, Christy said, "Dad called my mom 'milady.' Big difference is, when he did something crazy, my mom could and would bark!" Jordan smiled. Christy looked into Lady's eyes. "I guess I'm going to have to miss her all over again."

• • •

Skeeter confirmed for Ronnie that Michael Antonucci indeed held title to a small house on the island of Efate in Vanuatu. The property was within the city limits of Port Vila, the capital city, and home to about 45,000 islanders and expats, mostly from Australia and New Zealand, but a handful were likely from the US. Skeeter also delivered a package of information that would tie the noose around Dommerich Worldwide and its North America subsidiary, along with Michael Capshaw, Nelson Becker, and perhaps even Gunther Soldinger in Munich.

"This is how your guy embezzled huge dollars from Dommerich and managed to push through approvals on more than two dozen pharmaceutical and pesticide products with the FDA and EPA," Skeeter told Ronnie. "I need you to try and follow this."

Ronnie wasn't insulted. "Okay."

"First, Capshaw and a couple of scientists he'd re-cruited directly from the FDA and the EPA—with Dommerich dollars, of course—formed a Delaware shell corporation holding at least six product testing facilities in locations throughout the US. I've sent you the names and locations of the companies and of the other principals.

"As each place came online, Dommerich started pushing out products for animal testing and then for human evaluations. Of course, Dommerich paid for everything! It appears they even paid in-house FDA and EPA people to fast-track agency approval of the testing facilities. The way this all works, Capshaw takes half the pie for himself, and the guys in the trenches get paid nicely to make sure the products pass muster. That way, when they're sent on to either the FDA or the EPA, their evaluations are pretty much guaranteed, because the people at the agencies know the people doing the testing. And a few of the people at the agencies themselves are in Dommerich's pocket. It's a sweet deal for everyone, except us, y'know, regular people."

"So, if I understand correctly, Dommerich controls the process all the way through until the products go to their respective government agencies," Ronnie said. "This violates every idea of independently ver-ified testing expected by the EPA and the FDA, not to mention the public."

"It was a perfect closed and locked chain," Skeeter said. "Except for the ownership and profit distribution arrangement, it appeared the labs performed exactly as they should. Formulations with problems were sent back to Dommerich. If the problems could be resolved, fine, if not, either people got paid off or the product disappeared. The only time I can find something going really wrong was with Choralizine, and, as you found out, that was a problem with the labeling indications. And to Dommerich's good fortune, the FDA took a lot of the fall for that."

"It would be interesting to know if the person or people at the FDA who bit that bullet ended up with jobs at one of these test facilities," Ronnie said.

"You're learning, grasshopper," Skeeter said. "I'll check that out."

"So, when Capshaw is arrested, this whole house of cards falls to pieces," Ronnie said. "Of course, we can't use any of this without . . ."

"No, you can't, but they don't know that," Skeeter said. "If it was up to me, I'd push this out even before you have Crapshaw, or whatever that creep's name is. He's toast because he profited personally from the testing process. That's a mad conflict of interest. I'll have his financials from Vanuatu soon as I find a minute to dig 'em out. That'll end him. Once you put the whole testing story into print, it should end Dommerich, once and for all. Cool, huh?"

"Very cool, buddy."

"You know, you're gonna owe me big time when you get my bill, right?"

Ronnie hadn't given that minor little detail a moment's thought. "Uh, yeah, right. Yeah, we'll figure that out. Where are you two these days?"

Skeeter Bates laughed. "See ya, pal!"

• • •

In some strange way, Michael Capshaw was enjoying being on the run. For the first time in forever, his only concern was the problem right in front of his eyes. No FDA or EPA bullshit. No spreading money around like manure in third world shitholes from Africa to South America. No having to put up with Nathan Becker's constant whining.

No Nancy. That was the only downside.

He knew the FBI was hunting Michael Capshaw. Right now, and for the foreseeable future, he was back to being Michael Antonucci. Nobody knew Michael Antonucci.

He briefly thought about his mother. *Yeah, fuck her, too*, he thought. *She made her own bed.* She wasn't going to make the trip with him to paradise or purgatory or wherever the hell he was headed in the middle of the Pacific Ocean.

Seeing signs for Chicago and for O'Hare, he made a snap decision. *Fuck O'Hare. Feds will be all over O'Hare.* He stayed on I-90 when it became the

Addams Tollway. He ran every toll with impunity. He passed through Hoffman Estates, blew by O'Hare, and took the south exit ramp onto I-55.

His new plan was to get to St. Louis. He hadn't been there in a really long time, and he'd never been behind the wheel of a car while he lived there. But he still knew something about the place.

He planned to dump the Jag someplace where it would not attract attention, such as a hotel or mall parking garage. He'd spend a day or maybe two and then buy a ticket for LAX. When he was ready, after however long he decided to kick it in Los Angeles, he'd buy a ticket to Honolulu. Then he'd catch the first flight that would get him to Port Vila. Once he landed there, he'd take his shoes off, put his feet in the sand, and stare out at the big, empty . . . next.

Michael Antonucci was as naturally high as he'd been in years. He'd figured it out. He was . . . he was good.

• • •

Hallie Garard had secured enough agents to keep an eye on virtually every terminal gate at O'Hare International where Michael Capshaw might secure passage on a westbound flight. It was a budget buster, but the stakes were high, and she had her boss's support, who had his boss's support, who had the director's support. She was golden.

"I gotta ask, Hallie," Will Cushing said, "what if?"

She snapped her head around and took in the veteran agent. "What if? What if? I'll tell you what if, Will," she said. "If we happen to miss him at O'Hare, which, I admit, is a distinct possibility, we will absolutely, positively shut this fucker down somewhere else. Maybe the West Coast. Maybe Honolulu. And if I have to go to Port Vila in Vanuatu myself, on my own dime, I will bring Michael Antonucci Capshaw back and put his ass in an orange jumpsuit. This soulless bastard isn't going to cost me a minute of sleep. It's not a question of if, just when and where. That's what if, my friend." She gave him a tight smile.

He couldn't help but smile back. "Damn, but you are one badass badass, Special Agent Garard," Cushing said.

She decided to check in with Ronnie. "What's happening, Dr. Cooper?" she said when he answered.

"As of now, you are what's happening, Dr. Hofstadter," he said. "What's new on your end of this operation?"

She filled him in on their current lines of thought. The Bureau had O'Hare blanketed. If Capshaw showed up there, they'd scoop him up.

"If not?"

"As I just told my friend Will Cushing of the Minneapolis field office," she said, "who just asked me the same fucking question, he's going down. It's just a question of when and where. Remember, we know his Antonucci identity, and we know his ultimate destination."

"We do," he said. "We also know Vanuatu won't extradite him."

"Boy, aren't you just a little slice of joy and happiness, Sheldon," she said. "What's the matter, Amy cut you off?"

"Seriously, things here are good, and thanks for asking. Jordan's having his stuff trucked down. Christy is spending a lot of time with Jennie and Stacy. Second installment is ready to go. Just waiting on the final takedown."

"I know," she said. "He's holding most of the cards right now. He's got money, a fast ride, and several different ways to get where he's going. Shit, he could go to Mexico and leave from there. We can't cover everything."

"No, you can't, not really," Ronnie said. "But my guy told me that pretty much every flight from pretty much anywhere in North America to Vanuatu is going to have to stop either on the West Coast or in Honolulu, either to refuel or to change planes."

Hallie was silent, rolling those points west over in her mind.

"You know, Leonard, I don't see this asshole taking some leisurely road trip to get where he's going," Ronnie said. "If it were me, and I know it's not, I wouldn't bank on any other country giving a rat's ass about

Capshaw or Antonucci or whatever he's calling himself. You've got field agents everywhere on the mainland and in Honolulu, right?"

"Right."

"He knows you're after him, right?"

"Of course, he does. He's running."

"Until you know otherwise, I'd probably focus on LAX and Honolulu, Hallie," Ronnie said. "Maybe it's a day, maybe it's a week. Maybe he stops somewhere and shaves his head, tries to change his appearance. He's got the whole West Coast to jump off from. There are too many points of departure to watch them all closely. My bet would be, and I'd bet big on this, your best shot is either LA or Honolulu, either when he gets there or when he gets ready to leave."

"You know, I've never been to Hawaii," she said.

"Aloha, Leonard," Ronnie said.

Chapter 27

Michael arrived early enough on Sunday to make a stop at the St. Louis Galleria in Richmond Heights. A quick visit to Nordstrom produced a pair of Ralph Lauren jeans, a pair of light brown Cole Haan loafers, a gorgeous silky tropical-patterned Tommy Bahama shirt, and a new pair of Wayfarers for the sunny days ahead. He checked into the Renaissance Hotel near STL, had a light dinner, and turned in.

After a quick breakfast on Monday morning, he decided to put the Jag on the second level of the parking garage amid a bunch of other guests' cars. He left the keys on the seat and the door unlocked. He stared at it for a moment. *Maybe I should just drive to the West Coast. After all, what's the rush?* He mulled that over for a full minute before he returned to his room, collected his bags, and boarded the hotel shuttle to the airport.

Michael stretched out in his seat in the first-class cabin on American Airlines' only nonstop that morning between St. Louis Lambert and LAX. So far, no hitches, no glitches. He hadn't shaved in two days. A kind of hipster stubble had appeared on his face. He planned to let it grow and see how it turned out. *A good LA look*, he thought.

• • •

"Hallie!" a Minneapolis field agent called out. "A Michael Antonucci purchased a one-way ticket, nonstop, St. Louis to LAX. Flight took off . . . twenty minutes ago. Scheduled to arrive at LAX . . . 10:55 a.m. their time."

"Bazinga!" she said.

• • •

Hallie called the FBI's LA field office. It was only going on 7:30 a.m. there; day-shift agents would be just arriving.

"Beltran," the voice answered.

"Good morning, Special Agent Beltran," she said. "Special Agent Hallie Garard, IATF, calling from Minneapolis."

"Is that in the United States, Agent Garard?" he said.

"Hardy har har, Beltran. We need a full-court press

at LAX by about 10:30 a.m. your time. Target's flying American from STL. Scheduled arrival time is 10:55 a.m. I'm sending pictures, flight info, et cetera. His name is Michael Capshaw, traveling as Michael Antonucci. Maybe five eleven, 170 pounds, black hair, brown eyes, good looking, I guess, in a sleazy sort of way. He will definitely be well-dressed."

"What's he done?" She snorted.

"What hasn't this creep done? Two counts of kidnapping, conspiracy to commit two murders, maybe more, embezzlement, interstate fraud. That enough for you?"

"Yeah, that'll do. I've got your number. SAIC will holla back at you in an hour."

"You are the man, Beltran. Thanks. Call me when you have the son of a bitch in handcuffs. I want to fly out and pick him up myself."

"Oh, this is personal. You got it, Garard. Stay warm up there."

"It's June, Beltran, even in Minnesota. Weather's actually pretty nice up here."

• • •

Michael Capshaw stepped off the Boeing B767 in Los Angeles and was greeted at the gate by a team of federal agents and LA County deputies. He was taken into custody quietly and without incident.

Other agents drove him to the FBI's LA field office

on Wilshire Boulevard. He was photographed, fingerprinted, and booked on the preliminary charges of flight to avoid prosecution and using false identification to purchase an airline ticket.

He talked to no one, and no one questioned him. He was fed lunch at 1:15 p.m.

At 4:45 p.m., Special Agent Hallie Garard, accompanied by Special Agent in Charge Will Cushing of the Minneapolis field office walked into the LA field office.

"Hello, Michael," she said through the screen of the holding cell.

"Special Agent Garard," he said. "Not nice to see you again. You know, I was this close . . ."

Hallie smiled and shook her head. "You were never close, Michael," she said. "You stopped being close when you bribed federal agency employees. We collared those clowns yesterday." She looked at her notebook. "A guy named Jack Winter had a whole lot to tell us, Michael. So have your GSA security guys in Paraguay, including the two who snatched Christy Calder off the street last year. I doubt there's ever been a sleaze bucket in the history of sleaze buckets whose goose is more fully cooked than yours. Just so you know, Michael? Whatever future you imagined for yourself? Not. Gonna. Happen."

"Lawyer, Hallie. Lawyer."

"As many as you'd like, Michael. Unfortunately, I

can't represent you. That would be a conflict of interest. But don't you worry, this country's crawling with lawyers just itching to help you empty whatever legit bank accounts you may still have."

• • •

Ronnie reached out to Skeeter for what he hoped would be the last time on this assignment.

"You get him?" Skeeter asked.

"FBI's got him, not me. He's toast."

"Well done, grasshopper."

"Need one more thing, if possible."

"Anything's possible, my man."

"Any way to find out where former Paraguayan president Acosta hid the money Dommerich paid him for rights to deforest a big chunk of jungle?"

Skeeter was silent for a moment. "Yeah, I remember that. I'll let you know. Again, good work, man."

"Yeah, you too, buddy."

• • •

Even though Jordan Censell had been collected by agents of Dommerich in Orlando and brought to Minneapolis, the federal prosecutor assigned to handle the criminal portion of the cases involving Michael Capshaw and Dommerich Worldwide believed the crime of kidnapping, if they ever could make one, began when Jordan was put on the plane to Paraguay. It would be a tough case to make because Capshaw's people would argue that they had simply been reuniting him with his daughter.

But then, they'd have to explain everything else regarding that daughter.

In any case, Ronnie Levitt's second and third installments on the coup in Paraguay and the takedown of Dommerich North America established the basis for what everyone believed would likely be the *Chronicle*'s and Ronnie's next Pulitzer nomination.

The folks on Susie Q Court formally met Nelson J. Calder, Christy Calder, and their Basenji, Lady, at a backyard pool and grill party hosted by Doug and Stacy Peterson. There they all got to hear, firsthand, everything that had transpired involving Ronnie, Hallie, and the man they called the Professor.

Alberto couldn't fully grasp Hallie as an FBI agent or that Jordan formerly was with the Defense Intelligence Agency. He also had trouble with a dog that didn't bark.

"What kind of dog don't bark?" he kept asking.

Doug and Stacy got a full debrief from Ronnie before the festivities began. They all wished Hallie were there, even Alberto, but a box truck had arrived a day earlier and collected everything from inside her house. They all noted that the house between the Petersons' and Mikey's now featured a "For Sale" sign in the front yard.

Ronnie and Nelson Calder slipped away from the

party and walked across the cul-de-sac to Jordan's house. There was still a little unfinished business between the neighbors.

They walked silently into the back bedroom. Things had been cleaned up from the mess Jordan had left for Ronnie and Hallie to pore over.

Ronnie sat on the chair in front of the pull-down desk in the wall unit containing the Murphy bed and a host of now-empty shelves and drawers. Jordan—Nelson was sitting on the bed. Lady was where she had been when Ronnie first broke into the room.

"What was up with living like this?" he asked.

Nelson laughed. "I suppose, in hindsight, it wasn't ever really necessary, but my thinking after Christy was snatched in Asunción wasn't all that clear," he said. "That guy . . . mowing patches of dirt, quoting literature, acting like a lunatic, was my own kind of cover for whatever I imagined in my addled brain I might have had to do in order to get Christy back home."

Ronnie nodded. "But you couldn't live like a human being?" he asked. "You bought a whole house. Why live with Lady in just one room?"

"I know, it seems nuts," he said. "But from the day I moved in until the day I left for Minneapolis . . . You know it's only been about two weeks, right? Since they picked me up and took me to see Capshaw?"

"Yeah. Tell me about it. Two really busy weeks."

"All I did from the day I moved in was work on this," he said. "I didn't really want to form attachments. I didn't see anything beyond my own grief. For those purposes, this arrangement worked for me. You went through the diaries, right?"

"I did," Ronnie said.

"Life, for me, after the DIA, was in the dirt. Mushrooms. You know, you'd be amazed . . . Once Leslie died, it became about why. For me. For Christy, she gave up what I have to believe was a promising career in the law. I mean, who goes from practicing law in Chicago to digging wells in southern Mali, for Chrissake?"

Ronnie had, over the years, spoken to men who went to Vietnam. Some of them had had a *Deer Hunter* kind of experience. One day they were immersed in their mundane American civilian lives, the next they were getting shot at, ten thousand miles away, by short people wearing black pajamas and wielding automatic weapons.

"Knocked you and her for a loop," was the best Ronnie could come up with.

"Yeah," Nelson said, getting wound up. "I went after those demigods in white coats with everything I had. 'It's unfortunate, Mr. Calder,' they told me. Unfortunate, my ass. Your damned anesthesiologist is a drunk. You knew it, yet you covered for him, let him work, and now my wife is dead.

"I was so fucking angry, Ronnie. I didn't need their money, but I wanted them to pay for what they did. Revenge, I guess. I found a lawyer who absolutely, positively hated doctors, hospitals . . . the whole damned industry. You know, they wanted to settle with me for a quarter-million dollars, right out of the box. That told us, my lawyer and me, that they were just getting started. Ultimately, we got them to agree to $6 million, four for Christy and me and two for the lawyer." He nodded his head and pointed to himself. "If you ever need a malpractice shark, I know a guy."

He talked about moving to Florida in anticipation of Christy's return from Mali. It was supposed to be a new start for both of them. She could have easily gone back to Chicago, he told Ronnie, but when he'd visited her in Mali, she let him know that she probably wouldn't be doing that.

"Too close to Indiana, I guess," he said. "I'm pretty sure we'll be working through a whole lot of that now that we're both home, safe and sound."

"Then came Paraguay," Ronnie said.

"When Christy got taken in Asunción, that was, at least for me, a bridge too far," he said. "I couldn't get out of my own way, Ronnie. I took a three-day trip down there, realized I was way out of my depth, came home, and started doing research. I was, almost from day one, certain Dommerich was somehow involved."

"Where does Jordan Censell come in?"

Nelson laughed. "I'll get to that, I promise," he said. "It's not a big deal. All part of that persona I adopted. Frankly, I'm surprised you haven't figured it out."

Ronnie looked at his neighbor through brand-new

eyes. "I told Jennie, after I came home from work, the guy I talked to that Saturday morning was different from the guy we knew," he said.

"Yeah, I know. Look, Ronnie, I had no idea what was going to happen once I came face to face with Michael Capshaw," he said. "In my mind, it actually was an end game of sorts. Knowing what we all know now, it's entirely possible I could have been thrown from that really nice Gulfstream jet somewhere over southern Illinois. I just wanted you and Special Agent Garard . . ." He shook his head. "She'd been here all of a week before I made her as a fed."

"I know. She said it takes one to know one," Ronnie said.

"I guess. I'm glad she had you working with her. I need to thank her for taking care of Lady."

"Yep," Ronnie said, "she was all over that from the minute they met."

"Do you get what I'm telling you?" Nelson asked.

Ronnie stood and walked to the door of the room where Nelson Calder/Jordan Censell had spent months working his mostly fruitless alchemy on behalf of his only living family.

"I guess it makes sense," Ronnie said. "You went through all this changing your identity, adopting a persona stuff because you were facing so much uncertainty. Why set up a house? Why make friends?"

"Why think for a minute about living a normal life? There are any number of ways this whole thing could have come off the rails," Nelson said. "I tried the Peace Corps. I tried the State Department. I tried my congressman. I tried everything, and while I was trying to work through whatever passes for normal channels, I did research. Gotta say, man, the internet is an amazing and frightening thing, Ronnie."

Ronnie smiled. He thought about Skeeter Bates and Honey, working their own kind of witchcraft on behalf of all make and manner of underdog. "It is," he said. "I'm surprised you couldn't leverage your DIA connections."

"I probably could have, I guess. I . . . I just didn't want another disappointment from our wonderful government. You'll come to understand this, but I'm a 'ready, fire, aim' kind of guy. I've always had impulse control issues, and when I feel like I or someone I care about has been wronged, I just . . . I don't know. I just do stuff." He paused for a moment. "I really hope all of this is behind me, behind us. I want to help Christy find her own footing again. Not that she needs me for that. I'm glad you'll all get to know her now. She's really the goods."

"Seems like it, Jordan, er, Nelson. Guess I'm going to have to get used to you having a real name."

Nelson smiled and went to one of the bookshelves in the room. He selected a paperback book and handed it to Ronnie. "Hallie mentioned you had . . . have good taste in literature." Ronnie looked at the book, *The Count of Monte Cristo*, then looked at Nelson. "Jordan

Censell is just an anagram of Nelson J. Calder," he said. For a time, I considered calling myself Edmund Dantes, or some anagram of his name. Dantes is the hero protagonist of that book, a man wronged—so wronged—by people he should have been able to trust. He spends the whole rest of his life getting his revenge. That's kind of my story. I felt doctors, hospitals, government agencies, Congress, big business, they all, in my mind, had kicked me and people I love right to the curb."

Ronnie nodded. "In the end, though, it was a tenacious FBI agent and a CIA agent, both government people, who brought you and Christy home. It was even a state court who gave you something at least resembling justice for what happened to Leslie."

Nelson Calder nodded. He put the book back on the shelf and turned to his neighbor. "I've been in the revenge business long enough, Ronnie," he said. "Come on, let's go back to the cookout." He walked over and embraced Ronnie. "It wasn't just the FBI and CIA, man. It was also a damn fine, hardworking reporter. Thank you."

Ronnie and Nelson embraced. "Just promise me one thing, neighbor," Ronnie said.

"Anything, man," Nelson said.

"No lawn mowing on Saturday mornings before at least nine o'clock!"

Epilogue

A week later, Hallie checked in. She was in New York, taking care of some family business.

"Capshaw is trying to throw his bosses, Becker and Soldinger, under the bus," she said. "They, I am told, are returning the favor. These guys . . ."

"Well, all I can tell you is everyone on Susie Q misses you," he said. "Especially a sweet brown-and-white Basenji."

"Yeah, I'm sure," she said. "How are the Calder's?"

"They're good. Thankfully, they're resodding the lawn," he said. "I actually got to sleep in for a couple of Saturday mornings."

"Sounds like all is well in suburbia, Sheldon," she said.

"How's all this going to shake out?"

"Who the hell knows? These guys have more five-hundred-buck-an-hour lawyers on speed dial than Goldman Sachs," she said. "If I had to guess,

Capshaw's going to be in his late sixties if he ever gets out of federal prison. Becker is going to do maybe six, seven years for the five-mil bribe. One of our financial fraud guys says Dommerich is probably going to end up being broken apart. Some other pharma companies will buy their good patents. Stockholders will get dumped on. The big guy, Soldinger, is under indictment in Germany."

"Sometimes the system works," Ronnie said.

"You know, believe it or not, Sheldon, most times the system works," she said. "Listen, I can't be quoted, you know, you being one of those media devils and all, but I really enjoyed working with you on this. Far as reporters go, you are definitely one of the good ones, man."

"Shucks, ma'am, you're gonna make me blush. You take care of yourself, Leonard. Say hi to Penny."

"Her name's Emily. See ya, Sheldon."

• • •

Four Months Later

It was a typical autumn afternoon in Orlando, warm, but not the scorching summer heat. Ronnie was at his desk directly in front of the wall of offices in the back of the air-conditioned newsroom at the *Chronicle* when Elvis, the security guard in the lobby, buzzed him. "Hey, Mr. Levitt, you got a visitor."

"I'm right in the middle of something, E," he said. "I think you're gonna want to come down here."

Ronnie held his exasperation in check. "Maybe you can just send him up?"

"It's not a him. Definitely not a him."

"Okay, Elvis, can you send *her* up?"

"Okeydokey, Mr. Levitt. She's on her way."

• • •

Elvis hung up his phone and pointed to the staircase. "Hope you're ready, hotshot," he whispered to the back of the vision making her way up the flight of stairs from the lobby to the newsroom.

• • •

Ronnie went back to what he was doing. Years ago, Ronnie's first editor had told him that a daily newspaper is a custom manufacturing facility turning out a brand-new product every single day. The man was right.

It was nearly 4:00 p.m. and the room was buzzing with reporters, photographers, and editors all nailing down stories and pictures for the next day's edition. Ronnie was going through some photographs of the subjects of his latest investigative piece when an uncharacteristic quiet fell over the room. He looked around and spotted a woman making her way through a dozen rows of desks and cubicles in the general direction of his domain.

Every eye in the almost half acre of real estate that comprised the *Chronicle*'s newsroom was attempting to capture the magnificent creature moving down the center aisle. She didn't exactly walk. It was more like she glided. Long dirty-blonde hair, stunning blue eyes, Daisy Dukes at the top of long bare legs, and wedge sandals on her feet. She was wearing about half a T-shirt that read, "The opposite of poverty isn't wealth. The opposite of poverty is enough." Under the T-shirt, everything was moving. She approached him.

"Ronnie?" she asked, smiling. He stood.

"Yes, ma'am, I believe so. And you are . . . ?"

She smiled and handed him a manila envelope. He couldn't take his eyes off her. She licked her lips, leaned in, and kissed him on the cheek. She whispered, "Phillip said to tell you thanks, and this one is on the house. Read everything before you do anything. Be sure to follow the instructions." She turned, looked back at him, gave him a broad smile while wiggling her fingers, and walked back the way she'd arrived.

A few old-guard reporters broke into polite applause.

Ronnie stood, staring, like everyone else, as Honey stepped onto the down escalator and vanished from view, a mirage. He took in and let out a long deep breath. He now understood how and why his source could so easily be distracted.

As his fellow reporters began hazing him, he broke the seal on the envelope. Inside he found an ancient flash drive and a single sheet of paper with one line written in a woman's hand: "Insert the drive. Click the link. Read fast. Destroy the drive. Shred this."

Ronnie inserted the drive and clicked the link. A text file opened, and a timer appeared in the upper right-hand corner of the screen on his laptop. It began a sixty-second countdown.

"Dommerich sent $5 million to a numbered account in a Panama City, Panama bank. There is now $3 million in the account, but for some strange reason it cannot be accessed. Computer glitch. Shit happens. ☺ It should demonstrate for prosecutors the lengths to which Dommerich went to get what it wanted.

"The other $2 million appears to have vanished. Y'know. Into thin air. No idea what happened. ☺ Check out these pictures. Keep in touch. S and H."

Ronnie scrolled. The first photo was of a silver forty-four-foot trailer hitched to an old Kenworth 900. It was captioned "Before." The second was of a brand-new, top-of-the-line black-and-silver bus-length RV. It was captioned "Now."

One of his fellow journalists was making his way toward Ronnie's desk. Reporters—God bless 'em—always have questions. Ronnie processed what he had read and seen, smiling broadly. The timer ran down to 00:00. Everything on the screen disappeared. He couldn't help himself. He started laughing. It would have been like *Mission: Impossible*, except there wasn't any smoke, or music. He removed the flash drive and put it in his pocket for future disposal.

He turned his back on his advancing colleagues, sat down, stifled a laugh, and, as instructed, inserted the sheet of paper into his shredder.

End

Acknowledgments

The author would like to thank so, so many people who have supported this effort, including but not limited to the Katz, Medlar, Foster, Diehn, and Van Oss families; friends and colleagues in western North Carolina and central Florida; professors and fellow students from Valencia College, Rollins College, and Western Carolina University; and even a few OLD friends from Brooklyn, New York, and the United States Air Force. Some may recognize pieces and aspects of themselves on these pages, while others may wonder why they've been forgotten. They haven't.

Thanks to Robert Kenney of Thoughtful Editing, Victoria Griffin, and Nora Smith from Blue Pen. Thanks to Ron Rash, Pam Duncan, Bob Morris, Ilyse Kusnetz, and Steven Cooper for their wisdom, advice, counsel, and encouragement over the years. And thanks to my colleagues in Highlands, North Carolina for their generous support and feedback.

Special thanks always to Lynn, partner, best friend, and muse, for putting up with all the hours of closed doors, quiet keystrokes and noisy grumbling from the back room.

About the Author

Bruce F. Katz – Bud to his friends – is author of the business biography, *When Your Name Is On the Door*, along with novels, *The History Lesson* (YA), *The Filthy Five*, and *The Family Jewels*. He grew up in Brooklyn, New York and served four years in the U.S. Air Force. He was graduated Magna Cum Laude from Western Carolina University with a BA in English. A retired strategic communication, mass media, advertising and public relations executive, he lives with his wife, Lynn, a former defense and aerospace industry executive, in Highlands, North Carolina.